AUTHOR	CLASS
SEED, S.	AF
	ADVENTURE

TITLE

HEART SWAP

FABULOUS
THINGS

FABULOUS THINGS

KELLY BRAFFET

review

First published in Great Britain in 2005 by
Review

An imprint of Headline Book Publishing

10 9 8 7 6 5 4 3 2 1

Cataloguing in Publication Data is available from the British Library

ISBN 0 7553 2153 7

Typeset in Garamond by Avon DataSet Ltd, Bidford-on-Avon, Warks
Printed and bound in Great Britain by Mackays of Chatham plc, Chatham, Kent

Headline's policy is to use papers that are natural, renewable and recyclable
products and made from wood grown in sustainable forests. The logging and
manufacturing processes are expected to conform to the environmental
regulations of the country of origin.

HEADLINE BOOK PUBLISHING
A division of Hodder Headline
338 Euston Road
London NW1 3BH

www.headline.co.uk
www.hodderheadline.com

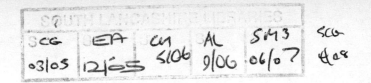
This is for my parents, Jim and Theresa,
and also for Casey, who put Bunny on the roof.

When the moon came they set out, but they found no crumbs, for the many thousands of birds which fly about in the woods and fields had picked them all up. Hänsel said to Grethel, 'We shall soon find the way,' but they did not find it.

Jacob and Wilhelm Grimm, *Hänsel and Grethel*

1

The worst hangovers come on the sunniest days. Even at sixteen I knew enough to expect that. The day when Jack drove me into town to buy aspirin, the sun was shining and the sky was the brilliant blue of a crayon drawing. Late summer in western Pennsylvania is muggy and oppressive enough to make your head spin even on a good day, and the air conditioning in the truck hadn't worked for years. My stomach rolled with each curve and dip in the road, and my head was impaled on a hot hard spike that made my eyes throb. I felt weighed down by the heat and barely alive.

'Josie,' Jack said. 'Okay?'

'There's a jackhammer in my head,' I said. 'Other than that, I'm fine.'

'Someone's grumpy.'

'You're not helping.'

'I'm driving you to get aspirin, aren't I?' he said.

We turned onto the highway, the sun hit us head-on, and I didn't bother to answer. Jack took a pair of sunglasses from above the sun visor. He had the radio on. The beat was jarring and obnoxious and the announcer's voice sounded like metal on asphalt. The glare off the road made my eyes hurt, and underneath the sourness of my whiskey-burned stomach the old familiar dread was taking shape.

I hated going into town. Town people *stared*.

Meanwhile, there was Jack, undamaged and cool as you could possibly please behind his sunglasses, just as if we hadn't been up till dawn drinking everything but the drain cleaner under the sink. That was my brother: it was like he was his own species, one that had sneaked a couple of thousand extra years in while evolution was looking the other way.

'You never feel a thing, do you?' I said.

'Not like you do,' he answered.

I leaned my head back against the rear window and closed my eyes. The truck hit a pothole and my head bounced hard against the glass.

'I want a pair of sunglasses,' I said.

Which was how it came to pass that instead of getting the trip to town over with as soon as possible, the way we usually did, I found myself wasting precious time at the revolving display rack in the drugstore, picking up and discarding one pair of sunglasses after another as I tried to find some that would hide me from the world and still leave me able to recognize myself in the mirror. Jack was standing by the paperbacks, reading the back covers of the novels.

There had been a woman standing at the cash register when we came in. The bell over the door jingled as she left, and Jack was suddenly standing at my elbow.

'You've got an audience,' he said, and I froze, the pair of glasses in my hand halfway to my face. I thought he meant the woman. Like I said, people in town *stared*.

'No, it's okay,' he said. 'The kid behind the counter.'

I put the glasses on, turned the rack slightly so that I could see the boy in the mirror, and looked.

The boy behind the cash register was about my age, with

2

longish hair and thin, rangy limbs. He wore a black T-shirt and jeans underneath his blue store apron. Jack was right, he was staring; but as I turned my head to get a better look he bent hastily over the magazine that lay open on the counter in front of him, as if he'd been reading it all along, and started flipping through the pages too quickly to see what was on them.

'So?' I said to my brother, who looked so easy by comparison in his old stained shirt and sleep-twisted hair.

Jack turned back to the rack of glasses and started to spin it lazily. 'He's been looking at you since we came in.'

'That's ridiculous.'

Jack said, 'We're undeniably charismatic,' and picked a pair of sunglasses at random. Then he told me to go ask my new boyfriend where the aspirin was. I said I knew where the aspirin was, but he squeezed my elbow and said to trust him, so I did.

When the boy saw me coming, he pushed his glasses up his nose and ran his hands through his hair.

'Aisle five,' he said when I asked about the aspirin. I noticed, almost clinically, that his glasses hid a nice set of eyelashes, for a boy. They weren't as thick as Jack's, but they were straight and dark. His long, thin fingers, tapping on the counter, were tanned to a rich golden brown.

He was making me nervous, this boy, watching me too closely. I realized that I was turning the sunglasses Jack had given me over and over in my hands, and stopped.

'They'll look good on you,' the boy said shyly.

I knew I was supposed to say something in return, but I didn't know what. So I just smiled. The smile felt strained on my lips.

Jack saved me by coming up behind me. 'I found it, Jo,' he said and held up the bottle of aspirin. He took the sunglasses and put both items on the counter. The look on his face was distant and bored.

The boy's movements were studied, too casual, as he rang them up. His eyes kept darting up at one or the other of us. Usually me.

'You're those Raeburn kids, aren't you?' he asked as he gave us our change.

'No, we're the other ones,' Jack said and handed me the sunglasses as we turned away.

As the door jangled behind us, the boy called, 'See you around?' as if it were a question.

Back in the battered blue truck, Jack used his keys to break the seal on the aspirin. He pulled out the wad of cotton stuffed in the top of the bottle and threw it out the window. Shaking out four tablets, he handed two of them to me and took the other two himself.

I wished that we'd thought of getting something to wash the pills down with and dry-swallowed them.

'What was all that about?' I said when I could talk.

Jack stretched his arm across the back of the seat and tugged lightly on my plait. His green eyes were amused. He said, 'He likes you.'

'You're still drunk,' I said.

'He couldn't take his eyes off you,' Jack said. 'But he could barely talk to you, and he was afraid to look you in the eye.' He winked. 'Broadcasting loud and clear, little sister.'

I pulled my knees up and braced them against the dashboard. I could still feel the pills in my throat.

'He doesn't like me,' I said. 'He doesn't even know me.'

'He doesn't need to,' Jack said, pinching my thigh. He started the truck's tired old engine. 'You're good-looking. You take after me that way.'

'Ha,' I said, watching Jack, the good lines of his profile and his hair, warm and golden in the afternoon sun.

'I know, it's hard to believe,' he said. 'Are you going to try on those sunglasses I bought you?'

I'd forgotten them. They were sleek and narrow and the lenses were a deep, smoky grey. When I put them on the world went mute.

'Look at me,' Jack said as we pulled up to a stoplight.

I did.

He smiled. 'Beautiful.'

We lived about fifteen miles outside Janesville, on a winding road that led through a scattering of houses collectively called the Hill. In the nineteenth century, the Hill had been purchased, parcelled, and developed by small-time industrialists from Pittsburgh, forty miles or so to the south. They came north to try to escape the toxins that their steel mills and coke ovens disgorged into the air, and when the wind was blowing in the right direction, they succeeded. When the wind was blowing in the wrong direction, they took their families and headed up to Presque Isle to take in the cleaner breezes that blew off the surface of Lake Erie. These folks weren't Mellons, Carnegies, or Fricks; they were Smiths, Johnsons, and Browns. A century later, each of them was as long forgotten as the next, but their houses still stood: decaying old palaces that were never as grand as they wanted to be, with overwrought architecture that was both confused and confusing. Corinthian columns supporting veranda roofs trimmed with pale pink Victorian gingerbread. That kind of thing. Some of them had been kept up – there was even a 'Historic Homes of Janesville' tour, which split the town's less-than-hearty tourist trade with a lacklustre establishment called the Janesville Shipping and Transport Museum – but most of them were like ours: too expensive to maintain and too ugly and weird to sell. Every now and again we found outraged fliers tucked into our mailbox about some developer who was trying to buy a chunk of land and put in a crop of split-levels. Not being particularly community-minded, we never did anything about them. Somebody must have, though, because none of the new houses were ever built.

None of the ten or so houses on the Hill was visible to its neighbours, but most of them faced the road with vast green lawns and maple trees whose leaves swayed gently in the breeze. Our house was higher up the mountain and deeper into the wilderness. It sat at the end of a long, twisting driveway, hidden from sight by a tall overgrowth of spruce until you were nearly at the front porch and shadowed by two huge old elms that were the last Janesville survivors of Dutch elm disease. It was always late afternoon under those trees, and the path leading up to the porch was always ankle deep with dead leaves, even in the summer.

Jack and I lived there, for the most part, alone. Our father, whom we called Raeburn, taught physics at a small college three hours away. Too far to drive every day, he said, but the house had been in his family too long to sell and he'd never give up the tenure he'd spent so many years earning. So he kept a room at the college's faculty house and lived there during the week while Jack and I stayed home together.

Once, one of the men who taught with Raeburn stayed the night with us on his way up to Canada, and he asked how we managed, staying by ourselves all the time and not going to school. Raeburn told him that since he wasn't around, we'd cut four days out of five anyway, so why bother? 'The American public school system is a doomed institution,' he told the man. 'All they'd learn at that assembly-line idiot factory is how to sink to meet the lowest common denominator. If they study with me, they'll learn things they need.' A nice theory, but the truth is that we rarely if ever actually studied *with* him; when he left the house every Monday morning, there were two piles of books on the kitchen table, with lists of assignments tucked between their pages, to be finished by the time he returned. When he was home, he preferred to spend his time locked in his study, listening to the radio, so actually studying *with* him was restricted to the two or three gruelling hours that the three of us spent gathered in his study on Saturday afternoons. Raeburn's version of education was grim and absolute: hard sciences, mostly – physics, mathematics, chemistry – with some fringe politics and economic theory thrown in, to show us what colossal messes human beings could create when they attempted to form an organized society.

We were alone a lot, but we had always been alone a lot, and Jack said that we were the sort of people who always would be. Crazy Mary – which was what we called the mother we'd briefly shared – left my father when I was two and my brother was four, and took Jack with her. I didn't see him again for four years.

But then one morning when I was six years old, a strained-looking social worker showed up on our doorstep with one hand holding an inch-thick stack of paperwork and the other holding – barely – my squirming and fighting brother. I hadn't even known that I had a brother – I only vaguely knew that I had a mother, and still wasn't entirely clear how I was related to the man who called himself my father – and now there Jack was, in the flesh, and he was the first person I'd ever seen who was even close to my size, and besides, he *looked* like me. He had the same wide, smooth forehead, pointed chin, and tawny hair, although his hair had been cut brutally short somewhere along the line. There was an ugly gash near his left ear that had been stitched up with spiky black thread. He looked straight into my eyes and I looked straight into his, which were strikingly green, and we knew each other instantly.

Later, when we were left alone together while Raeburn went through the paperwork with the social worker, eight-year-old Jack reached out and took a lock of my hair between his fingers. The housekeeper Raeburn paid to take care of me had long since given up on my hair; it was snarled and matted and it hadn't ever been cut, but Jack didn't seem to notice. He looked at the greasy golden hank as if it were something miraculous.

'You have hair like Mary's,' he said, his voice full of wonder. Then his expression changed, became firm and efficient. 'But you need to brush it.'

'I don't know how,' small Josie said. It's the first sentence I can actually remember speaking.

'I'll show you,' Jack said, and he did. Ten years later, I was probably the only sixteen-year-old in America who still gave her hair the legendary hundred strokes each night, and sometimes during the day, because Jack loved to watch me do it.

Raeburn told me that Jack had come to live with us because my mother was dead; it was Jack who filled in the blanks by telling me that my mother and his mother and Mary were all the same person. 'We're on our own now,' he said. 'Just you and me.' The world I lived in was a third again as big as it had been a week before; I no longer felt alone, but I read the solemn look in his eyes and nodded soberly.

Not long after that, the housekeeper was fired – I'd hated her anyway, and much preferred spending time with my new brother – and the stacks of schoolbooks began. By the time Jack and I were teenagers, we had come to a silent understanding with Raeburn: as long as we spent the weekends pretending to pay attention, Raeburn couldn't have cared less what we did with ourselves during the week. And what we did, left alone in our decaying old house, was this: ice-skate in winter and stargaze in summer, get stinking drunk on cheap whiskey and cheaper wine, smoke cigarettes in bed, smoke pot on the front lawn, climb trees, walk in the woods, daydream, sleep, fight, scream, laugh, and do whatever else we wanted to do. I used to think that was all we'd ever do.

'Take functional relationships,' Raeburn said, his mouth full of half-chewed chicken wing. 'We design the experiments that define them, we give them names, we spend centuries proving and re-proving them; but we don't *create* them. They are entirely separate from us. They're like invisible machines, but far more intricate and fine than anything we could ever build. I am talking, children, about *constants*.' He brought one hand down hard on the table, making the cutlery jump. 'John.'

Jack, on my left, was staring blankly at the table. He looked up when our father spoke. Raeburn liked us to dress for dinner, so he was wearing a jacket and tie despite the heat. His eyes, the same green as the beer bottles we'd buried in the trash that afternoon, were shielded and cold. They might as well have been closed.

'Give me an example of a constant.' A piece of breading from the chicken fell onto Raeburn's shirt as he spoke. He didn't notice.

'Gravity,' my brother answered.

Raeburn shook his head. 'You might have been half right sixty years ago, before space travel and experimental antigravity aircraft. The U.S. government has successfully defeated gravity.

Bully for it.' He belched and dropped the chicken bone, picked clean.

I kept my eyes on my own plate, with its untouched drumstick and soggy heap of broccoli. When we'd returned from the drugstore, Raeburn was already there, even though we hadn't expected him for another couple of hours. He'd brought a whole chicken home with the regular groceries. Jack had cut it into pieces and I had fried it at the stove, despite the summer heat. It didn't take long, in the full stench of cooking meat and hot grease, for my hangover to resurface. By the time I put the frozen spears of broccoli in a pot of water to boil, my legs were shaky and the hair at the back of my neck was damp with sweat. I'd wiped the sweat away with a cool rag when I was upstairs dressing for dinner, but my stomach rebelled anew at the sight of the separated chicken leg on my plate, the white knob of bone glistening through the cooked tendons. It didn't look like food. It looked like a piece of a dismembered corpse. Eating it, I knew, was a practical impossibility.

And yet somehow I couldn't look away from it. Maybe I was making sure it didn't move.

'Josephine,' Raeburn said. 'There are many wrong answers and only one correct one.'

There are actually over a dozen universal physical constants, but it didn't matter. There was never more than one correct answer with my father. I knew this one; if Jack hadn't convinced me to do his physics for him, he would have known it, too. I tore myself away from contemplation of the thing on my plate and said, 'Hooke's Law.'

'Which is?'

'The ratio of a weight on a spring to the elongation of the spring.'

Jack's eyes flickered at me.

'The relationship of weight to tension. Good.' Raeburn picked up a fork, speared a limp piece of broccoli, and stuffed it into his mouth. 'Always constant. Always the same. Nature makes sense, children. Logical, concise, direct. It's humanity that's fucked it all up.'

'Gravity is a natural constant,' Jack said.

'Not once we've violated it. Then it becomes another part of the universe that we've irrevocably destroyed.' My stomach lurched dangerously. 'We've made all the technological advances we can make without dooming ourselves; all that's left to us is destruction. This is our dusk, children. This is our twilight.' He paused. His eyes were sparkling and his cheeks flushed. Our father liked nothing better than contemplating humanity's imminent self-destruction. He gloried in it.

One of Jack's hands fell casually beneath the table and I felt a light pinch through my crisp wool skirt. I grabbed for his hand. The tips of my fingers brushed his skin as he pulled it away.

Raeburn looked from Jack to me and back again. He grunted and took the other chicken wing. 'One of my students – an exceptionally perceptive young woman, Margaret Revolt – she used the most wonderful phrase in her final paper last term. "Anything that humanity does from here on out," she wrote, "is a wave at the band as we leave the dance floor." Brilliant,' he said and tore the wing into two pieces.

Under the table, Jack's hand crept back into my lap and found my hand.

'Josephine,' Raeburn said, 'you're not eating.'

I tried to pull my hand away. Jack wouldn't let go. 'I know. I'm sorry,' I said. 'I'm not feeling very well.'

My father stared pitilessly at me and said, 'Will starving yourself make you feel better?'

I didn't answer.

'Eat, girl,' he said.

The dismembered chicken leg lay, lifeless and greasy, on my plate. I picked it up and began to eat.

After dinner Raeburn sent Jack to put gas in his Buick and went to bed early with a bottle of brandy and a hand-rolled cigarette. I stayed downstairs to clean the kitchen. I moved slowly; my stomach felt swollen and hot and I could still taste the grease from the fried chicken. I could still feel the squeak of the meat between my teeth.

Eventually all the dishes were dried and put back in the cupboard, the table and countertops were wiped down with a wet rag, and the garbage was bagged and placed outside on the back porch, where it would ripen in the heat overnight. By Monday night, when Raeburn had left, the kitchen would reek of rotting chicken parts. I tried not to think about it and crept upstairs to bed.

I hung my blouse and skirt carefully in the closet, where they wouldn't be wrinkled, and let my bra fall to the floor. Raeburn didn't care what our bedrooms looked like as long as the rest of the house was clean. One of Jack's T-shirts was balled up on the floor next to my bed and I put it on. I turned off my light and stretched out on my unmade bed, pulling the sheet over me so that I could feel the cool cotton against my legs.

My stomach moved inside my gut. I lay motionless and waited for it to decide what it wanted to do, either throw up or calm down or leap out of my body in one sick, throbbing piece. At some point I must have fallen asleep, because when Jack pulled back the sheet and put an icy bottle of beer against my bare leg, I woke with a start.

'Drink this,' he said. There was no moon outside and all I could see of him was the glimmer of starlight picking out his profile. 'You'll feel better.'

My stomach was still queasy. I shook my head.

'It's cold,' he said. 'Come on, Jo. Hair of the dog.'

'More like feather of the chicken,' I said, but I took the bottle from him anyway.

'Move over,' he said.

Carefully, I sat up against my wooden headboard, which was blissfully cool, and pulled my knees up to my chest. Jack stretched out with his head beside my ankles and his boots hanging off the edge of the bed. I took a tentative sip of the beer. When my stomach didn't immediately object, I took another.

Jack reached up, took my ankle in one of his hands, and moved his head into my lap. His hair was soft and clean and tangled and it smelled of the night air. He'd driven to the gas station with the car windows open.

After a while, he said, 'Three days left.'

'Two full days, one morning.'

I felt his head move in my lap as he tilted it back to look at me. 'I think you should make friends with that kid from the drugstore.'

I stared at him in surprise. 'A town kid?'

'The *pharmacist's* kid,' Jack said. 'Josie, do you have any idea what's behind the counter in the back of that store?'

'Allergy medicine and antibiotics?'

He squeezed my ankle. 'All I'm saying is, the pharmacist's kid might not be such a bad person to have on our side. We should go back there.'

'How about the next time we're out of aspirin?'

'Sooner than that. This week, maybe.' I felt his head move

again and he said, 'And maybe you, my sister, could try your hand at flirting.'

'You must be joking,' I said.

'Why?'

'I can't flirt with him. I don't know how.'

He grinned and said, 'Sure you do.'

'Jack,' I said. 'The only boy I've ever talked to is you.'

'O ye of little faith. Don't worry, it'll come naturally. Besides, I've talked to town kids. I promise you that either one of us is smarter than that kid's entire family put together. You can talk circles around him, Josie my love.'

'Talking and flirting are not the same.' And I can't do either, not with a town kid, I almost said. But instead I concentrated on my hands working in his hair, unknotting it.

'For you, they will be,' he said. 'You had him the moment he saw you.'

But first there was the weekend to get through.

Jack and I sat with Raeburn in his study, a dark, book-lined room with one small dirty window and a stale, claustrophobic smell. A sepia-toned globe lay pinioned in its wooden rack before us like a giant egg waiting to hatch. Long outdated, it had originally belonged to my grandfather; ostensibly we were studying geography, but the point had long since been lost, which was the way Raeburn's lessons usually ended up. It's a wonder either of us ever learned to think coherently.

My brother, bored, slouched next to me on the couch, digging at the engine grease under his nails with the point of a compass. I was staring out the open window. It was raining outside and the air coming through it was moist and warm and clean-smelling.

'There is history here,' Raeburn said. 'Rhodesia. Persia. The

Ottoman Empire. All false constructs, created by the human urge to carve, to parcel, to own. Even our United States is a construct – and a recent one at that.' He gave the globe a desultory spin. 'All of the creations of man are ephemeral. They'd pass away in their own time even if we didn't do our best to destroy them.'

His dry, droning voice choked the room like a noxious cigar. I thought drowsily about wet leaves: not old, mouldering leaves like the ones that rotted beneath our porch, but fresh, supple, green leaves, washed and shining with rain.

'Fascinating,' Jack said.

Raeburn took off his glasses and stared at us, his watery eyes narrow and annoyed. 'The point,' he said, 'is that you may as well learn the capitals for a country that no longer exists as for one that does. Does it matter to the peasant whether he lives in Persia or Iran? Does the government that rules the city help him find food in the country?'

Jack made a noise of disgust and resumed cleaning his fingernails. Raeburn's lips went thin and tense.

'I want you to learn these things – all things – so that when you go out into the world, you aren't at its mercy,' he said. 'So that you will be armed with information, and able to defend yourselves.' The narrow line of his mouth grew tighter as he watched Jack dig under his thumbnail with the compass.

'Put that damn thing down,' he burst out finally and knocked the compass out of Jack's hands. It hit the dingy wooden floor with a clatter. I jumped. A drop of blood, rich and dark, welled up from Jack's thumbnail.

Jack wiped the blood onto his white shirt, leaving a rusty smear. 'How much use do you think your peasant would have for all of this information you're arming us with?'

'And you'd rather have what?' Raeburn said. 'A cigarette?'

'Maybe a good heavy rock,' Jack said. He reached down and picked up the compass again. 'Or a gun.'

Raeburn sighed and rubbed his forehead. 'Try to understand. There is a greater philosophical issue at work.' My father, I knew from old photographs, had once been as good-looking as my brother. Sometimes I could see Jack's face in his, particularly when he was scornful or annoyed. He looked very like Jack now.

For a moment the three of us sat in silence.

Then Raeburn said, 'Fuck this. I'm tired of wasting my time. I'm tired of you. Get out of my study. Go away.'

He didn't have to ask us twice. As soon as we were both standing in the hallway on the other side of the closed door, the soft voice of the radio announcer began to speak behind it. One of my most enduring memories of my years on the Hill is the calm, tuneless drone of news radio.

There were two miles of forest between our house and our nearest neighbours. When we were younger, when Jack was eleven or so and I was around nine, we spent most of our time playing in that span of woods. We climbed trees, we built forts, but mostly we played a game called Run. Jack made it up. The theory was simple: I ran. Jack, in my memory all knees and angular elbows, chased me. We did try it the other way around once, but I lost heart too quickly.

But Jack could, and would, chase for hours. The game ended when he caught me, which was usually when I was too tired to run any more; and then we would retrace our steps back to the house. As we walked, he'd say, 'You could have hidden under this branch, in the hollow here. Or, look, if there were leaves on that tree I wouldn't be able to see you from the ground. How would you get up there? See, you could climb this little tree, and then jump over on that branch, and then—'

Now, after all these years, I still couldn't walk in the forest without looking for hiding places. The rain stopped just after we left the house, and the forest was beautiful, all grey-green and sparkling with raindrops. So when Jack said, 'What do you think,' I had absolutely no idea what he was talking about.

'What do I think about what?' I said, and he scowled and said, 'You haven't heard a damn thing I've said for the last five minutes, have you?'

'Sorry. I was daydreaming.' My toe caught a hidden rock and I stumbled.

'You're still daydreaming. Watch where you're going, will you? I'm not carrying you back to the house if you break an ankle.'

'I'm not going to break anything,' I said, but I watched my feet more carefully.

Soon Jack veered off to the left, straight through the undergrowth. I followed him as best I could. It was hard to see the ground through the thick weeds. After a few minutes of hiking through the rough, we found ourselves standing on a narrow path beaten through the brush, choked off by the high bushes growing on either side of it. It was the only path to the pond. Nobody else knew it was there. We were sure of that, because we'd made it.

Jack walked in front of me. Watching the way his shoulders moved beneath his T-shirt, I stumbled again.

'Okay?' he said without turning around.

'Yes. Jack?'

'What?'

'I don't see why we need that drugstore kid.'

Jack pushed his way through the undergrowth, held a branch

aside so that I could pass, and then we were at the pond.

What we called the pond was deep enough for Jack to jump into the deepest part of it without hurting himself, but too small for us to get any kind of a race going from one side to the other. The soft mud on the bottom rose steeply to the shore on either side, so all that the pond was really good for was crouching in. On hot days, that was enough. But the mosquitoes could be awful.

Now, though, the sun was bright and warm. The mosquitoes had retreated to the still, shady places in the shadows of the trees, and the air had a fresh, damp feel to it. There were rocks on one side of the pond, where the spring was, and they caught the sunlight in the late afternoon. Jack took off his T-shirt. There was enough room on the flattest part of the biggest rock for the two of us to sprawl out, side by side.

Jack flicked an ant away and said, 'It could be useful to have a reliable source for real drugs. Think about it. When was the last time you saw a doctor? I haven't seen one since I came to live here, and I don't think you have either. One of us could get sick. But that kid could get us antibiotics, painkillers – hell, birth control pills, even,' he said.

I rolled onto my stomach and pulled my T-shirt up so that the warm sun hit my back. I turned my face away from him, towards the pond. The sun was beginning to turn the warm gold of late afternoon, and the shadows of the trees were long across the surface of the water.

'Admit it,' I said. 'You want a new way to get high. All of this antibiotic, birth control stuff is a cover. You want the good stuff.'

I heard Jack move behind me. There was a small splash, like a fish jumping, and then I felt him move my T-shirt higher on my back, pulling it up so that my shoulder blades were exposed. His hands were cool and wet with pond water. Slowly, he began to rub my back. I closed my eyes.

He dribbled water down my bare legs and said, 'Consider this. Friday afternoon. Raeburn comes home in a foul mood, as usual – snarling and sniping at us, telling us how stupid and worthless we are, ranting and raving and throwing things – and there, in the middle of it all, there's you and me, Jack and Josie. We dropped a couple of Valium a few hours back and we're feeling no pain. We couldn't care less.'

'And then he throws a plate at me and I'm too doped to duck,' I said. 'Sounds great.'

'I'll catch it before it hits you. Throw it back at him.'

I turned over. The sun was behind him.

'We could drug his coffee,' I said. 'Then he'd leave us alone.'

'That's my girl,' Jack said and touched my face with his cool, wet hands.

The morning Jack came back, when the social worker was gone and the three of us were standing silently on the porch staring at one another, Jack gazed up at Raeburn and said, calmly, 'Mary says you're a crazy son of a bitch.'

Jack was obviously repeating something he'd heard from Mary. Even so, Raeburn flinched. But his voice was as calm as Jack's when he answered, 'Your mother was an ungrateful, degenerate slut.'

Young Jack gave him a belligerent look. 'You better not be crazy with us,' he said. My six-year-old heart thrilled at being included. Raeburn told us to go away and I remember looking back at him as we left the porch. His eyes were tightly closed and he was rubbing his forehead as if it was hurting him. His hair was thick and dark back then, and he didn't yet wear glasses. He couldn't have been more than forty.

It made perfect sense to me then that my mother had taken Jack and left me behind. Jack was incredibly angry, even then, but he was also smart and funny and beautiful, in a savage, hard-edged way. I wasn't any of those things, but Raeburn hadn't abandoned me; he had kept me and fed me and taught me multiplication tables and ancient Greek, and if everything he'd done for me had taken more time and determination than love, all the facts seemed to suggest that I really ought to be grateful for what little I'd gotten.

As I grew older, I abandoned this theory. By the time I was sixteen, I knew that even though it was our mother that we called Crazy Mary, both of our parents were mad. My brother Jack was the first person ever to treat me with love or gentleness. He became my world.

By the time we headed back, the sun was starting to set and it was already too late for us to make it home for dinner. Raeburn didn't like waiting. After we'd battled our way through the undergrowth, though, Jack said, 'Wait,' and stopped.

'We should go,' I said. 'We're late already.'

'Smell that?' Jack said.

I did. 'Something's burning.'

'It's a barbecue,' Jack said. 'Come on.'

He turned in another direction, away from our house. We crashed through another patch of brush and found ourselves standing on another path; not as clear as the one we'd made to the pond, this was more of a track. We followed it for several hundred feet and then Jack turned to me and said in a low voice, 'Quiet.'

'Where are we going?'

'Show you something,' he said and set off down the track

again, moving more quietly this time. I followed him and tried to do the same.

Suddenly I stopped, alarmed.

'I hear voices,' I whispered to him.

He motioned to me to shut up.

A few more feet down the track, there was a huge copse of spruce like the one that surrounded our house. Jack crouched down and led me between the bushes into a kind of natural den. There was a hole that we could see through in the branches ahead of us. On the other side of the hole was a big house, like ours; but unlike ours, this one was cheerful and well tended. There was even a swimming pool a bit farther down the slope, a blue plastic ring that sat on top of the grass like a discarded toy. A low net stretched across part of the lawn, and two children in bathing suits stood on either side of it, playing badminton with small, brightly coloured rackets.

'I won, I won!' cried the girl, who was bigger.

'Didn't,' the boy said. 'I was sneezing. Do-over.'

'Baby,' the big girl said. She picked up the birdie, which looked like a dead parakeet, and hurled it into the air. A neat swipe with her racket sent it over towards the boy, who hit it this time.

On a wide wooden deck behind them, there was a man standing near an outdoor barbecue. A woman pushed the door open with her backside and came out of the house, carrying a plate. As she set it down next to the grill, the man said something to her, and she laughed.

I reached for Jack's hand.

Suddenly the little boy shrieked. He was holding one hand to his eye; the birdie lay at his feet.

'She hit me!' he wailed. 'She hit me with the birdie!'

'Not on purpose!' the girl said indignantly.

'Let it go, and come eat,' the woman said.

The girl tossed her hair and followed the boy up the steps to the deck. The woman pried the boy's hands away from his eye, looked, and hugged him. Soon they were all seated around a wooden table on the deck, with plates of food in front of them. In the deepening twilight, we could still hear the sounds of their voices drifting across the darkening lawn.

Jack let go of my hand and pointed back to the trail. My legs were cramped from crouching so long, and raw from the rough rock at the pond, but I made it out to the track, and then back through the brush to the main path. Jack walked behind me.

Raeburn was sitting on the front porch, smoking and listening to his portable radio. He barely glanced up when we came out of the woods. An announcer's voice was talking about politics: somebody had a meeting with somebody else, and they were going to sign something, and the voice didn't think they should.

'I've eaten,' Raeburn said curtly.

'Sorry we're late,' I said. It was the first thing either of us had said since leaving the hedge.

Jack pushed past me and went into the house.

Raeburn's eyes flicked up at me. 'I'm listening to this,' he said. 'Go clean the kitchen.'

I followed Jack inside and found him standing motionless in the doorway between the hall and the kitchen. I touched his back and said, 'What's wrong?' Then I looked over his shoulder and saw what he saw.

The floor was covered with food. The milk from the refrigerator, the flour and sugar and cocoa from the cupboard, the pasta and the rice from their jars on the counter: all of it mashed into a thick, gooey paste that covered the linoleum. The bread had been pulled out of its plastic bag, slice by slice, and ground into the mess underfoot. The condiments from the refrigerator door, the pickle relish and the mayonnaise and the mustard, had been thrown onto the floor in their jars. Shards of glass sparkled like diamonds in the muck. What couldn't be broken had been dumped. What couldn't be dumped had been broken.

Jack turned on his heel and pushed past me without a word. The expression on his face was dangerous. I let him go.

Slowly, I picked my way across the floor to the cupboard under the sink, where I found a dustpan and a rag. I used the rag to push the mess into the dustpan. There was an acrid chemical smell in the air, strong enough to make my eyes water, but I didn't identify it until I carried the first dustpan full of ruined food over to the garbage can and lifted the lid. There were three empty bottles of cleaning fluid lying on top of the garbage inside.

I sighed and found a pair of rubber gloves under the sink.

After a while, Jack came down and helped me. Cleaning the kitchen took us three hours, and the spoiled food filled two big garbage bags.

We were almost done when Raeburn appeared in the kitchen door, red-eyed, with a glass of whiskey in his hand. He stood and watched us for a few minutes.

'You're thinking now about the nature of my parental responsibility towards you,' he said finally. His words were slurred. 'But you'll soon realize that my parental responsibility is not the issue. Food is the issue. The parental responsibility construct is of no consequence.'

I didn't look up. Took a rag from the cupboard and began to wipe up the last smears of food on the floor.

'Doesn't matter whether we're in Persia or Iran,' Raeburn said. 'You're still going to bed hungry. Do you understand? Finally, do you understand?'

2

Everything in the kitchen had to be replaced, so Raeburn left us a hundred dollars on Monday. Jack made me ask him for it. 'He won't give it to me,' he said.

'He won't give it to me, either,' I said, but he did. I had to plead for it, though. We both knew he'd leave me the money in the end, but he wanted me to beg. When I gave the money to Jack, he counted it and stuffed it into his back pocket.

'And she says she doesn't know how to flirt,' he said.

I turned away.

The nearest place to eat was a bar that served takeout sandwiches during the day, fat overstuffed things with coleslaw and French fries right there between the slices of bread. We drove to the bar in the clothes we'd slept in and ordered four of them, three fried chicken and one fish, and devoured them in the truck. There was mayonnaise and grease-soaked paper everywhere. I ate one chicken sandwich and half of the fish; Jack ate the rest. They were disgusting. They were wonderful. When we were done, we went back up the Hill and took showers. I washed my hair and brushed it until it gleamed.

Then I put on a pair of shorts and a T-shirt, what I always wore during the summer. Jack took one look at me and marched me back into my bedroom, where he made me change into a different pair of shorts and a different T-shirt.

'What's the point?' I said.

'The point,' he said, 'is that the first time, you looked like you were wearing your brother's old clothes. Now you don't.'

'I like my brother's clothes.'

'I like you in my clothes, but take my word for it. No, don't plait your hair,' he said. 'Leave it down.'

'It's too hot,' I complained, but I did as he said.

This time, Jack made me go into the drugstore alone.

If I was lucky, I thought, it would be the boy's day off and I could just buy toothpaste and leave. But there he was, sitting at the counter with his hair in his eyes, looking bored. He was wearing a green cardigan sweater against the chill of the air conditioning, the kind that Raeburn sometimes wore in the fall.

As soon as he saw me he jumped to his feet.

'Toothpaste?' I said, managing to smile.

'Aisle six,' he said. 'One aisle down from the aspirin.'

He remembered us, then. The smile eased into my face a bit.

I walked to the aisle, chose a tube of toothpaste, and walked back. I could feel him again, watching me too closely. The scrutiny hadn't grown any easier to deal with. The muscles in my legs still didn't seem to remember which way to move.

As he rang up the toothpaste, the boy said, shyly, 'Your name is Jo?'

'Josie,' I said. 'Well, Josephine, but—' I shut my mouth fast, in case I was babbling. I kept my eyes wide and my hands away from my hair, and tried to pretend that nothing I said really mattered to him. It was like talking to Raeburn.

'Oh,' he said. 'I heard your brother call you Jo the last time you two were in here. I'm Kevin.'

We stood for a minute. The drugstore was so quiet that I could hear the hum of the fluorescent lights above me. I was waiting for him to talk; maybe he was waiting for me.

'Your brother drives a blue Ford,' he said. 'I see you two together a lot.'

'We are together a lot.'

'But you don't go to school.'

I shrugged.

'That must rock,' he said.

'I wouldn't know. I've never been to school.'

'Believe me, it rocks,' he said. 'School's a drag.'

'That bad?' I said.

'Yes,' he said. Now it was his turn to shrug. 'Or – I don't know. It's getting better, because I've got two free periods this fall, plus the jazz band. Other than that,' he shook his head, 'it pretty much sucks.'

I tried to look sympathetic, but I had no idea what he was talking about. 'How much time do you have left?'

'Two years.'

Behind him, through the store's front window, I could see Jack's golden head inside the truck, waiting for me. Waiting for me as I flirted with a high school boy, I thought, a little bewildered. Was I doing a good job? How was I supposed to know? It would be easier if there were a meter that you could look at, like the temperature gauge in the truck.

Then Kevin said, 'So what about you?'

'What about me?' I asked and smiled as if I'd said something witty.

Kevin smiled back and said, 'What do you like to do?' His throat moved as he swallowed hard. 'Do you like to go to the movies?'

'Sometimes,' I said, although I'd only been a few times. The smile on my face was beginning to feel strained. 'Not really.'

'Me neither,' he said, too quickly for me to believe him, and we stood in silence for another minute before he asked, 'Do you ice-skate? Because the rink is open year-round now.'

I was a good skater. Jack and I went every winter, as soon as the pond froze. The ice was always thin but we went anyway. The town rink, though – I'd seen the crowds outside the town rink on Friday nights. 'I'm not very good,' I told him.

'Neither am I,' Kevin said.

I was confused. 'So why did you ask?'

He shrugged and looked depressed. 'People do it,' he said. 'What about music?'

I finally figured out what he was trying to do, and thought: coffee, ice cream, a bottle of rum in the alley – anything, but ask me something I *know*. Then I heard the bell over the door jingle and Jack was there to save me.

'What's taking so long, Jo?' he asked, but his voice was friendly. He looked at Kevin. 'Hey.'

'Hey,' Kevin answered, and they introduced themselves. I stuck my hands in my pockets, fast, before anyone noticed that I'd been wringing them. Jack's grin was just enough, not too much. Someone who didn't know him would never have seen how intent and calculating his eyes were.

'We were talking about music,' I said.

'Oh, yeah?' Jack said easily. 'What kind?'

Kevin coughed and looked embarrassed. 'We hadn't gotten that far yet. But I'm into jazz, mostly, right now. The old stuff.'

'Like Coltrane?' Jack said.

'I don't know much about Coltrane.' Kevin looked as relieved as I felt to have something to talk about. 'But what I know, I like.'

Jack grinned. 'I just picked up *Blue Train* down at Eide's. Great stuff.'

'Eide's is awesome,' Kevin said. 'They've got everything down there.'

The rest cascaded into place; my brother was a master. Before Kevin could figure out right from left, he had accepted an invitation to come up to the Hill on the following Monday night to listen to Jack's new Coltrane album. All I had to do was stand there, smiling at Kevin and nodding enthusiastically when it seemed appropriate. I didn't know who Coltrane was, or what Eide's was, or what was going on, but Kevin's eyes kept drifting towards me and that despairing look was gone. By the time we'd said our farewells, he had begun to look hopeful, even excited.

I was surprised to find that Jack actually had the album they had talked about. He dug it out from under his bed when we got home. There was a black-and-white photograph of a dark-skinned man with a saxophone on the cover. The plastic sleeve had a price tag stuck to it that said 'Eide's'.

'What's Eide's?' I asked Jack.

'Big record store in Pittsburgh. It's where all the cool kids go to buy their vinyl.'

I stared at him. 'How do you know these things?'

Jack shrugged. He was looking at the back of the album cover. 'That ratty green sweater he was wearing, it had "dumb white jazz fan" written all over it.' He glanced up at me. 'White boy jazz fans tend to be heartbreakingly sensitive. Maybe he'll write you a love poem or two.'

I pointed to the album. 'But how do you know about Eide's? When were you in Pittsburgh buying records?'

'Not records,' he corrected. '*Vinyl*. When was I in Pittsburgh buying *vinyl*.'

'When?' I repeated. 'When was it?'

'Drove down there one day when I was supposed to be getting the truck tuned up.'

'You randomly drove down there,' I said, 'and happened to find the cool kid record store. Randomly.'

'I had that job there for a while. You remember. I told you about that.'

'That was in Pittsburgh?' I said, disconcerted.

He nodded.

I didn't know what to say. 'Well, what if the truck breaks down?'

He threw the album down on his bed and took a cigarette from the pack on his dresser. 'The truck is in better shape than Raeburn thinks.'

He lit the cigarette and pitched the match out the window into the still water and rotting leaves in the gutter. I studied my bare toes. There was dirt in the crevices around my toenails.

Finally Jack said, 'I can't take you everywhere,' and I said, 'I know.'

The next Monday, Kevin McNerny showed up at our doorstep at eight o'clock, as arranged. Standing on our porch, his face so hopeful, he looked alien and out of place. For an instant I panicked. I almost told him to turn around and go home. I almost told him to leave us alone. Letting him take even a single step into our house was unthinkable. This was our house; this was where we *lived*.

Then he told me that my dress looked nice.

'Thanks, it was my mother's,' I said and let him in.

The parlour was ours. Raeburn taught lessons there during the winter, when the light was a little better than in his study. Other than that he never used it. As I led Kevin in from the front hall, I could practically smell the curiosity coming off him in waves. And sure enough, even after the two of us were sitting on the dusty couch, he was still poking around the room with his eyes, inspecting and collecting everything that he saw. For a moment I let myself look through his eyes as if I didn't see the room every day of my life: the fraying, cloth-covered books in the bookcase, the dingy floral wallpaper, the shelves full of odd things that we'd brought from elsewhere in the house. But then I thought, let him look. We've got nothing to be ashamed of.

When he finally looked back at me, he blushed and looked embarrassed. 'I've never been in one of these old houses before,' he said. 'My mom went on that historic homes thing last spring when my aunt was visiting, but I didn't go. Do they all look like this?'

'This is the only one I've ever been in,' I said.

'Are you on the tour?'

'We're not really an open-to-the-public kind of family.'

'No, I guess you're not.' He smiled. He had a nice smile, with straight white teeth. Some of my hostility melted away. 'Well, I bet that none of those houses have as much cool stuff in them as yours does, anyway. Where did it all come from?' He stood up and walked over to the bookcase and took down a tarantula the size of my head, sealed in glass and framed in wood.

'My grandfather, mostly. That spider is older than both of us put together.'

'Wow.' Kevin sounded awed. 'Was he a collector?'

'Sort of. He was a trader – he sold curios and things – and we ended up with some of the leftovers. I don't really know anything else about him.'

'He was a smuggler,' Jack said from the doorway, three bottles of beer dangling by their necks from one hand. 'Used to ferry whiskey down from Canada during Prohibition. After that, I think he switched to art and artefacts.' He crossed the room and handed a beer to Kevin, who seemed delighted to get it.

'That's awesome,' Kevin said.

'Is it true?' I asked Jack.

'Nearly as I can figure. You like our house, Kevin?'

'It's great. Looks like it should be haunted. Is it?'

'Only by us,' I said, and we all laughed.

We were good that night. My job, Jack had told me before Kevin arrived, was to make the boy fall in love with me. By the time Kevin left, I think he was a little in love with both of us.

'It's great that you guys get along so well,' he said, a little drunkenly, as I walked him out to his father's car. 'But I guess you sort of have to, don't you?'

'He's my brother.'

'Yeah, but you should see me and my little sister.' He shook his head. 'That kid drives me nuts. If we had to spend more than fifteen minutes a day together, neither of us would survive.'

'I think it's different with us,' I said, and he said, 'I think it is, too.'

When he was gone, Jack and I sat together in the parlour and finished the beer. He was sitting in the old horsehair armchair, next to the fire; I was stretched out on the sofa.

'Say whatever you want about little Kevin McMonkey,' he said. 'At least it's something different, right?'

'He's nice.'

Jack rolled his eyes. 'So are puppies.'

Kevin came up again the next night and half-scolded us for letting him drive home drunk. Jack said, 'All right, then. I promise not to get you drunk,' and disappeared upstairs.

I said, 'I'm glad you came over.'

Kevin blushed.

In a few minutes, Jack was back with the cigar box where we kept our pot.

'Jesus,' Kevin said. 'You two have any other tricks up your sleeve?'

'This cashes me out,' Jack said, grinning, as he started to crumble the dried leaf between his fingers, 'but I think Josie might have one or two surprises left in her.'

'Ignore my brother,' I said. 'He's a garden-variety madman.'

'My sister, of course, is a rare and precious blossom,' Jack said, looking me in the eye as he deftly rolled a joint thicker than a pencil. When he was done, he passed it to Kevin. 'Guests first. I think this is half oregano, but it'll have to do until we can find something better.'

'No complaints here,' Kevin said, and didn't cough on his first drag, which surprised me. After a few minutes he said, 'This is good. Where did you get this?'

'I know a guy,' Jack said.

A million years later, the night rubbed smooth and silky by the pot, I was sitting on the rug in front of the fireplace in the parlour. It wasn't anywhere near cold enough but we'd built a fire anyway, and we were lucky we hadn't set ourselves ablaze doing it, stoned as we were. My legs were stretched out in front of me where the firelight could bathe them in a warm, flattering glow. I had good legs, I thought, admiring the way the shadows flickered in the hollows at the sides of my knees.

My gaze drifted up and landed on Jack. He was staring at my legs, too. He caught my gaze, smiled, looked away.

Kevin sat near me in a battered green leather armchair. It was the chair Raeburn always chose, and there was a painting of a naked woman with blue skin hung on the wall directly opposite it. Kevin gazed thoughtfully at the painting for a few heartbeats as he sucked on our second joint and exhaled.

'What the hell is that?' he said, nodding at the painting.

'It's Art.' That was how I thought of it, with a capital letter. 'Raeburn's father bought it in Spain.'

'Spain?' Kevin blinked and passed the joint to me.

'Spain, Portugal, Brazil. I forget which. Ugly, isn't it?'

Jack spoke up: 'I think the guy who painted that was doing a lot harder stuff than this,' he said, and we laughed for a long time and the subject drifted away.

Suddenly Jack was gone and Kevin was sitting next to me on the hearthrug and if I hadn't been so stoned it might have been awkward. Then he kissed me. The fire had burned down to embers, and as Kevin touched my breasts through the thin cotton of my dress – delicately, as if he was afraid they might bruise – he told me that he was crazy about me and I kissed him and it seemed so good, so innocent. We lay together in front of the fire for a while, and at some point Jack came back; he and Kevin talked but their voices were too low for me to hear clearly and I don't remember when Kevin left. When I opened my eyes again, it was Jack who was sitting next to me, smoking a cigarette and staring into the fire.

'I kissed him,' I said, because I felt I had to.

'You were supposed to,' my brother said.

That week was registration week at the college where Raeburn taught, and every fresh-scrubbed new face was another reason for him to long for the end of the world. The first thing that he told every incoming class was that they knew nothing. He knew everything. All questions were pointless.

'It's ludicrous,' he said, hunched over my algebra book on Saturday afternoon. We were alone in the study; the night before, Raeburn had kicked a hole in one of the porch steps, and Jack was outside fixing it. 'They stand there in front of me with their sincere, thoughtful little questions and their sincere, thoughtful little ideas. As if an eighteen-year-old girl who'd never been out of the Allegheny Valley could possibly have *ideas*.' He pushed his glasses up his nose, gestured angrily at me and said, 'Look at you. You don't have *ideas*. At least you're smart enough to know it.'

There wasn't much I could say to that.

'At least you understand your limitations.' He shook his head. 'Forget it. Back to work. Factors of polynomial equations.' He tapped a pencil against the book in front of me.

'I understand the answer once I see it,' I said. 'I just don't understand how to get there.'

Raeburn's pencil kept tapping, tapping against the open pages of the book, faster and faster.

'Your generation gives up too easily,' he said. 'When I was eighteen, if someone had offered to challenge my brain, to *expand* it, I would have been grateful. Grateful! Even that mother of yours knew enough to appreciate the chance she was being given. Now when I tell these students about my class, all I see in their eyes is fear. Fear and laziness. And then they scuttle off down the hall to study physics for goddamned poets with Ben Searles.'

He jumped to his feet and began pacing restlessly. 'They should be afraid. Knowledge is an awesome force. They should absolutely be afraid. But that fear should urge them to conquer, not retreat.'

His huge feet thumped against the rug, one after the other, back and forth, back and forth. Outside, Jack began hammering a nail into the porch step, slightly out of sync with Raeburn's stride.

I knew Ben Searles. Jack and I had met him at one of the faculty functions that we occasionally attended with our father, the brilliant physicist with the two beautiful, well-mannered children. Searles, who was young and good-looking and immensely popular, had been teaching at the school for about five years. Raeburn had hated him from the start.

'It doesn't make sense,' I said, trying to bring him back to the algebra. 'There's no process. It all seems like guesswork.'

'You're scared, girl. You're so paralysed with fear that you can't even make a simple deductive leap without a *process* to guide you.' Raeburn stopped pacing and turned to stare at me. His eyes were sharp, interested. 'Josephine,' he said. 'Let's examine a hypothetical. Let's say that you're given a choice: study with me here at home, or go to the idiot factory and be spoon-fed theory like puréed vegetables. What do you choose?'

'You,' I said.

Raeburn shook his head. He stood over me at the table, his hands outspread on its surface; his shoulders, his chin, his eyebrows, every point of his body fixed on me.

'No, you wouldn't go,' he said. 'You'd never dare to put yourself at the mercy of the outside world.' A slow, bitter smile twisted his mouth. 'But let's say you were normal. Let's say you were a normal girl with a normal upbringing. Dollhouses, ballet lessons, a mommy who bakes cookies, and the kind of older brother who takes you out into the backyard to teach you how not to throw like a girl. Cheerleading, prom queen, the entire kit and caboodle of the American dream: never an unhappy day in your life and never an original thought in your skull. And you head off to college, expecting the world on a platter and Most

Popular Girl all over again, and instead you find yourself confronted by me.' He leaned in close. His face was inches from mine. I could smell the burned tobacco on his breath and see the unshaven stubble on his face. 'What do you do?'

The hammering outside stopped and the room was suddenly very quiet. I had to look away from him, back down to the maths book. I was unaccustomed to my father's direct attention. 'I don't know,' I said. 'I've never been that way.'

Raeburn's eyes narrowed. Then he threw his head back and laughed, a giant uproarious sound that broke the tenuous stillness of the afternoon. He looked familiar when he did that; he looked like Jack.

'Thank God for that,' Raeburn said. He pulled out the chair next to me and sat down again. 'Because if you were, the instant you were confronted with anything the least bit challenging you'd run right down the hall to that pernicious fungus Searles, Mr Rock 'n' Roll Physicist, to have your brain stuffed full of more strained peas. A waste of time and a waste of money.' He leaned back and smiled, and I had to look away again. It was unpleasant when Raeburn smiled. 'You wouldn't learn a thing, but it would have a good beat, and you could dance to it.' He tapped the book in front of me again. 'Let's talk about polynomials. Think, Josephine.'

I picked up my pencil again and he put his hand on mine.

'It's easier to spot the checkmate when you're not one of the players, Josephine,' Raeburn said. 'I don't think you know how lucky you are.'

Outside, Jack started hammering again. Between thuds I could hear him whistling a tune from the Coltrane album. My pencil went to work. The part of my mind that had no interest in factoring equations went far away.

* * *

Later that week, when Raeburn was gone, Jack and I discovered the roof.

Finding anything new was special. We'd lived in that house all our lives – well, I had – and sometimes I felt that I could close my eyes and describe in sharp detail the contents of every cluttered shelf and every overstuffed closet. All the rooms that we didn't use were filled with sealed cardboard boxes. Some of the boxes were packed with yellowing tax records and phone bills, pointless details that had been saved for no reason that I could see, but some of them held things that I thought were amazing. Cheap jewellery. Engraved cigarette lighters. Hairbrushes with blond hair twined among the bristles. Mary's stuff. When she left, Raeburn must have thrown anything of hers he found into the closest box, and then put the box away where he wouldn't have to look at it. The afternoon we found the roof, we also found a shoebox, tucked carelessly on top of a pile of empty suitcases in a third-floor bedroom closet, that held nothing but a crumpled piece of tissue paper and a package of guitar strings. Jack said the strings had been Mary's.

'She played the guitar?' I asked.

'Sometimes.' Jack tossed the strings back into a corner of the closet. 'I don't remember.'

It was a few minutes later in that same room that Jack moved a big cardboard box from the top of a stack of other boxes and we found ourselves looking out of a dormer window that we hadn't ever noticed from the ground. Jack stuck his head out, craned his neck around to see the rest of the roof, and said, 'Let's go exploring.'

I followed him out the window and onto the steep shingled slope. We crabwalked across the slope, moving parallel to the edge of the roof, until we came to another slope that ran at a right angle to the one we were crawling on. We climbed over the top and down the other side, and discovered a gentle slope that overlooked the elm trees in the front yard.

We went there every night that week. I loved lying on the roof and watching the stars, but I hated getting there. If not for Jack climbing ahead of me and leading me over the roof, I never would have dared.

At night, on the roof, the elm trees were silver with starlight and there was a breeze that was so cool and fresh and steady that I said it felt like it came straight from the stars. Jack said being on the roof made him feel less like he lived at the bottom of a hole. I said that what I really liked was the feeling that I was exposed and hidden at the same time.

'It's like another world,' I said.

'You're awfully dreamy tonight for a kid who never read a fairy tale,' Jack said and lit a cigarette. 'What are you, in love?'

'Please.' I took the cigarette from him.

We lay together for a long time without speaking, watching our cigarette smoke climb into the air. I thought about fairy tales: what Jack had said wasn't true. He'd told me some when we were children. Like 'Rapunzel', with the prince whose eyes are scratched out by thorns after the witch catches him in the tower. He wanders blind in the desert until finally he finds Rapunzel, and her salty tears wash the blood out of his eyes and his sight is restored. I always remembered that one: probably because of her long golden hair, and the way that Jack liked to pull on my plait when he told it.

Eventually, still watching the sky, I asked Jack if he thought we were lucky.

'Depends what you mean by lucky,' he said.

'Lucky. Possessed of luck. Fortunate in the hand that life has dealt us.'

He exhaled a long column of smoke the same colour as the clouds. 'Does it matter?'

'I've been wondering. Trying to figure it out. It's hard because I can't think of anything that's all good or all bad, you know?' A cool breath of air blew across me. It was a humid night, even though it wasn't hot any more, and the breeze felt good. I closed my eyes. 'Do you think anything is either all good or all bad?'

'What about Kevin McNerny?'

I laughed. 'Christ. He's neither.'

'You like him. So doesn't that make him good?'

I shrugged.

'He stares,' I finally said. 'I don't know what he wants from me.'

'I do.'

I thought about this. 'No. If it was only that – I could deal with that. But there's more to it. That's the thing.' The cigarette was back in my hand now, but it had burned down almost to the filter. I sat up, pitched the butt over the side of the house, and watched the orange spark arc towards the ground. 'Everything is like that. Raeburn's a lunatic, but he's gone four days out of seven and we can do anything we want. I hate doing algebra, but I'd hate school more, I think. And when Crazy Mary left—'

I stopped.

'Go on,' Jack said. His voice was completely neutral and I knew I was treading on dangerous ground.

I tried to choose my words carefully. 'If she hadn't taken you away from us, everything would be different. If you'd never lived in Chicago and I'd had a mother, we'd both be completely different people. Raeburn might be a different person. We might not even live here still. Or if she'd left later, or taken both of us, or left both of us behind. I remember when her leaving seemed like the unluckiest thing that had ever happened to me. But maybe it wasn't, because if she hadn't, I wouldn't be me.'

Jack was very still beside me.

'Do you have another cigarette?' I asked him, just to say something.

'You think it's lucky that she left?' he said.

'Maybe. Because you had a completely different life than I did. And then you came back, and now you're here. And that was lucky. For me, at least,' I added.

'You think it was lucky that I came back here?'

'Of course.'

'I came back here because she died,' he said. 'You think that was lucky?'

I rubbed my palms against the rough surface of the roof. 'If she had to take you with her when she left, it's lucky that you came back.'

'That's not an answer.'

I stared at my toes, pale and blue and indistinct against the dark shingles.

Finally I said, 'It was lucky for me. It was the luckiest thing that ever happened to me.'

I didn't look at him. I didn't want to see the expression on his face. The night was very quiet. In the distance, on the highway that led to town, a pair of headlights moved slowly and I thought, those people are different from us, those people don't know we exist.

'I don't see any fireflies tonight,' I said after a while. 'They must be gone for the year.'

'When I was a kid,' Jack said, 'when I was bad, you know what Crazy Mary would say to me? She'd ask me if I wanted to go live with my sister. "I'll send you back there," she'd say. "I didn't have to bring you with me." And I always shaped up right away. The way she said it was like it was the worst thing in the world. Living with my sister.'

I tried to remember her. All I could come up with was a face-less mannequin, like the ones in the department store window downtown, wearing the few scraps she'd left behind: the blue dress I wore when Kevin came up, a pair of pearl earrings, a scarf. The mannequin's wig would be blond, because the hair in the hairbrush was blond, and because Jack and I were both blond and Raeburn's hair had been dark before he went grey. But the face was a void.

I added the guitar to the picture, sitting in a case at her feet. When I lay back again, the warm crook of Jack's arm was there to catch me.

The next night, Jack asked Kevin about the drugs, point-blank.

'Well,' Kevin said and looked thoughtful. We were sitting on the front porch, watching the stars move above the elm trees and drinking a bottle of rum. Kevin and I were on the old porch swing, and Jack was perched on the railing. I'd stretched my legs across Kevin's lap. His head was turned towards Jack, but his eyes kept drifting back to me. His expression was perpetually amazed, as if he didn't quite believe in me.

'Well,' he said again and took a swig from the bottle. 'The good stuff's all locked away in my dad's office. All the stuff on the shelves, it's like, laxatives and zit pills and stuff.'

'Allergy drugs and antibiotics,' I said.

'That doesn't make much sense,' Jack said. 'What if some housewife forgets to refill her Valium prescription and your dad's sitting at home having dinner?'

Kevin shook his head. 'There's another pharmacist who comes in at night. I don't have anything to do with the prescriptions, except handing them across the counter sometimes. Seriously, he'd kill me if he caught me messing with the drugs. The government makes him count everything.'

'Well, I wouldn't want to get you in trouble or anything.' Jack sounded genial enough, but there was an edge underneath the friendliness, like a knife blade wrapped in velvet.

'I think it would be more hassle than it's worth,' Kevin said. 'I mean, you guys don't seem to have any trouble getting pot. If you want something else, can't you get it from whoever you go to?'

'Who *do* you go to for pot, Jack?' I asked.

'My sources are somewhat limited in that area,' Jack said, ignoring me. 'Highly unsatisfactory. Look, just think about it. That's all I'm saying.'

'I'll think about it,' Kevin said, 'but things are what they are, man.'

Jack nodded as if he'd already stopped caring. A few minutes later he asked me to come into the kitchen with him, to help him look for the other lighter. When we were alone, he opened a bottle of whiskey and poured himself a shot. He didn't look at me.

'Get him to change his mind,' he said in a low voice.

'You heard what he said. Things are what they are.'

Jack turned on me. 'What the fuck are you, some sort of Greek chorus? Make things change.'

He grabbed the bottle and went upstairs. Leaving me alone.

For a moment I stood there, waiting until I felt that I could muster a pleasant expression. Then I went back out onto the porch. Kevin was still sitting on the porch swing; as I sat down next to him, I heard Jack's window slide open high above us, and music started to play, faintly.

Kevin was quiet for a moment. Then he said, 'That isn't jazz.'

'What?'

'The music. I thought Jack was a jazz fan.'

I listened. It was Wagner. Jack liked Wagner.

'Just because a person likes one kind of music,' I said, 'that doesn't mean they don't like another.'

Kevin shrugged. 'I guess so. My God, you're beautiful in moonlight,' he said.

'You mean in the dark?'

'You know what I mean,' Kevin said and kissed me. When he kissed me, I felt like I was letting a thirsty man drink me. He told me that he'd been dating a girl named Kathy before he met me. He hadn't seen her since the first night he'd come to the Hill. So he had options, even; but he still wanted *me*.

He made me feel like an active participant in the life lived by the rest of the world, and I liked kissing him. All the same, there were snatches of music from Jack's room drifting through the cooling night air and I couldn't help but picture him sitting alone on his bed, smoking and taking long pulls from his bottle with his eyes closed and the music thrumming and soaring around him, while downstairs Kevin slid an awkward hand underneath my clothes to touch my breast.

'Stop,' I said, pulling away. I crossed my arms.

Kevin looked confused and terribly young. His hair was beginning to clump with sweat and his collar was askew. 'What's the matter?'

'I can't do this.'

His face grew cautious. 'Why not?'

'I just can't.'

We sat in silence for an impossibly long time.

Finally Kevin said, 'Josie, I really like you.'

'I said no.'

'Jesus, Josie. I said I liked you, that's all.'

'Sure it is.'

He let out a long, controlled breath. 'Give me a break, Josie. I said I liked you and that was what I meant. That was *all* that I meant.'

'You don't like me,' I said. 'You don't know me. You only met me two weeks ago.'

'So what? How long does it take to know you like someone?'

'I'm not even sure you do like me. You might like the package, but you don't like me.'

Kevin shook his head wearily. 'I'm sorry, Josie, but I don't have any idea what you're talking about.'

'You like us,' I said, gesturing around me. 'You like the way we live. But you don't have to actually live the way we live, do you? You drop in and have some fun and leave, and we're the ones who have to clean up afterwards.' I pushed my hair – it was as sweaty as Kevin's – back out of my face. 'It doesn't have anything to do with us.'

Kevin stared out into the trees. His face was blank and unhappy. His father's station wagon was parked out there. I wondered if he was thinking that he should get in it and drive away.

'I'm right,' I said. 'I know I am.'

'Yes and no,' he said.

'Yes and no.' I heard the chill in my own voice and stood up to leave. Forget the drugs, I thought. Jack will get over it.

But Kevin grabbed my hands and pulled me back down onto the porch swing.

'Josie. Yes,' he said, 'you're right. I didn't grow up here. I don't have to live here all the time. But I wish I did.' There was envy in his voice. 'You have no idea the bullshit you don't have to put up with here. Yeah, maybe your old man's a son of a bitch. But so is mine. So are a lot of people's. You only get yours three days a week and the rest of the time you can do whatever you want. It's like *Pippi Longstocking* or something.'

I stared blankly at him.

'The kids' book,' he said.

'When I was a kid I read Euclid. In Greek.'

'There you go.' He sounded angry. 'You think my parents would sit down and talk to me long enough to teach me Greek? Hell, no. I don't know *anyone* who has parents who would do that, except you.'

The summer that Raeburn decided that I needed to read Euclid in the original, I spent eight hours a day, seven days a week, at the kitchen table, doing nothing but Greek: Greek sentences, Greek flash cards, Greek grammar. I didn't go outside. I didn't take naps. I took ten minutes for lunch and two bathroom breaks. That was how I learned Greek. I was six at the time.

'You have no idea what you're talking about,' I told Kevin.

'Neither do you,' he said. 'Yes, I like hanging out here. But you know what else? This is all we ever do. Most couples go to movies. Most couples do things. Most couples see people. We sit in your living room and drink beer with your brother. I mean, I like him and all, don't get me wrong, but' – his grip on my hands softened – 'you're the coolest girl I've ever met. If you'd lived next door to me my entire life, I'd still be crazy about you. Do you think I'd put up with this if I wasn't?'

I didn't say anything.

'If you weren't here, I wouldn't be here, either,' he said. His voice was quiet. 'It's all you.'

We stared at each other for a minute. The light from the parlour window was reflected on his glasses, so I couldn't see his eyes.

Upstairs, the music stopped.

On the porch, in the dim light from the windows, Kevin brought my hand up to his mouth and kissed it. Then he pulled on my arm, gently, so that I had to move towards him, and he kissed my mouth.

'You have the most beautiful hair,' he said.

In a matter of minutes we were back where we'd started, as if the whole tortured discussion had never happened. He took my hand and put it on his penis, hard inside his army pants. I moved my hand and his breath caught.

When the front door opened, he was as close as the rickety porch swing would let him get to lying on top of me, one hand fumbling inside my jeans and the other deeply twined in my hair. I saw Jack's shadow, cast in a square of yellow light on the ground, out of the corner of my eye. Kevin panicked and jerked away from me, but somehow his hand tangled itself in my hair and pulled. It hurt. I was startled. I shrieked.

Jack moved so fast I barely saw him. He was just a silhouette, standing motionless in the doorway, and then he had Kevin by the shirt and bent backward over the porch railing.

'Jack,' I said, and Jack hissed, 'Did you hurt her? Did you hurt my sister, you scrawny high school *fuck*?'

'It was an accident!' Kevin cried. He was babbling. 'I swear, man! I didn't mean it!'

'Jack,' I said again, louder. My scalp was throbbing a little, but the shriek had been more surprise than pain. 'Let him go. I'm fine. I'm *fine*.'

Jack looked at me for a long moment. His hands were still holding double fistfuls of Kevin's shirt. Kevin's face was frozen in a mixture of embarrassment and fear. I was afraid he might cry.

Then Jack let him go.

To Kevin's credit, he didn't run, although he looked like he wanted to. His face was pale and his glasses had been knocked crooked. As he straightened his shirt, he said, 'I didn't mean to hurt her. You startled me, that's all.' His voice was trembling.

But Jack wasn't even looking at Kevin. He was looking at me.

'Go home,' he said.

'Yeah, okay,' Kevin said, and then, 'I'm sorry, man.' He stepped down off the porch, his black T-shirt quickly disappearing as he walked towards his father's car, parked among the dark trees. The station wagon's engine roared to life, and for a moment Jack and I were bathed in the brilliant white flash of its headlights. The look on my brother's face was stony and frightening. Neither of us moved as the engine's hum faded into the night.

Until, incredibly, Jack began to laugh. 'Well, that put the fear of God into him.' He sat down hard next to me. The porch swing bucked wildly.

'I don't think it's God he's worried about.'

'Not my problem.' Jack gave me a critical look. 'You could at least button up your shirt, Jo.'

I did as he suggested. My hands were shaking slightly. 'You scared him, Jack.'

'A little fear will do him good,' he said. 'Did he hurt you? Really?'

'Not much. But he didn't mean to hurt me at all. Couldn't you figure that out?'

He reached out and put a finger on the tip of my nose. I tried to ignore it. He kept it there.

'Stop it,' I finally said.

'You need to be careful, smaller sister,' he said. 'Don't give Monkey-boy anything until he gives us something. Too much too soon, and the game's up.'

'I don't care about the drugs.'

'I just walked in on my little sister with some guy's hand down her pants.' Jack's tone was conversational. 'I don't particularly care about the drugs right now, either.'

'Good, because you probably scared him away for good.'

I felt his burning green eyes on me, piercing into me. 'I mean it, Josie. Don't fuck him.'

'That's up to me.' My voice didn't sound nearly as brave as I'd intended it to.

'Is it?' Jack said.

We sat in uncomfortable silence. Somewhere an owl hooted, and I could hear distant cars cruising by on the highway.

Jack grabbed my hand and kissed it. Just like Kevin had. 'Baby sister,' he said. As quickly as I shook him off, he had my hand again and was stroking my palm. 'Poor smaller, weaker sister, with her big mean brother—'

'Who can't make up his mind about what he wants—'

'Only a promise. That's all I want. Your most solemn, sacred promise not to deliver until Monkey-boy does. Baby sister can wait that long, can't she? For her mean old brother?'

'Shut up. You're being a dork.'

'Dork. That's very expressive.' He shook his head sadly. 'Two weeks with a high school superstud and she drops fifty IQ points.' He moved to tickle me. I squirmed away, and then I was laughing in spite of myself. We were laughing together.

Finally, I said, 'I like him.'

'Then you can have him,' Jack said simply. 'I want you to have everything you want.'

Kevin didn't want to come back. Not at first.

'Can't we do something else?' he said during one of the many phone conversations we had that week. 'Can't I take you out to dinner? Maybe you could come over to my house. My mom's a good cook.'

The last thing I wanted to do was sit at a table and eat meatloaf with Kevin's parents, so I kept reassuring him that Jack wasn't going to kill or maim or otherwise injure him. Jack was always close by during these conversations. He was usually laughing.

'Let him stay gone if he's so determined,' Jack said after a week of this. 'It's not as if he was doing anything for us, anyway.' Then he smiled wickedly. 'Well, I guess he was doing something for you, wasn't he, little sister? Or was it the other way around?'

'Stop it.' I spoke quietly, with a big smile. We had long since discovered, Jack and I, that the best way to keep your voice low and calm while saying nasty things was to force your words through a smile. Raeburn was home and in a rage. He'd locked himself away in his study, so Jack and I were sitting in the parlour, dressed in our dinner clothes. We had been playing chess but we'd started arguing instead, and now the pieces lay forgotten on the table. 'If you hadn't scared him off, he might have done something for us.'

'You don't get it.'

'I get that he's terrified that you're going to bash his head in.'

Jack shrugged. 'Maybe he's right.'

'You won't,' I said. 'You wouldn't.'

'The point, dear sister, is that he thinks I will.' Now he was smiling, too. The effect was disconcerting. 'He thinks I want to kill him because I caught him in a compromising position with my only and beloved sister. If you ever do get the pathetic little shit back up here, he's going to bend over backwards to make sure that he stays in one piece. Thus, success.'

'What if he doesn't come back? What if you've driven him away for good?'

'Thus, success. But of a different sort.' He picked up one of my rooks, which he'd taken earlier and left lying on its side, and stood it upright.

'You're jealous.'

'Of Kevin McMonkey?' he said with contempt. 'I don't think so.'

From another part of the house there came a tremendous crash that made us both jump, and we heard Raeburn bellow, 'John! Josephine! Come here!'

We instantly forgot that we'd been fighting. I looked at Jack and he looked at me. Neither of us was smiling now.

'For Christ's sake,' Jack muttered. 'What now.'

We found Raeburn sprawled across the carpet in the study. His briefcase lay open and upside down beside him, and the floor was strewn with papers covered in rows of text and equations and Greek letters. There was a bottle of Jack Daniel's lying on its side next to the mess. One of Raeburn's shoes lay abandoned near his chair – the foot it had covered looking small and vulnerable in its yellowing cotton sock – and his glasses were missing; his blue plaid shirt hung unbuttoned, exposing his white undershirt. Raeburn was making hysterical gasping noises, like an asthmatic in the middle of an attack. He seemed unable to catch his breath. He was laughing.

'Children. Come in. Come in and have a drink.' With great

concentration he managed to lift himself onto his chair. 'Josephine, get glasses.'

Jack picked up the bottle and glanced carelessly at it. 'Better get another bottle, too,' he said as he sat down on the worn couch. 'This one's empty.'

There were three clean glasses and a bottle of vodka in the liquor cabinet. I brought them to the table next to Raeburn's chair. Jack was sitting with his foot propped up on his knee and his arm spread out along the back of the couch, as cool and comfortable as if this were all entirely normal. And in fact it happened once a month or so: after downing most of a bottle of something high-octane, Raeburn would do the unthinkable and develop an interest in us, said interest usually limited to finding more alcohol and pouring it down our throats. Jack thought these little parties were amusing. I found them harrowing. It was the only time I didn't like to drink.

I sat down on the couch with my brother and pulled my skirt primly over my knees.

Raeburn filled the glasses to overflowing. His hand was unsteady as he raised his glass into the air. Neither of us moved.

'Come on, come on,' he said impatiently.

Jack reached over, picked up a glass, and handed it to me with exaggerated gentility. He took the last for himself and we raised them. Mine was so full that the liquid sloshed over the rim, sending a cold rivulet of vodka running down my arm towards my elbow.

'Here, drink,' Raeburn said. 'Drink to yourselves. The two of you – you insane fucking children – you're the world's only hope, God help it.'

The vodka burned my throat and settled like liquid fire in my stomach. The chemical smell of it was thick in the air. I'd never liked vodka.

Raeburn laughed again. The noise grated like a nail being pulled.

'Would you like to hear what your father did this week?' he said. 'You never ask. Aren't normal children interested in their father's work?'

'Sure,' Jack said. His voice was cheerful. 'How was the office, Daddy?'

'Ghastly,' Raeburn said. He was too drunk for irony. 'I am surrounded by sycophants. Idiots, sycophants, and toads.'

'Who?' I asked.

'The board. The fucking Executive Board of Academic Appointments. They've announced this week that Professor Ben Searles, the Rock Star Scientist himself, may he slowly be irradiated by his own experiments, is going to be considered for tenure this year.' Raeburn poured himself another glass of vodka. 'And he'll get it, too, may his teeth fall out and his limbs wither one by one.'

'I thought Searles was harmless,' Jack said.

'Searles,' Raeburn said clearly, 'is a human plague who spends more time on his hair than he does on his research. The boys love him because he wears motorcycle boots to class, the girls love him because he's got dreamboat eyes, and the board loves him because the girls love him – and it's so very exciting to have such a high percentage of female students concentrating in the sciences!' He snorted. 'He's a mediocre scientist and a worse teacher, and if he's granted tenure I'm stuck with the ridiculous fool for the rest of my career.'

I took a tiny sip of my vodka. 'Maybe he'll leave.'

Raeburn's empty glass fell to the floor. It landed on the thick carpet with a dull thud. As he bent over to pick it up, he said, 'What an intelligent idea, Josephine. We'll make a scholar of you yet.'

'Maybe he'll drop dead without warning,' Jack said.

'Only if I kill him,' Raeburn said. 'Not that it matters. The world's doomed anyway. Maybe I'll get lucky and he'll live through the nuclear firestorm when we blow ourselves up. Just Ben Searles and millions of mutated cockroaches.' He smiled radiantly. 'That clever Margaret. Do you know what she did? She's gone and enrolled in one of his classes. To see the devil firsthand, she says. To campaign against him from the inside. Clever little minx.' His eyes focused on me. 'Sometimes, Josephine, I think I ought to bring Margaret here to meet you. You might benefit from knowing her.'

'Oh, by all means, bring her up,' Jack said with a slow, ugly grin. 'I'd love to meet her.'

Raeburn leaned forward in his chair, his face a malevolent mixture of loathing and glee. 'You, she would eat alive,' he said to Jack. 'She would destroy you. She is a pragmatist. She is a logician. She has a mind far superior to any I've seen in years.' He poured himself another glass of vodka – the bottle was now half empty – and raised it, presumably in a toast to the incomparable Margaret Revolt. 'The last student I had who showed so much promise was your mother. For all the good it did her.'

'Mary was one of your students?' I said.

Jack answered: 'Absolutely. Flourished under his care like a hothouse flower, didn't she, Daddy?'

Raeburn drained half the glass at one gulp. He gave me a pitying look. 'She was brilliant. Not as brilliant as she wanted to be – not as brilliant as she thought she was – but brilliant. God, when I was young I had such grand plans. Such grand plans. I was going to change the world. Tear it down and build a new one. Some help she turned out to be. I should have known about the two of you. The moment I saw you lying in your cribs. I looked deep into your eyes, and there she was, looking out at me.'

He raised his glass. Jack's face was expressionless.

'We have to fight it,' Raeburn said. 'Fight the idiots, the Searleses of the world, fight your crazy fucking mother who almost managed to ruin everything—' His words were beginning to slur together. 'You must take advantage of this – of the world that I've given you. I made it, children. I made it for you.' He stared into his glass.

When his bladder let go, we knew he was passed out for the night. Jack's hand found mine and we left our father alone then, with the dark stain of urine spreading at his crotch. Jack led me to his room. Lit a cigarette. Took off his shirt.

'I never knew Mary was one of his students,' I said.

'I never told you,' he said.

The first night that Jack and I were alone again, I managed to convince Kevin that it was safe for him to come around. I used the phone in the kitchen. Jack watched from the counter, his beer dangling between his legs. The windows behind him were blank with darkness and it was as if there were no world beyond the two of us in the kitchen. I had to close my eyes against him.

'Forget Jack. I want you to come up. Jack will be fine. Everything will be fine. I want you to come,' I said again, sounding more desperate than I meant to. 'I want to see you.'

After a long pause, Kevin said, 'I want to see you, too.'

'Come up tonight.' I hung up.

Jack jumped off the counter. 'You should have told him to bring drugs. No admission without Percodan.'

I was mixing rum and Cokes in the kitchen when I heard Kevin pull into the driveway. Jack met him at the front door and held it wide open; from the kitchen I could hear snatches of what Kevin said as he apologized for touching me. The phrase, 'I would never do anything to, you know, take advantage of your sister,' came through clearly from the other room. A bubble of nervous laughter burst from between my lips. I'd been looking forward to seeing Kevin, to basking in the simple, obvious glow of his adoration. Hearing him plead with my brother for the right to touch me came close to ruining it. In fact, for no good reason that I could think of, it made me angry.

Jack must have said something that made everything okay, because I heard the door close with their laughter on the inside of it. 'Josie, look who's here,' Jack said as they came into the kitchen. It was early September, the first day that really felt like fall, and Kevin wore the same thing he always did: his black denim jacket, army pants, a T-shirt from a rock concert. He looked so vulnerable and harmless, standing there next to Jack with his skinny body and his skinny arms and his hair that fell wherever it wanted to. It was easy to forgive both of them for everything. In fact, as Kevin planted a chaste kiss on my cheek and Jack said, 'My sister makes the best drinks,' there was a moment when I was completely happy, completely satisfied, surrounded by people who were there because they loved me. Then I saw Jack watching me with Kevin, a vaguely amused expression on his face, and I was embarrassed and angry again.

Jack played it well that night. He was his charming self, but beneath his friendliness he was just standoffish enough to make Kevin uncomfortable. I don't know if Kevin even realized why he felt uncomfortable.

But there we were, playing three-handed gin rummy an hour or so later, when Kevin said, 'I was thinking about what you said, Jack.'

'What did I say?' Jack said around the cigarette in his mouth. He didn't look up from his cards.

'About my dad,' Kevin said. 'About the pharmacy.'

'Yeah?' Jack said, as if he'd forgotten the subject entirely. 'What were you thinking about that?' He picked a card out of his hand, stared at it for a moment, and then put it back in a different place.

'I was thinking maybe I could see what I could do,' Kevin said. He looked back and forth between the two of us with big, earnest eyes. 'Maybe I could pinch a pill or two off the top of the filled prescriptions. Before they go out. Nobody ever counts them once they have them.'

'If you want to.' Jack sounded as if the whole subject bored him immeasurably. 'I wouldn't want to cause you any trouble.'

There was a slight emphasis on *trouble*: slight, yes, but very definitely there. Kevin answered, 'I'm not afraid of a little trouble.'

'Never said you were,' Jack said.

I put my cards on the table. 'Gin.'

Jack dropped his own hand and grinned broadly. 'Martini. Kevin, my friend, would you like a martini?'

The subtext was gone. Kevin relaxed and said, 'Indeed I would,' which sounded so much like something Jack would say that I did a double take.

'My sister makes the best drinks,' Jack said again.

By the end of the next week, Kevin was coming up every night, sneaking out of the house after his parents went to bed and staying until two or three o'clock. As far as Kevin was concerned, everything was fine.

But I was worried about my brother. Kevin had brought him a few Valium and a handful of Tylenol with codeine, and Jack and I had taken them and – I suppose – enjoyed them; the Tylenol made me vaguely nauseated but I never said anything about it. Jack seemed bored. Having ostensibly gotten what he wanted, he had less and less to say to Kevin, and soon he was sitting through his visits in silence, watching us. After a few hours he would drift upstairs without so much as a see-you-later. I couldn't get out of my head the image of Jack sitting alone on his bed, propped up against the wall, smoking a cigarette while Kevin and I shared our fumbling kisses.

Things weren't much better when it was Jack and me alone. He didn't want to let me out of his sight and he didn't want to talk. We walked, we played cards, we did calculus, all in a thick silence. Nothing I said or did, or didn't say or didn't do, broke through it. But every night, soon after I'd gone to bed, Jack would come to my bedroom and lie next to me, throwing his arm across me as he'd done since we were children. Sometimes his need, his anger, whatever it was, came off him in waves and I knew we would be awake for hours. Sometimes he just seemed to want me next to him, and on those nights we lay silently until one or the other of us fell asleep. It was a funny thing about my bed. When I lay in it alone, it seemed too big; with Jack there, it seemed too small.

By contrast, being with Kevin was a relief, blissfully uncomplicated, though Jack was watching over us like a sparrow hawk, listening for our movements from the next room, or just outside. If Kevin noticed, he didn't seem to care. Once or twice we took his father's car, drove to some deserted spot, and spent an hour kissing frantically. I came home those nights with sore lips and damp underwear, feeling rumpled and sticky. Jack was always waiting: staring at me, through me, as if he could somehow see where I'd been and what I'd been doing.

I never did meet Kevin's parents. He didn't mention them

again. Maybe he'd decided I wasn't that kind of girl; ironic, considering how staunchly I kept my promise to Jack. Kevin got nothing from me. The line I drew was so hard and fast that I wanted Jack to challenge me on the subject so that I could explain to him how faithful I'd been, how steadfast and loyal. But he never asked. In fact, he never said anything at all about Kevin, until one Saturday afternoon when Kevin rang the doorbell and Jack refused to open the door.

'Why are you being like this?' I said. I wanted to scream it, but Kevin was on the other side of the door, ringing the bell over and over again.

'Why are you being such a love-struck little girl?' Jack said. 'I didn't think I had the kind of sister that would fall over backwards as for the first guy who stuck his' – Jack's lip curled – '*tongue* in her mouth.'

'Don't start.' My teeth were clenched.

'Tell him to go home. Tell him you don't want to see him any more.'

'I won't.'

'You want me to tell him?'

'This was your idea!' I said. I was almost crying with rage. 'This was *all* your idea!'

'It was my idea to milk Monkey-boy for some cheap drugs.' Jack's voice was cold. 'It was not my idea to sit upstairs by myself all night while he fucks my little sister on the family couch.'

I could hear Kevin calling, 'Josie? Jack? You guys home?'

Jack stared at me and I started to shake.

Suddenly Jack smiled. 'Just a sec, Kevin!' he called merrily through the door. 'Having some trouble with the lock, here.'

'No problem.' Kevin sounded relieved.

Jack stepped away from the door, close to me. I tried to move back. There was a wall in my way.

'You do this to me every night,' he said quietly. 'Every single goddamned night. I'll let him in. But this is the last time.'

'Fine.' I was furious.

He pushed me to the wall, standing against me so that I couldn't move away, and took my head in his hands. Each of his fingers was a hot hard bolt pressing into my skull. He pulled me towards him so that our foreheads were touching, so that all I could see was his face.

'Did he tell you he loves you?' His voice was acid with contempt. I could smell whiskey on his breath. 'Did you *believe* him?'

'Let me go,' I hissed. I tried to pull away.

He held me harder. 'I am the only person who has *ever* loved you. The only person in the entire goddamned world.'

Then he dropped his hands and stepped back. I stood trembling against the wall. He reached out and smoothed my hair down where he'd rumpled it. Then, calmly, he said, 'Now let Monkey-boy in and let's get this over with.'

He turned away without another word and left me standing there alone.

I waited until I heard him climbing the stairs. Then I opened the door. By then I had my breath back, but my hands were still shaking.

Kevin put his arms around my waist and kissed me as if he were back from the wars. I did my best to respond. 'Where's Jack?' he said as he let me go. 'Wasn't he down here?'

'He went upstairs,' I said. 'He's not feeling well.'

We went into the living room and I put the Coltrane record on, but I had trouble making conversation. I was trying to decide whether I felt too weird, whether I should plead sick, too, when Jack came in carrying a bottle of Smirnoff.

'Just came to keep an eye on the circus,' he said, his voice dripping with fake cheer.

I ignored him. Kevin's smile was only slightly uncertain. He said, 'I guess you're the ringmaster, huh?'

'Naturally.' Jack sat down in Raeburn's armchair. 'And Josie here is the monkey handler. Hey' – as if he'd just thought of it – 'I wonder what that makes you, Kevin.'

Kevin half-laughed and glanced nervously at me.

I took his hand. 'Lion tamer.'

Kevin laughed again, more normally this time. 'Maybe I'm the guy who gets shot out of the cannon.'

'Or the last little clown in the clown car,' Jack said.

'Yeah,' Kevin said. 'Sure.'

Then we sat, the three of us, in the parlour. Jack was silent, taking shots of vodka straight from the bottle and staring at us, his green eyes hostile and intense. I rubbed my arms where he had grabbed them.

Kevin broke the silence. 'Josie. Didn't you want to show me something upstairs?'

'I'll meet you up there,' I said.

He nodded and left. Jack and I sat and stared.

'You hurt me,' I said.

Jack took a long pull at the bottle.

'He's waiting,' he said.

Fifteen minutes later, Kevin and I were in my bed under the covers, naked and fumbling. The things he did were clumsy and well intentioned. I think it was the first time he'd ever been naked with a girl. I didn't ask. Jack was playing *Tristan and Isolde* at top volume in his room. The floor of my bedroom shook with each crescendo.

I thought of Jack. I thought of his strong hands and his green eyes; I thought of him fuming and rage-filled in his bedroom on the other side of the wall. If he was hurting, I was glad.

When Kevin fell back panting and sweaty, we lay without speaking for a few minutes. It was nice to lie together. Some of my fury dissipated. But the space that was left was filled with feelings that I liked even less.

'Something's wrong, isn't it?' Kevin said.

'Something is, yes.'

After a small silence, he said, 'I don't think I'd better come up here for a while.'

I shifted so that I could put my ear against his chest. I said nothing for a minute. I could hear his heartbeat hidden under the music like a secret message.

'We've lived here for so long,' I said. 'Just me and him.'

He nodded. A drop of sweat traced its way down my back. We didn't say anything else. Isolde wailed in the next room.

Kevin got up and began to put his clothes on. I watched him from the bed.

'I'll walk you down,' I said when he was done, standing up. I didn't bother to cover myself. I was shivering and sticky and I didn't care.

At the front door, Kevin turned to me. 'There's a bonfire Friday. It's a pep rally sort of thing. Come with me.' His words were rushed, as if he were trying to get them all out before he changed his mind.

'All right,' I said. He kissed me and left.

I went back upstairs and crawled into my clammy bed. I expected Jack, but instead I heard the music cut off, the front door slam, and the truck engine start up outside.

Jack returned hours later and woke me. He brought a bottle of wine and gave me the first sip. I'd been dreaming. I was still half asleep. He never said he was sorry for anything, and I never asked him to.

3

Friday was cold. Jack and I had been up all night so I slept most of the day. Around three I shook myself awake, left Jack – who was still sleeping – and went downstairs to make some coffee. For a long time I sat on the front porch and watched the clouds move.

At five I went back upstairs. Jack was awake now, but still in bed, smoking a cigarette and throwing darts at the dartboard that hung from his bookcase. His room was hot. When he saw me standing in the doorway, he moved his legs to make room for me at the foot of his bed.

'Open a window,' I said. 'It stinks in here.'

Jack dropped the darts on his pillow and reached for the window. The sheets had been bunched under him and had left dull red lines on his back. 'Raeburn home?' he said, handing me his cigarette.

'Not yet,' I answered, and we smoked in silence for a few minutes. His blond hair was thick with grease and stuck up at weird angles from his head. He looked like a rumpled lion.

'Can I borrow your leather jacket tonight?' I asked eventually.

'Why?'

'Because it's cold.'

'You have a coat.' He threw his blanket onto the floor and stood up, rooting through a pile of clothes on the floor until he found a pair of jeans.

'Mine smells like wine.'

'So wear a lot of perfume.'

'Just let me borrow it, okay?'

'To go to that bonfire thing?'

I nodded.

'No,' he said, pulling on a sweater.

'Why not?'

Jack took a drag from his cigarette. 'Maybe I don't want Kevin McNerny's monkey hands all over it.' He sat down in the old armchair we'd dragged down from the attic and watched me. His eyes were steady and their full force was formidable.

Finally he spoke. 'You know, Raeburn left those quadratic equations that I was supposed to do.'

'So?'

'When's he getting home?'

'I guess six. Like always.'

'Time's it now?'

'Five.'

My brother had a roundabout way of making a point.

'Those equations are weighing on my mind. Maybe if they were done, I'd be able to think about whether or not I wanted to let you take my jacket.' Jack picked up a half-full coffee mug, sniffed at it, and took a drink.

'How many problems are there?'

'I don't know.' His eyes glittered. 'More than you can do in an hour.'

'I hate quadratic equations.'

'I hate Kevin McNerny.' Jack stepped close to me, reached out, and brushed something off my cheek. He smelled like whiskey and stale cigarettes.

I sighed and said, 'Brush your teeth.' Then I went to find my calculator.

* * *

Raeburn came home cackling and blissful. Because of the equations, I hadn't had time to fix anything except spaghetti for dinner, but for once he didn't seem to care.

'It's a paradox,' he told us, and laughed. 'If my enemy does something explicitly self-serving, it's unethical; but if I do the same thing, it's strategy. We have to make our own opportunities. The world does not deliver kindnesses.' He picked up his fork and put it down again. There was a dreamy look on his face.

'I've solved the Searles problem,' he said. 'We've had the most brilliant idea, Margaret Revolt and I.' He threw down his napkin and pushed away from the table. He hadn't eaten anything. 'I believe I'll go have a celebratory drink. I don't suppose there's any of my brandy left, is there?'

'Some,' Jack said.

'Excellent,' Raeburn said cheerfully. A moment later we heard the study door slam shut.

'Is Monkey-boy waiting for you?' Jack said.

'He won't be here for another twenty minutes.'

'Then you have time to do the dishes.'

'Thanks a lot.'

'Love must suffer,' Jack said. He turned around in his chair, folding his arms across its high wooden back, and watched as I carried the dirty plates to the sink.

'At least I won't be sitting here all night listening to Raeburn describe what it will feel like when my atoms start to split,' I said as I scraped Jack's plate into the garbage. 'And I'm not in love.'

'Only fucking him, then?'

'None of your business.'

'I'd say it is.' He stood up. 'I'd say it's very much my business who you have sex with.' He pushed the chair into place and left.

When I was done with the dishes I went to my room, changed into jeans and a sweater, and tied my hair into a ponytail. I used some of Crazy Mary's left-behind lipstick and powder. Then I changed my mind about the hair, let it down again, and went to see Jack.

He had taken off his tie and was lying on his bed. 'Look at you,' he said when he saw me standing at his door. 'What time is the sock hop, anyway, kitten?'

I stuck my hands in my front pockets and then took them out and slid them into the back ones.

'Quit fidgeting,' Jack said.

'Come on,' I said. 'I did your stupid equations.'

He didn't move. 'Take it.' He gestured towards his leather jacket, which was slung over the back of the armchair in the corner. Jack had brought the jacket home a few years earlier. It had once been black, but by the time he bought it, it had been fading to brown and was half beaten to death. Now it was three-quarters dead, but the sheepskin lining was intact and warm and it was his only prized possession. I picked it up and put it on. It was too big and smelled of old leather, cigarette smoke, and the cologne he sometimes wore. Jack's face was completely blank.

'Jack,' I said, and stopped. I didn't know what I was going to say, anyway.

'What?'

'Nothing.'

'Better get going,' he said. 'You'll be late.'

When I left, Jack was with Raeburn in the study, laughing about something. Raeburn already sounded drunk. I used the back door in the kitchen and took the path that cut straight through the woods to the main road. There was an old family cemetery back there, one or two graves. The white headstones were worn smooth and they gleamed in the fading daylight.

Kevin was waiting for me at the bottom of the driveway in his father's car. He told me that he liked my jacket, and we drove off down the highway.

We didn't look at each other. The engine hummed.

'I'm glad we're doing this,' he said. 'None of my friends quite believe in you.'

'I know how they feel.'

'You don't believe in them either, huh?'

'Exactly,' I said, although he was wrong. I watched the highway roll under the front wheels.

At the next stoplight, Kevin leaned over and gave me a quick kiss. While I rode to the high school in Kevin's father's Pontiac, I was thinking of Jack and Raeburn drinking brandy in the study. I knew that if I looked through the back window I would be able to see our attic window above the trees. I told myself I wouldn't look back, but eventually I did, and there it was, harmless-looking in miniature and a long way behind me, on top of the Hill.

Kevin put a hand on my knee. 'You okay?' he said.

'Sure,' I said and pulled Jack's coat closer around me.

'Good.' Kevin turned the radio up.

The high school was built over an abandoned strip mine. The main building, which sprawled around an open courtyard, was tucked onto a series of plateaus carved into the side of the hill, artificially flat stretches of land that had once held the mine's cranes and loaders. The parking lot where Kevin left the car was at the edge of the uppermost plateau. Looking through the chainlink fence that separated us from the steep drop, I could see the tennis courts and the track spread out beneath me in the dusky valley, each on its own level with its own set of splintering railway sleepers serving as steps to the levels above and below it. The air was thick with smoke and music and voices.

Kevin led me around the front of the school, to a place where there was a wide notch cut out of the half-mile or so of forest that separated the school grounds from the main highway. The bonfire was already raging in the centre of the notch. The lawn between the fire and the place where we stood was choked with cars. Each car had four or five kids draped over it, soaking in the light and heat of the fire like lizards. Some of them greeted Kevin with a nod or a 'What's up?' or a 'How's it going?', glancing at me with lazy curiosity and then looking away. Only a few stared.

'How do you like being the mystery woman?' Kevin whispered.

'Call me Mata Hari.' My hands, in Jack's pockets, were clenched into fists.

'She is *bootifahl*,' Kevin said, in a fake accent that wasn't French and wasn't anything else, either. 'But she is *deadlee*.' He leaned in close, grinning, a possessive arm slung around my shoulders. A kid with spiked blond hair was watching us blankly from the hood of a car.

Kevin tried to kiss my cheek.

Annoyed, I said, 'Stop.'

He pulled back. 'What?'

I thrust my fists deeper into the jacket pockets. 'Nothing.'

'You're nervous.'

'I'm not nervous. I'm tense. There's a difference.'

All this time we were walking, weaving our way towards the bonfire. Some of the cars were parked so close together that we actually had to climb over the bumpers where they touched. I could hear at least three different radio stations playing. The music was jumbled and discordant. My ankle turned in a hollow in the ground and I swore.

Kevin peered down at my foot. 'You okay?'

I shook his hand away from my elbow and said, 'You live in an ant swarm.'

'Relax, Josie.'

'How do you deal with this? All these people?'

He shrugged. 'I've known some of them since kindergarten. They're okay, most of them.' My distrust must have been written on my face, because he let go of my hand and said, 'Of course, you're probably safer back home with your psychopath brother. My friends are over there.' Before I could say anything, he was headed towards them. There was nothing for me to do but follow.

By the time I caught up, Kevin was deep in conversation with a boy wearing a Miles Davis T-shirt. The shirt was about three sizes too big. I heard the boy say, 'Hey, it's the invisible girlfriend.'

'What do you know? You do exist,' a girl said, grinning cheerfully at me. She was wearing a pair of work boots that didn't look like they'd ever seen a day's work.

I said, 'In the flesh,' and tried to smile back, wishing that I really was invisible – or at least that I hadn't pissed Kevin off. Then at least I'd have one friend in that teeming crowd. But he took my hand to help me up into the back of the red pickup truck as he told me their names, which slid through my brain like water.

Work Boots said, 'I've seen you around town with your brother. You really don't go to school?'

'I really don't.' I was still grinning like an idiot.

'Isn't the school board up your dad's ass about it?' T-shirt said.

'We're home-schooled. It's all legal.'

'I wish my parents would do that,' Work Boots said. 'I hate school. It's so pointless. The teachers are dumber than we are.'

Kevin leaned in. 'You know Josie was studying Greek when she was six?'

'No kidding! Our school doesn't even have Greek,' Work Boots said. The three of them examined me as though I were a specimen under glass.

Finally T-shirt said, 'Not having to go to school would totally rock. Kevin says you guys have a hell of a time up there with your brother.'

Kevin's smile vanished.

'Well,' I said. 'Things get a little intense sometimes.'

'Insane, huh? Right, Kevster?'

He mumbled, 'Shut up,' and looked away from me.

'Your brother's cute,' Work Boots said.

'I guess so. He's my brother; it's hard to tell.'

Kevin forced a laugh. 'I think you're a little young for him, Amy.'

She tossed her head and said, 'You're as old as you feel.'

An image came unbidden to my mind: Amy's immaculate work boots lying among the overflowing ashtrays and crumpled clothes that always covered the floor next to Jack's bed while above them, his lean body moved over her compact round one and she moaned softly—

My stomach lurched. I said, 'Well, get Kevin to bring you up sometime,' knowing that he would never do it. Just then, the marching band, which had been standing idly in a rough circle a few feet away, broke into something strident and loud, and a pack of cheerleaders tumbled and handsprung their way into the clearing, and I learned that the Tigers – or maybe it was the Titans, I couldn't quite make it out – were going to go, fight, win, killing the Lions and going all the way, that's right, all the way. The cheerleaders barked out questions like drill sergeants. Kevin and his friends seemed to know all the correct responses.

'Assembly-line idiot factories,' Raeburn said in my head,

'producing assembly-line idiots capable of assembly-line thought. You two are better than that.'

Someone in a tiger suit bounced into the midst of the cheer-leaders, eliciting a massive burst of enthusiasm from the crowd. Around me, a sea of entranced faces eagerly watched each sharp, martial movement. Fists punched the air. Feet stomped loudly in time with the music. Kevin put his arm around me, pulling me close. I tried to smile.

There was a commotion on the side of the clearing closest to the parking lot. The crowd parted and an old car, rusted and covered in primer, was pushed into the centre of the crowd by a group of huge boys wearing football jerseys over faded jeans or sweatpants. More boys sat on top of the car, waving their arms in the air and shouting 'Yeah!' and 'Oh, yeah!' and occasionally '*Fuck* yeah!'

'What's going on?' I asked Kevin.

'The car smash. They do it every year.'

Work Boots – Amy – leaned over and said, 'It's mostly an excuse for the seniors to show off what big, tough men they are.'

'My dad says whoever donates the car gets a tax write-off,' T-shirt said.

As if by magic, a sledgehammer appeared in the hands of each of the riding, shouting boys. Someone blew a whistle and they started to smash, blows raining down on the already dead car. Glass shattered. Metal buckled. It was like bumper cars on the autobahn, like a war, like someone being killed, and still there were fenders to be hammered flat and bumpers to be ripped off and held aloft like trophies. Something shiny flew through the air. It was one of the side mirrors, thrown clear of the carnage.

I tapped Kevin on the shoulder. 'Doesn't anyone ever get hurt doing this?'

He smirked. 'A few years ago some kid got hit in the kidneys. If they're stupid enough to do it they deserve what they get.'

The band played and the fire roared, and somewhere out of reach of its flickering red light, my brother sat in a room with my father and they drank brandy by the light of a smaller, more private flame.

The pep rally ended when the car was reduced to naked, twisted metal. The cheerleaders closed things up with a few more rounds of 'Go! Fight! Win!' but the kids were already leaving by then, trickling off in ones and twos towards the parking lot. Kevin's friends wanted to go to a coffee shop in Janesville, so we all piled into the red truck, which belonged to T-shirt – or, more likely, to his father. Kevin sat in the back and Amy and I squeezed together in the cab. Amy was sitting in the middle and she and T-shirt were laughing about something, some story about Kevin that I think was being told for my benefit.

My face ached from smiling and I couldn't quite figure out what to do with my arms. They seemed too long and I moved them restlessly from the open window, which was too high, to the armrest, which was too low, to my lap, which felt too timid. The air outside, which made my hair lash at my face as it blew in the open window, smelled of smoke and cold weather and carried with it the clear tang of water. I envied Kevin sitting by himself in the truck bed.

I moved Jack's jacket around me. His scent surrounded me like an aura.

Amy said, 'So we're all of thirteen years old, Lisa's parents are right upstairs, and Mr Smooth Moves in the back, there, decides that it's time for his first makeout session and pulls her into the bathroom.'

T-shirt said, 'This is so classic.'

'Like you're any better, Mr Back-Seat-of-the-Bus – during a band trip with six sets of parents in the front and everyone we know watching.'

'All I'm saying is, I didn't get caught.'

Amy shook her head dismissively and turned back to me. 'Anyway, so naturally Lisa's mom comes downstairs to see if we want more chips or something like that. And she's like, "Where's Lisa?" and we're like, "Uh, we don't know, Mrs Nath." And Lisa's in the bathroom with Kevin, listening to all this, so of course she opens the door and comes out, like, "I'm right here, Mom," like nothing's going on. And Kevin follows her.'

The two of them burst into laughter. I wondered who was watching the road.

'What?' Kevin called through the sliding panel in the back window. 'What's going on?'

They only laughed harder. They were still laughing when T-shirt pulled into a parking place in front of the coffee shop and turned the engine off. 'Caught!' he said, too loudly in the sudden silence. '*So* caught!'

'I guess that pretty much did it for the party, huh?' I asked.

'That party and every other party from now until we're all dead,' Amy said as she climbed out of the truck after me. 'Lisa still has to swear in blood, practically, just to get out of the house, and it's three years later, for God's sake.'

Kevin jumped down from the tailgate. 'What are you guys telling her?'

'Oh, nothing,' T-shirt said. 'Only the legend of the Bathroom Bandito.'

Kevin blushed. 'Yeah, well, I was thirteen.'

'You were a dork,' Amy said.

'You still are,' I said. Kevin's eyes darted towards me, and Amy crowed with delight.

'See,' Amy said. 'She's a smart one. She knows the score.' She threw her arm around my shoulder. 'They're all dorks, aren't they, Josie?'

'Not my brother.' I reached up to adjust the collar of Jack's jacket and make Amy move her arm.

'Jack's cool enough,' Kevin said carefully.

'My older sister used to see him down at Eide's all the time,' she said. 'She says he's the coolest guy she's ever met. Smart and funny and just *awesome*.'

'Jack worked at Eide's?' Kevin asked me as we entered the warm coffee shop.

'For about fifteen minutes.'

'I didn't know that.'

'It was literally about a week.'

'What happened?'

They had asked for a social security card and a driving licence, and Jack had neither. 'He didn't like it,' I said shortly. T-shirt and Amy were ahead of us, following the waitress. I moved quickly to catch up.

'Ask him if he remembers my sister,' Amy said as we slid into the booth. 'Beth Furlough. She had a huge crush on him.' Amy's words were authoritative, as if she were repeating Delphic prophecy. 'She used to say that she wouldn't be surprised if he turned out to be someone special, like a rock star or a secret agent. Something.'

'Okay, we get it.' Kevin looked disgusted. 'Jack Raeburn is good-looking. So is his sister. Can we drop it?'

'I was just saying.'

'And saying, and saying, and saying,' T-shirt said, rolling his eyes.

She sniffed. 'Not my fault if he's the only interesting thing in town.'

I hugged his jacket closer as the waitress came to take our order. The others ordered coffee and French fries and hot fudge sundaes. I got coffee.

They were capable of amazing amounts of talk, those three. On and on and on they went: about Amy's boyfriends, about T-shirt's girlfriends, about what a drag living with your parents was, and how cool college would be. Amy said she wanted a car for her birthday, she didn't care what kind, and they talked about that. T-shirt said he was thinking about joining the soccer team and they talked about that. I sat and looked at the veins on the backs of my hands. At one point Kevin turned to me and asked, 'You okay?' I nodded and he didn't ask again.

They weren't unusually dumb, or unusually superficial, or any other kind of unusual. They were normal, nice kids from normal, nice families. Jack and Raeburn were right; we weren't like them. I had nothing to say to them. I wanted my coffee to have whiskey in it and I wanted my brother, and nothing else was all that interesting.

T-shirt and Amy dropped us off at the high school around eleven-thirty. There were two cars in the empty, moonlit parking lot. One of them was Kevin's station wagon. The other was a battered blue truck.

Kevin dropped my hand. Together, we stared across the dark lawn at the parking lot in silence.

I heard him swallow. 'Did I keep you out too late?' he said.

'Violating the strict Raeburn curfew, you mean?'

'Well, your dad's home . . .'

'And by now he's passed out in the study. Let's go the other way.'

We walked towards the clearing, where the bonfire had been. The scent of the night air was still good.

'Shit, Josie,' Kevin said. 'What's he doing here?'

We had reached the soggy black scar where the fire had been. The moonlight glinted off Kevin's glasses. He was scared. He kept running his hands through his hair, turning his head nervously.

I took a deep breath. Now I smelled char and Jack's coat and the coffee on my own breath. I looked at Kevin, who was a nice boy who liked to wear army pants and rock star T-shirts, and an eerie calm slid over me.

'I'm going to go back alone,' I said. My voice was steady. 'Stay here. Give us a chance to leave.'

'Wait a minute,' Kevin said.

I turned to go.

Jack was standing there watching us, with his hands in his pockets. He was blocking the way to the parking lot. His face was turned towards the sky.

'Hey, little sister,' he said, staring into the cloudless sky.

'What are you doing here?'

'Waiting for you.' He looked at me. 'Nice jacket.'

'Thanks.'

Then he looked at Kevin.

Kevin made a strangled noise in his throat and bolted forward. I'm not sure what he was doing. Maybe he was hoping to get in the first punch. Maybe he was trying to run.

Anyway, Jack caught him.

The last time I saw Kevin McNerny, he was lying where Jack had thrown him, face-down in the ashes of the dead bonfire. I could hear him drawing long, sobbing breaths through his broken nose.

He was trying, weakly, to get up, or at least to get his face out of the soot.

Jack's T-shirt was stained with blood and there were a few splattered drops on his cheek. We drove home in silence.

I went straight up to my room and closed the door behind me. Turned the light off and lay face-down on my bed.

The leather jacket was in a heap on the floor, where I'd dropped it.

A few minutes later, my bedroom door opened and shut again. I heard the flick of a lighter. My thin mattress dipped slightly as Jack sat down on the edge of my bed.

'So,' he said, finally. 'How was the sock hop, kitten?'

I rolled over and pulled myself up to sit against the headboard. By candlelight, I saw that Jack had changed his shirt and washed the blood from his face. He was staring at me, his expression calm, and rubbing his raw knuckles.

'Leave me alone.'

He went on as if he hadn't heard me. 'Let me guess. All the girls giggled about boys and all the boys punched each other in the arm and slapped each other on the ass and talked sports. You sat there and didn't say a word the entire night.'

'I talked.'

'Yeah? What did you say?'

I didn't answer.

'Because, by nature, we're great conversationalists, aren't we? Let's see. What subjects does one find in the incomparable Raeburn repertoire? You could tell them all about Kepler's theory of planetary motion; I'm sure Kevin's furry little forest friends would have been into that. Or you could break the ice with a few good jokes, maybe some wacky anecdotes? I know, you could tell them about the time at that faculty dinner when the dean of studies puked all over his shoes. They would have liked that one. High school kids like puking.'

'Stop it.'

He moved in closer, staring intently at me. 'Or you could tell them about the time you broke Raeburn's Italian barometer. That's a good one. Particularly the end.'

'Why are you doing this?' My voice was a hoarse whisper.

Jack didn't even blink. 'No, here's a better one. Did you hear the one about the guy who had a sister—'

I tried to get up but he blocked me with an arm.

'And she was the most beautiful thing he'd ever seen, with pretty blond hair and pretty green eyes, and he couldn't stand the thought of some asshole ever getting his hands on her, *hurting* her—'

'You told me to do it.' My hands were covering my face. He pulled them away.

'I told you to do it,' he said, his nose inches from mine, his eyes burning into me, 'because I knew you were going to anyway and you had to know what it was like, because you didn't know shit, little sister. And now you do, don't you?'

'Yes,' I whispered.

He sat back and watched me. 'There's a gap between us and them and you can't bridge it,' he said, his voice gentle now. He touched my hair. 'You're not like them and you're not ever going to be. We're different. We're better. We don't need anyone else. Okay?'

I nodded. 'You didn't have to hurt him.'

'He deserved it.'

'He wasn't that bad.'

We sat together and watched the moonlight move across the walls. I was thinking of Kevin crying in the ashes. 'He was going to hurt you eventually,' Jack said after a long while. 'He was going to hurt you worse than I hurt him.'

'He might not have.'

'Well, he won't now,' he said.

Not long after that, Jack and I were sitting on the porch swing on a warm evening, passing a bottle of wine back and forth and watching the moths fly at the porch light, when Jack said in an offhand tone that Kevin must not have been too badly hurt, since the police hadn't shown up.

I shivered. I hadn't thought about the police. I pulled at the cuffs of my sweater and asked if it had really been that bad. Jack shrugged.

'But I don't think he'd have ratted us out, anyway,' he said. 'If his parents squawked too much, he'd have made up some story. What else is he going to do? Say, "Mom, Dad, I've been sneaking out after hours to get stoned and fuck this girl, and now her brother's gone and beaten the shit out of me, so call the police quick"? No way. He could never admit he'd been so naughty. Might ruin Mommy and Daddy's good image of their little boy.' Jack grinned. 'He could say he'd never had sex with you, but he couldn't prove it, any more than he can prove that you're not fourteen.'

'That I'm not – oh.' I saw what he meant. 'But he wouldn't expect us to do that.'

'Sure he would,' Jack said, 'because that's what I told him we'd do, right before I kicked him in the face.' He slipped an arm around my shoulder and handed me the bottle. The wine was bitter and warm in my throat.

We fell asleep in the parlour that night. Jack was stretched out on the couch and I was curled up in Raeburn's chair under the ugly nude. I woke up sometime in the night. I was still drunk and my head was packed with steel wool. Rising from the chair, trying to be quiet so I wouldn't wake Jack, I made my unsteady way upstairs to my bedroom. My window shade was up. There was enough moonlight in my room to see my way to my bed and to the battered wooden box wedged tightly between my headboard and the wall. Jack didn't know the box existed; it was my only secret.

Carefully, I slid it out from its hiding place. The box held three things, treasures – relics, really – that I had found in the house when I was a little girl and hidden carefully away. There was a charm bracelet, heavy with tiny silver animals and keys and skulls and even a miniature crystal test tube, held to the chain by a thin silver band around its throat. There was a broken wristwatch, delicate and obviously intended for a feminine wrist, with a leather strap that still smelled faintly of the perfume, spicy and floral, that had been dabbed on the skin underneath it. There was a folded square of thick paper. The bracelet and the wristwatch had been my mother's; the piece of paper was me.

Magee Women's Hospital. Pittsburgh, Pennsylvania.

The writing was fancy. The embossed seal was round and smooth under my fingers.

Father: Joseph Raeburn.

Mother: Mary Elizabeth (Chandler) Raeburn.

I'd found the box long ago, shoved carelessly into the bottom of a closet, beneath an old boot and some moth-eaten blankets. My birth certificate was inside it. It was after the social worker brought Jack home, but not long after, because the housekeeper was still there to slap my face when she found me with the certificate in my hands, to tell me that it was important and I had no right to touch it.

But I knew better. I was seven years old, and I could read English as well as Greek, and the name on the thick paper was mine. The paper was mine. The paper was me. I kept it under my bed; I knew it was there.

Josephine Leigh Raeburn.

That night was the last warm night of the year. Soon we had the last of the warm days, and then that summer was officially over. The snow fell early, and we never spoke of Kevin McNerny again.

4

As Christmas neared, Raeburn grew secretive and distracted. The changes were small at first. Each week he came home a little later than he had the week before, and Friday afternoons soon became Saturday evenings. His eyes took on an unwholesome glitter, like marsh fire, and everything he did was infused with a horrible excitement, even when there was nothing in particular to be excited about. He began to grin.

He still left us piles of work, but didn't seem to care if we did it or not, and had no interest in going over it if we did. The phone would ring late at night and he would jump for it, snarling, 'Don't touch it!' as if we were in the habit of dashing for the phone any time it rang; then he would take the phone into the study and lock himself away, talking for hours to whoever was on the other end. I asked him once, without thinking, who the calls were from, and he snapped that it was none of my business.

Soon all of his weekends were spent behind the closed door of his study, working at the battered manual typewriter he'd had since graduate school ('Computers, children, are responsible for the mechanization of human intelligence'). His wild laughter and the firecracker sound of the typewriter keys drifted through the heating vents.

Jack said it couldn't mean anything good. He said it felt to him like the old one-two, that we'd somehow missed the one but he was watching out for the two.

It came, of course.

'The faculty family Christmas party is next Friday,' Raeburn said one night, during another interminable dinner. 'It's the sort of ridiculous function that I normally try to avoid, but this thing with Searles – I can't afford to be antisocial.' He gave us one of his new grins, humourless and unpleasant. 'We'll all be very charming. I'll find a motel room for the two of you somewhere in town. You can drive up in the truck.'

'I'm not going,' Jack said.

Raeburn gazed levelly at him. 'That's not an option,' he said.

'It is if I don't show up.'

I stared at the hamburger patty on my plate. Discussions that began this way in our house rarely ended well.

Raeburn's fork paused for only a moment in its journey from the plate to his mouth. Then it shoved a mouthful of peas between his teeth. 'You have somewhere else to be?'

Jack shrugged. 'Maybe I do.'

Raeburn laughed. 'Do what you like,' he said. 'But if I don't see you at that party, I'd better not see you back here either.'

The big muscles in Jack's jaw clenched tightly. I couldn't have moved if I'd wanted to.

'Do we understand each other?' our father said.

'Go to hell,' Jack said. His voice was low and dangerous.

Raeburn smiled gently. 'You sound like your mother, John. I hope you don't end up the same way she did.'

Our mother had killed herself two weeks before my brother came to live with us. Jack said, 'She ended up a long way from here.'

'Sure. Decomposing in a pool of her own vomit. Isn't that what the social worker said?'

This was true. It was also one of my father's favourite bedtime stories. It never lost its appeal for him.

'Dead in a gutter,' he continued, 'with the rest of the creatures that float on the surface. A little more residue making life slimy around the edges. A terrible waste, really.'

'Speaking of slime,' said Jack, 'fuck you.'

Raeburn pointed at my brother's face with the tines of his fork. 'Your mother never bothered to use her intelligence, either. She counted on the pretty blond hair and the ethereal bone structure and all of the other biological trinkets you two see in the mirror to make her way for her. You'd find yourself as lost in the real world as she did.' His fork moved to indicate the room around us, and the house, and, presumably, the world itself. 'I've built you two a lovely little pond where you won't ever become what your mother was. I've taken away that variable. And all that I ask of you is that occasionally you show up at a party and play nice for my colleagues.' He grunted. 'You should consider yourselves fortunate.'

I watched Raeburn's fork move from his mouth to his plate, again and again, while something there with us in the room formed a haze over the table, surrounding me, locking my muscles in place and forming a thin layer of ice under my skin. Jack, though – he was burning. I could feel the heat emanating from him. His hands gripped the edge of the table. The thought came to me dimly, through the icy fog in my brain, that he was using the table to hold himself down, that if he let go, the force of his rage would be all-consuming.

'Fortunate.' His voice was tightly controlled.

'I taught your mother and I taught you. There's not a thought in your head that I haven't put there.' Raeburn looked calm enough. But I saw the deliberate way he moved the food around on his plate. I heard the light, dangerous lilt in his voice. It was as if I were looking at a pressure gauge and the needle was trembling precariously at the farthest edge of the dial.

And on the other side of the table was my brother.

Don't, Jack, I pleaded silently. Just leave. Don't.

If it was a prayer, it was to him and for him, I guess; but more than that, it was for myself. At that moment, I didn't care about my mother, or how she'd died, or anything else. An argument between my father and my brother meant an inevitable firefight; in that house, even when the bullets were aimed at Jack they always seemed to pass through me first, and my father's temper terrified me.

Suddenly, without another word, Jack pushed away from the table, stood up, and left the room.

Raeburn's eyes – which were almost as green as my brother's, and had the same intensity – followed him. The fog drained away like thick liquid, and the sudden release of pressure made my ears ring. My stomach was still sick and twisted in knots, but I could move again.

Then the old man snorted. 'Your brother spent nine years too long with that woman. He'll always try to charm the world out of its basket and he'll die angry because it doesn't work, just like she did.' His expression now was indifferent. 'Just like that asshole Searles, with his wacky ties and his motorcycle boots in the classroom. People like that are incapable of imagining that there might be something they weren't born knowing.'

I stared down at my plate. The canned beets on it looked like chunks of raw meat.

Raeburn took a deep breath and let it out again. 'Humanity will not survive as a collective unit, Josephine. It is too deeply infected with stupidity. The only way to survive is to isolate yourself from the diseased cells. Move away from them as soon as possible. Remember that.'

Wiping his mouth, he stood up and shook the crumbs from his shirt. 'Maybe while you're in town, you can meet Margaret Revolt. She wants to, and I think—' He paused. 'She is a very clever young lady.'

Then he left. Distracted, heedless, he turned the light out as he went.

I pushed my plate slowly out of the way. Let my head fall to the table, my cheek against the cool wood. Sat like that, in the quiet. In the dark.

That night, around three in the morning, Jack woke me up when he stumbled over my shoes, which were lying in the middle of my floor.

'Just me,' he said, lifting up my blankets so that he could crawl under them. The burst of cold air made me shiver, and when he pulled the covers back over us I curled up close to his warmth.

He slid an arm around my stomach and laid his head on the side of my neck. His hair was damp with sweat.

Still half asleep, I said, 'Okay?'

'Fuck him.' His breathing was heavy and ragged.

Jack had nightmares. Sometimes they were so bad that he cried out in his sleep and woke up drenched in thick, clammy fear-sweat. Meanwhile, I usually couldn't sleep at all, and those were the hours that we spent together: when I couldn't sleep and he was afraid to try. I never needed to ask him what the nightmares were about. Mary had been dead all night and most of a day before a neighbour knocked on the door – a night and a day that

Jack had spent sitting next to her, waiting for her to wake up.

Now his arm was tight around my waist and his face was buried in my hair. I could feel the moistness of his breath and the prickly growth of his beard against my skin.

'Your dreams are about her,' I said.

'Josie, everything in this house is about her. Everything that happens.' His face turned, burrowed. 'You, me, Raeburn, all of it.'

His breath was a slight tickle on my neck as he spoke, and his chest swelled against my back as he inhaled. I was waking up now, groggy and unsettled. I nestled closer into the nook of Jack's body, closed my eyes, and wondered wearily if I would be able to get back to sleep.

Then I felt Jack's hand on my hair, smoothing it into a soft pile on the pillow, lifting it from the back of my neck. He kept stroking even when the hair was out of his way.

It sent shivers over my scalp. I felt my eyes close with contentment and, drowsily, I said, 'You never talk about her.'

'Sure I do.' Now his hand was buried in the pile of my hair, lifting it up and letting the strands fall through his fingers like water.

'Almost never.'

'He likes it when I talk about her. It's his favourite fucking subject.'

'I like it when you talk about her.'

'You don't know the difference. You never had her to lose.'

But he didn't say it unkindly. I said, 'I have you,' and felt his lips curve against my neck in the darkness. Soon he was asleep.

I woke up alone, with the bleak winter sunlight streaming through my windows. I listened to the quiet house and heard nothing: no music, no movement, no life.

I knew if I went to Jack's room, his bed would be empty and his jacket gone.

I hated days like this.

Sometimes Jack vanished. He'd be gone for a few hours, or maybe more than a few, and then he'd reappear, usually bearing a bottle of something or a stack of magazines for me. I didn't really care about the magazines, but when he brought them to me I always read them, because I was so glad to have him home.

Once, when he was gone nearly every night for six or seven hours at a stretch, it turned out he'd been working at the record store. After that I paid more attention to his disappearances, to see if they fitted into a schedule, but they never did. There was no pattern to them. Sometimes something had happened beforehand that depressed him; sometimes nothing had happened, and he was depressed anyway; sometimes everything seemed fine, and I never suspected a thing until I woke up to an empty house. There was just the vanishing act, and then his return, bearing gifts.

In the morning it was all right. In the morning I could pretend that the silence was actually peace and sit with my cup of coffee thinking calm, pleasant thoughts about the sheer freedom of getting to do exactly what I wanted. While the coffee brewed, I went upstairs for a book of word puzzles, which were more mind-numbing than any drug I'd taken. I spent two hours bent over the table, filling in little black and white boxes and breaking words apart. I smoked cigarette after cigarette, ate dry toast because we were out of butter, and drank coffee until my heart pounded and my nerves sang. When I'd exhausted the range of comfortable positions that the hard kitchen chair had to offer and the walls started to close in, I jumped up and began to clean: wiping down the counters, scrubbing the stove, cleaning the sink with scouring powder until my hands felt raw and chemical-soaked.

Then the kitchen had nothing else to offer me. I drifted from room to room, never spending more than a few minutes in any one, touching things, picking them up, putting them back down. From the front porch into the parlour and then into the study, the basement, the downstairs bathroom, the dining room that we never used. I climbed the front staircase, also little-used, and stood in turn in the doorways of the upstairs bathroom, the first spare bedroom (where most of Crazy Mary's few remaining possessions were kept under a well-picked lock and a badly hidden key), and then Raeburn's room, with its reek of stale laundry and after-shave. In each new room I felt more and more like an intruder.

I sat in Jack's room for a while, perched at the foot of his unmade bed and flipping idly through a science-fiction paperback that I found on the floor, but I couldn't read. I put on his Coltrane album, but that wasn't enough to distract me either, so I went back downstairs and did it all over again.

Then it was almost six o'clock. The sun was starting to set. Jack still wasn't back. I started to catch odd movements out of the corners of my eyes and feel breezes in still air. Strange voices seemed to be having low conversations in other rooms, out of my range of hearing. The house was full of peculiar odours: unfamiliar cologne, cigarette smoke.

I didn't deal well with being alone.

Eventually I fell asleep on my bed and dreamed that I was in a river, swimming. I didn't want to be in the river, but I was trying to get somewhere and the river was the only way to get there. The world on the riverbank grew more alien every time I climbed on shore until I couldn't climb out at all because I knew that nobody would know me, that nobody would even be able to see me.

By the time I saw the twin beams from Jack's headlights shine through the front window, sometime close to midnight, I'd finished crying and thrown up twice. I flew down the stairs and was at the door, near tears with relief, when he came in. His face was tired and he was holding a paper bag that smelled like Chinese food.

'Hi,' I said and threw myself at him.

He caught me, but only just, and then he pushed me lightly out of his way. His eyes were impatient.

I brushed at a stray piece of hair that had fallen in my eyes, rubbed my cold cheeks, and tried to look normal.

'You've been chewing on your fingernails,' he said.

'No I haven't.'

'They're bleeding.' He handed the paper bag to me and went upstairs.

I took the bag into the kitchen and unpacked the food. There was lo mein and sesame chicken and fried rice: he'd gotten me my favourite foods. I took two bottles of beer from the fridge, grabbed some forks, and carried it all into the parlour. His jacket lay across the couch where he'd thrown it. I took a packet of cigarettes out of the pocket – I'd smoked all of mine – and sat down to wait for him. By the time he came down in a pair of jeans, drops of water still clinging to his bare shoulders, I had pretty much stopped shaking.

He ate quickly, shovelling the food into his mouth. I wanted, as always, to tell him about how much the house scared me when there was nobody else in it, about the terrible silences, about the way I couldn't seem to stay still without the walls closing in on me, but – also as always – he never gave me a chance. He never even looked at me. It was as if I wasn't even there.

Until he said, 'You know, Josie, at some point you're going to need to be able to be by yourself.'

I tried to smile. 'I've got you, haven't I?'

Now he looked at me. The set of his mouth was hostile. 'You think I'm going to be here for ever? You think I'm going to waste my life sitting in this house holding your hand?'

Never, never had Jack spoken like this to me. There had never been any mention of leaving me, of wasting his life. I didn't know what to say; for a moment I sat in stunned silence.

Then I stood up. 'Fine. Don't, if it's such a waste of your time.' I turned my back on him and left the room.

Upstairs in my room, with the door shut against him, I stood in the middle of the floor, among the piles of clothes and textbooks and half-done pages of maths problems. I was so angry that my body felt like it was going to implode, or spontaneously combust, or draw lightning from the sky. I wanted to fight him, hit him, tear at those smug green eyes of his – but the house was no longer lifeless and empty. My room was bright with rage, but it was familiar and comforting.

An hour later, I was reading when he knocked on my door and came in.

He sat down on the edge of my bed. 'I'm an asshole.'

'Perceptive.' I didn't move over.

He lay down anyway, laced his fingers behind his head and said, 'What are you reading?'

'Ray Bradbury.'

'Deep.'

'It's yours.'

He smiled a little. 'Martians?'

'The end of the world.'

'Is that all,' he said and was silent for a while.

Finally, he spoke. 'This morning, when I was going back to my room, I pictured myself doing the same thing in twenty years. You and me and Raeburn, all still living here, everything the same, except now we're older. Can you picture that? Everything the same, except we've lived our whole lives here, in this house. With him.' He turned over on his side, propped his head on his elbow, and looked at me, his expression grave. 'I started thinking about what Raeburn always says, that nothing anybody does matters because we're going to blow ourselves to kingdom come anyway, and so forth.'

'So?'

'So?' Jack repeated and let his head fall wearily to my stomach. 'So, I don't know.'

'If he's right, it pretty much lets us off the hook, doesn't it?'

Jack's face crumpled. He looked tired and sad and very young. I touched his back and said, 'It's not that bad.'

'It's hell,' he said. 'We're in hell.'

Then he wrapped his arms around me and pulled me down, burying his face in my hair. We lay like that for a while. Eventually he lifted his face and said, 'But I have to admit, if I've got to be trapped here, I'm trapped with a pretty exceptional sister. Even if she is a weakling sometimes.'

'Thanks,' I said.

His finger traced my collarbone. 'I think I'd go crazy without you.'

It was as if my muscles had been clenched for hours and relaxed when he spoke. Forgiven; forgotten.

The year's first snowstorm began the day before the party. Jack, who'd been sullen and withdrawn for days, drove us to the college on roads frosted thick with a mixture of salt and ash, and, in places, with patches of treacherous, gleaming black ice. As we crossed the mountains, the snow came down in vicious little flakes. My dress and Jack's tux were in garment bags in the back of the truck. When the snow didn't stop we pulled over to the side of the road and covered them with the emergency blankets from behind the seat.

As we fought with frozen hands to push the seat back into place, the sky darkened above us. I didn't know if the darkness had fallen because of the time or the weather, and neither of us had a watch. I said, 'I think we're going to be late.' When we got back on the road Jack drove faster. He turned on the radio, but there was no reception: not in a snowstorm this high in the mountains. 'You try,' he said, and so I turned the knob back and forth. There was nothing to hear but static.

Meanwhile, the snow outside had turned to flashing, glittering shards of hail in the truck's headlights. They hit the windshield and ricocheted off into the darkness. The sound was like driving over gravel. There was an embankment to our right where the road had been blasted into the side of the mountain; on the left was only blackness and the pale trunks of the bare trees that covered the steep slope.

I looked at Jack. 'Storm's getting worse.'

'Try AM.'

I hit the button just as the rear wheels hit a patch of ice and the tail end of the truck lurched across the yellow line that was barely visible in the road ahead.

Jack twisted the wheel calmly in the opposite direction and we were straight again.

'Maybe you should slow down.' The words felt stupid coming out of my mouth.

'First I'm too slow, now I'm too fast. Make up your mind. What do you want?'

'To get there alive,' I said, and then the truck seemed suddenly to *lift* and was sliding above the tarmac in a soft frictionless glide that for the briefest of instants was actually gentle and easy. Jack swore and wrenched the wheel to one side. There was nothing calm about him this time, and all at once the road in front of us was gone and we were looking at the pale dizzying forest and then more road and more embankment and the terrifying black drop behind the thin white trees, spinning around and around us like some kind of nightmare kaleidoscope. The force of the spin was pushing me against the door and I was clutching at anything I could. Jack was still swearing and fighting with the wheel. His voice and his motions were desperate and then the wheels were spinning in the gravel of a sudden rare shoulder on the embankment side.

We'd stopped.

In the abrupt silence I could hear the truck's motor purring like a contented cat, and Jack breathing hard, and myself breathing harder. He was staring straight ahead of us, out into the swirl of ice crystals in the headlights.

Centripetal force, I thought, bizarrely. Not the spin pushing against the truck, but the truck pushing against the spin. One by one, I unclenched my fingers from the door. I'd been bracing myself against the floor of the truck so hard that my knees ached.

'Slick patch,' Jack said. When I didn't respond he said, 'I wouldn't have let anything happen. I'd never let you get hurt.'

'Just get us there,' I said.

'Your wish is my et cetera.' He drove slowly the rest of the way.

We went straight to the address Raeburn had given us for the motel, which turned out to be one of those places that rented rooms for thirty dollars a night or fifteen dollars an hour. Our room was squalid. When we turned on the light, the walls were crawling. Brushing my teeth in the bathroom, I took one look at the shower stall and decided that I was clean enough. Nobody had ever intentionally made a bathroom fixture that colour.

Jack was whistling as he dressed. For tonight, at least, the impenetrable melancholy that had been on him since his disappearance seemed to have spun itself away on that mountain road. 'You know what would be funny?' he said as he put on his tie in front of the spotted mirror. 'If Raeburn came by tomorrow and neither of us was here. Say, for instance, you were to catch the eye of our favourite up-and-coming physics professor and he were to invite you back to his charming little apartment for a quiet evening of gravity-testing.'

'What about you?'

'I hide in the closet and film it.'

I gave him a hard look. 'I think you're getting sicker.'

He grinned at me and stepped away from the mirror so that I could use it. 'Speaking of getting sick, if either of us tries to sleep in this room, ten to one we end up with dysentery.' He kicked the bed. The iron feet made a ghastly squealing noise against the dingy linoleum and I heard – or imagined – the skittering of a thousand tiny cockroach legs. I shuddered and turned to the mirror to put on Crazy Mary's pearl earrings.

Jack grabbed me from behind.

'Your mission,' he whispered into my ear, his breath hot, his hands on my waist, 'should you choose to accept it: use those deadly feminine wiles to seduce one Professor Benjamin Searles, soon to be tenured, and thereby secure a halfway decent place to sleep tonight while your lowly brother hovers outside the window with only the soulless mechanical hum of a video camera for company.' As he spoke, his hands slid up my sides to my bare shoulders.

I brushed him away. 'No, thanks.'

Jack dropped his hands and stepped back from me. 'Failing that, we can always drive home after the party if neither of us is too ploughed.'

'I'm not sure I trust you to drive,' I said as he turned me around and looked me up and down.

'Very nice,' he said. 'Beautiful.'

My dress was forest green velvet, with a low neckline and a lower back. The colour did nice things for my eyes, and the thick, clingy fabric did nice things for my body. It made me look older than sixteen. Jack had brought it home for me the week before.

'Thanks,' I said. 'Not so bad yourself.'

And it was true. The tux suited him; it made the burning spark in his eyes and the angry tension in the set of his jaw dashing. He appraised himself in the mirror, pushed a lock of his gelled hair into place, and nodded. 'Yeah. Not bad.' He held out an arm to me. I laced mine through it. I felt grand, female, beautiful. For once I didn't mind that people would be looking at us.

We didn't leave anything in the motel room and we didn't bother to lock the door behind us.

The party was being held in the president's mansion, which was the sort of place that our house on the Hill might have been, if anyone still cared about it. The walls of the library, where the bar was set up, were lined with books on handsome wooden shelves. Some of them were in languages and alphabets that I couldn't read. Our house was full of books, too – some of them beautiful first editions that had come down to Raeburn from his father. Most of them, though, were college textbooks, and except for Jack's science-fiction paperbacks and spy novels there was very little in the way of entertainment. But on one shelf of the president's library, I found Dostoyevsky, Dashiell Hammett, and volume six of the 1933 *Oxford English Dictionary*. It made me want to steal away and find a corner.

The rest of the house was full of carefully placed furniture, expensive rugs, and simple arrangements of fresh flowers. There was a huge heated tent over the lawn and garden, lit inside and out with strings of golden lights. Dozens of small candles floated on the reflecting pool. The year before, they'd had a string quartet; but even without live music it was a pretty good party.

We found Raeburn under the tent, talking to a stout man with wild hair and thick glasses. He taught physics, too, which I would have guessed even if I hadn't recognized him. None of them, Raeburn included, could ever remember to comb their hair. I think they all liked to imagine themselves as Einstein, too preoccupied with matters of the universe to think about trivialities like combs.

We were an hour late. Raeburn's eyes flickered dangerously when he saw us, but his smile was broad as he said, 'The return of the prodigals,' and kissed me on the cheek. 'Eugene,' he said to the fat man, 'you remember my children, John and Josephine.'

'Of course,' Eugene said, shaking my brother's hand. His eyes were fixed on me. 'Lovely. I hadn't remembered that you had such adult children, Joseph.' Raeburn assumed a modest expression, and Eugene continued: 'You're both very lucky. Not many fathers would take the time with their children's education that your father has with yours. I certainly didn't. You, John—'

'Jack.'

'Really?' Eugene blinked. 'Jack for John. I thought that was outdated. Were you a Kennedy fan, Joseph?'

'Their mother's brother was John,' Raeburn said shortly. 'Called Jack.'

'Hmm, well,' Eugene said. From the uncomfortable look on his face, I guessed that he'd heard about Crazy Mary. 'Jack, you're what? Nineteen?'

'Eighteen.'

'And you, my dear?' Eugene's small, watery eyes gazed at me from behind his glasses.

'I'm sixteen,' I said.

'Really?' Eugene did the blink again, pushing his glasses up for good measure. 'Really? I'd have guessed much – but you really must meet my son Martin,' he said hastily, glancing at Raeburn. 'He's around somewhere. I suspect you two would get along famously.' He scanned the crowd.

'Actually, what I'd really like right now is a drink. I mean, I'd like something *to* drink,' I added quickly and pulled a grinning Jack away as Raeburn glared at me.

'One look and he could tell that you and Martin would get along famously,' Jack said. 'You two must have a lot in common.'

'Maybe Martin has breasts, too.' I concentrated on following Jack as he forced his way through the crowd.

'I wouldn't be surprised, after meeting the old man.'

At the bar, a stylishly dressed woman, her hair dyed the same artificial shade of ash blond as most of the other older women at the party, looked at us closely and said, 'Why, you're Joseph's family, aren't you?'

'Have we met?' Jack said.

She laughed. Old or not, she was still beautiful. She had amazing skin: clear and smooth and tanned, in a healthy time-in-the-garden sort of way. 'Not that you'd remember. I'm Claire. My office is down the hall from your father's. Chemistry. I saw your picture on his desk,' she said. 'It was taken quite a while ago – but of course I recognized two such handsome kids. Your mother must have been quite a looker.'

What kind of person uses the word 'looker'? I thought, but Jack's expression warmed considerably. 'She was. She was beautiful.'

'I didn't even know her,' I said, surprising myself.

'That's so sad,' Claire said absently, without looking at me. 'You must be John.'

'So people keep telling me. Jack.' He pointed to himself. 'And Josie.'

Claire grinned an attractive gap-toothed grin. 'Well, Jack and Josie, I'm afraid you're the only two young people in a room full of old folks.'

'Eugene said something about a son,' I said.

She grimaced. 'Dear God, is Eugene trying to set you up with Martin? That's like him.' She rolled her eyes. 'Poor, deluded Eugene. He does keep hoping.' She winked at me. 'Let's just say you're not his type, dear, and let it go at that. And even barring that – but never mind.' She shook her head. 'I'm still not sure that physicists should be allowed to breed. Although you two seem to have turned out all right,' she said, looking at Jack.

'We're painfully average,' I said.

'I'm not sure about that,' she said, 'but you're identifiably human.'

'We have to go. Our father is waiting for us.' I pushed Jack into the crowd. When we were well away from her I said, 'My God, is there anyone here who isn't going to hit on us? Maybe you're right. Maybe I should try and land Searles.'

'It's all about sex, Josie.'

'What is?'

'Everything.'

Raeburn was talking heatedly about something when we got back. Eugene was still standing next to him, and a small crowd of men had gathered around the two of them. 'He is the personification of everything that's wrong with modern theoretical physics,' Raeburn was saying. 'What can possibly be left of quantum mechanics after it's filtered through a brain raised on thirty-second promotional spots? A music video, that's what. Lots of flashing lights and flashy clothes. A pseudo-revolution led by pseudoscientists who study the laws of the universe because "black holes are sexy".'

Jack nudged me.

'I'm not saying Ben's a brilliant theorist,' Eugene said placatingly, 'but he's a wonderful teacher. Even you have to admit that, Joseph.'

'I have to admit nothing of the kind. He's engaging. He's popular. But does that make him a wonderful teacher? It might make him prom king, but—'

'You're only jealous because you didn't get to stand up onstage wearing the crown, Joseph.' Claire appeared at Raeburn's elbow and put a consoling hand on his arm. 'Don't worry, darling. I promise I'll ask you to the next Sadie Hawkins dance.'

Everybody laughed. Even Raeburn. I shifted awkwardly on my too-high heels and wondered if all of his colleagues were blind not to have seen the flash of rage on his face when Claire spoke. Jack was watching Claire with open admiration. I decided that I didn't find her amusing.

'Really, though,' Claire continued. 'You're taking this all too seriously, Joseph. You're still the acknowledged mad genius around here. Rest on your laurels, why don't you, and leave poor Ben alone. He's a nice kid.'

Kelly Braffet

Raeburn smiled tolerantly. 'Poor Claire, led through the nose by
the ever-louder ticking of your biological clock.'

'Careful, Joseph,' Claire said. Her lips were tight. 'Your
desperation is showing.'

Eugene looked around nervously, seemed to see me, and
coughed. 'Well, then, Miss Josephine. Why don't you tell us what
grand plans you have for the future?'

'I haven't really thought that much about it,' I said. 'Maybe I'll
be a physicist.'

Jack stared at me.

'Like your father?' Claire said. 'Oh, that's sweet.'

Raeburn smiled and managed to look proudly at me. Well, at
least now we're both lying, I thought, and smiled back.

Later Jack and I smoked a joint behind the greenhouse, shivering
and up to our ankles in snow but away from the lights and the
people. I'd had quite a bit to drink by then, and the cold, fresh
air was good after the heat and noise of the party. The store of
sociability I kept in reserve for these occasions was exhausted. My
nerves were jangling. I wanted to be stoned. I wanted to go
home.

'What was that crap about wanting to be a physicist?' Jack said.
'You're no more a physicist than I am.'

'I don't know. That Claire person was getting on my nerves.'

He half-laughed. 'She's a sharp one, all right. Think you'll be
that sharp when you're fifty-two?'

'How do you know she's fifty-two?'

He shrugged. 'She and I had a little chat while Raeburn was
talking about what a firm grasp of string theory you have. Already
knowing what an impressive junior physicist you are, I didn't feel
a need to listen.' The joint crackled as he drew on it. He passed

it to me. 'That old bastard deserves what he gets, all that pompous garbage about pseudo-scientists, and black holes being sexy. What a fucking snob.'

I said nothing. Just took a long drag on the joint and waited for it to hit.

Jack kicked at the ground furiously. Then he looked at me and gave me a wan smile. 'I could kill him, Jo. Trotting us out like show ponies whenever the mood strikes him,' he said. 'I could kill him.'

'Well, don't,' I said. 'I don't know how we'd get out of that.'

Jack didn't answer.

Somebody was trying to get my attention. I was standing in a corner, trying to be furniture; I was thoroughly stoned and not a little drunk, and it took a moment before I understood that the voice was speaking to me. I turned around. A man with sandy hair tied back in a ponytail and wire-rimmed glasses stood at my shoulder. He was young, not that much older than Jack, and he didn't look entirely comfortable in his tuxedo.

'Your hair is about to catch fire,' he said and pointed to a small table next to me. On the table was a short, fat candle with three wicks, all of which were burning simultaneously. My hair, free of its plait for the night, had drifted perilously close to the flames.

'Oh,' I said stupidly.

The man said, 'Oh, indeed,' and moved the candle. The sober part of my brain sent up a signal flare and I realized who he was.

'You're Ben Searles,' I said.

'I am. Have we met?'

'Last year.' I remembered to stick my hand out so that he could shake it. 'I'm Josie Raeburn.'

'Joe Raeburn's daughter.' He gave me a careful look. 'I heard you and your brother were going to be here tonight. I should have recognized you.'

'How? It can't be from the photo on the Christmas card. They aren't even in the mail yet.'

He smiled. 'There's a family resemblance. But I'm glad to hear about the card. I was starting to think I was being snubbed.' He looked a little strained. 'You know, your father is a brilliant scientist. I actually wrote a paper on some of his work when I was a student. Condensed matter theory. Terrible paper on an interesting subject. I hear you're planning to go into the family business.'

'What? Oh,' I said. 'No. That's a rumour. I'm not sure how it got started.'

'So what do you want to do?'

'I was thinking about cosmetology.'

'Ah. Fringe astrophysics,' he said. 'Studying cosmets.'

I stared.

'Joke?' he said.

Then I got it and laughed – probably too hard. I was stoned, and what Raeburn had said was true: Searles really did have dreamboat eyes. When I could speak, I said, 'I didn't know you were funny. I've been hearing about you all night. Nobody said you were funny.'

Ben took a sip from his drink, which looked like Scotch on the rocks. 'I've been hearing about you since I started teaching.'

'Not from my father.'

He gave me a curious look. 'No. From everybody else on the faculty. Whenever his name comes up, somebody says wait until you meet his kids.'

'Wait until you meet us to do what?'

He shrugged. 'Everyone says you're – really something. Smart. Good-looking. All those things we like in people these days.'

Something about the way he said it made me think that smart and good-looking weren't what he'd heard about us at all. 'I imagine,' I said, 'that the things that you've heard about us are the same things we've heard about you.'

Ben smiled crookedly. 'Quite possibly.'

We sat in silence for a while. Across the room I could see my father talking to someone I didn't recognize.

'Your father's a brilliant scientist,' he said again.

'He's a raging son of a bitch,' I answered.

A few glasses of wine later, I went looking for Jack and found him standing on the front porch, talking to a girl. She was young, wore her dark hair in a severe bob, and had thick glasses. I didn't notice anything else about her before I pulled him back into the house.

'Please can we go home now?' I said.

Distracted, Jack ran a hand through his hair. 'Wait a few minutes. I was talking to—'

'I saw. I want to go home. I want to go home now.'

'Just wait.'

'No.' It was hard to talk. Everything seemed to be happening at a great distance. 'I'm stoned and I'm drunk and I'm starting to get paranoid. Please?'

'Five minutes,' he said and went back outside to the girl on the porch.

I waited by the door, growing more and more agitated. He didn't come and he didn't come and he didn't come. Meanwhile, my stomach was increasingly unreliable and my feet increasingly unsteady. The room was full of people in elegant clothes, light chamber music was playing somewhere, and I was standing next to a burning candle that was filling the air with a nasty sweet smell.

I couldn't avoid the people or the music, but I could get away from the candle. Fresh air, that was what I needed. Not the front porch, though. Not with Jack and that girl. I started to make my way through the crowd. It was harder than I thought it would be. Things were whirling. The air grew thick. The other door seemed to have disappeared, or the layout of the room had changed, because I no longer knew which way to go. I put out an arm to steady myself.

Unexpectedly, somebody took it. From somewhere on the other side of the fog I heard somebody say my name. I grabbed at the voice with both hands and fell over onto Ben Searles.

'Hi,' he said. 'You need some help?'

'Outside,' was all I could say.

'This way.' Gratefully I let myself be led through the crowd. I tried to lean on him so it wouldn't be obvious that I was drunk. Finally we came to a door and he opened it, letting in a wonderful blast of cold air. Then the thick, sweet smell of burning vanilla filled my nose and mouth. I opened my mouth to say that this was the wrong door. Instead I threw up.

Then I was on my knees, staring at an enormous puddle of red wine and stomach acid soaking into a beautiful, intricately patterned rug. The people near us looked alarmed and embarrassed, and moved away quickly. I heard Ben say, 'She's okay, but don't eat the oysters,' as he handed me a cocktail napkin. There was a little nervous laughter. I was wiping vaguely at my mouth and staring at the spreading pool on the floor, which looked exactly like I felt: soiled, used, vile.

'Okay?' Ben was crouched next to me. His polished shoes were perilously close to the vomit puddle. For some reason that made me feel worse and tears welled up in my eyes.

'It's okay,' he said. 'Can you get up?' He put his arm around me and lifted me to my feet. Somewhere between the floor and his shoulder I started to feel dizzy again and my eyes closed. My head fell against his chest and I thought, dimly, this is all very inappropriate.

I heard Raeburn's voice. 'What is this? What's wrong with her?'

I didn't open my eyes. Ben's shirt smelled nice, like an extremely clean forest.

'It's okay, Joseph,' he said. 'She's not feeling well, that's all.'

And then Jack's voice cut through the fog like a bell. 'I'll take her.'

Ben said, 'She's okay,' but I made my eyes open, found the tuxedoed, golden-haired blur that was Jack, and put my arms out towards him like a child. I saw the face of the girl from the porch drifting over his shoulder and then I was in a cloud of Jack-smell, with his good, strong arms around me, and my eyes closed again.

Raeburn sounded formal and aloof. 'I can't even begin to tell you how embarrassed I am, Searles. I'm sure we can handle her from here.'

'Just get her home, she'll be okay.' Ben sounded easy and light.

'I'll take care of it.' Raeburn was still smooth, still polite. He took my arm and pulled me away from Jack and I was on my own again, trying to stand, with the only certain thing in the world the bright burst of pain where his fingers dug into my flesh.

Searles turned away.

Raeburn started to pull me outside, half carrying, half dragging me.

'In front of all my colleagues, Josephine?' His voice was an angry hiss. 'In front of everyone I know? Do you think I don't have enough to worry about from these people?' His grip tightened. 'Where did you get it? Who gave it to you? Was it Searles?'

'They aren't exactly checking ID,' an unfamiliar female voice said. 'She could have gotten it anywhere.'

'What she didn't get herself I got for her,' Jack said. 'For Christ's sake, let go of her. She's sick enough.'

I was conscious of wintry air on my bare legs. We were outside now. 'Excellent,' Raeburn said. 'You've gotten your sixteen-year-old sister drunk in public.'

'As opposed to in private, where it's okay.'

Raeburn swore and pushed me towards Jack, who was warm and stable in the cold white world. 'Take her if you want her. You've already ruined her.'

I started to cry. My legs lifted off the floor, and then I was being carried away and placed in the truck, carefully; Jack's coat was tucked around me, something soft was put under my head, and all the while I heard Raeburn's voice from very far away saying cruel things until finally the door closed.

Later, at home, Jack held a glass of water up for me to drink.

'Jack.'

'Hm?'

'They were talking about us. All of them.'

'Well, they are now,' he said calmly.

'Who was that girl?'

'What girl?'

'On the porch.'

He stroked my hair. 'I'll tell you about it when you're sober.'

I felt very warm and faraway. 'Jack?'

'Hm?'

'Changed my mind,' I said. 'You can kill him.'

The next day, fighting my hangover in bed, I pulled the

wooden box out from behind the headboard, took out my birth certificate, and tucked it underneath my mattress, where I could reach down to touch it. Then I lay back, sweating and sick.

His part is finished, I thought. He no longer matters.

Christmas passed the way it always did in the Raeburn household, which is to say without notice. The notion of the three of us sitting together in the same room, exchanging gifts and singing carols, was ludicrous. But late on Christmas night Jack produced a brick of hash and said, 'Ho, ho, ho.'

'Joy to the world,' I said.

We deserved any fun we had. Any time the college wasn't in session was hell for us. Summer was the worst – by July our father had usually descended into a depression that approached psychosis, and we made it our business to be somewhere else whenever possible – but winter break was no picnic either. Our long driveway wasn't ploughed unless we arranged and paid for it in advance. So once the snow fell, and it was just the three of us there in that isolated old house, Jack and I retreated to the attic.

Raeburn never came up there, and Jack had set apart a corner with an old couch, a hot plate, and a space heater. There we sat, through those long, dark winter weeks, and played cards or read to each other or smoked joint after joint until neither of us felt like talking. Jack and I never had trouble amusing ourselves. God knows we'd had enough practice.

This winter wasn't as bad as some. Raeburn didn't talk to either of us for a week after the Christmas party, which was some relief, but whatever ace was up his sleeve was entertaining enough to dull the edge of his cabin fever and too good to keep to himself. On those rare occasions when the three of us met for dinner, our father would chortle and snort to himself with the smugness of a person who wants to make sure you know that you're not being told a secret. He kept the study door locked tight now.

Finally, finally, Raeburn called the snowplough. After it came and went, he threw some clothes in the back of his car, mumbled something incomprehensible, and disappeared down the road. The bar that sold sandwiches also sold pizza and six-packs; Jack and I gave Raeburn a twenty-minute lead and went in search of one of each. When we came home, we moved back into the parlour, which was flooded with bright winter sun. It was as if the very air in the house was celebrating with us. Late that night we went for a long drive on the twisting back roads outside Janesville; the air was bright with starlight reflected from the snow, and the world seemed beautiful.

For about a week.

Raeburn came home that Thursday because the first week of the semester was registration week and there was nothing for him to do at the college. It was only the second week in January, but the snow was melting and patches of green grass were showing through the white. Jack and I were in the parlour, playing double patience, and we heard the motor long before we saw the motorcycle on our driveway through the bare trees. I remember thinking that anyone who would ride a motorcycle in January, early melt or no early melt, had to be either crazy or desperate; so I wasn't surprised when the rider, who was wearing a leather jacket and jeans and must have been freezing, pulled off his helmet to reveal long hair and wire-rimmed glasses.

'It's Searles,' Jack said, although I could see that for myself. A moment later we heard Ben pounding on the front door and screaming our father's name.

'Should I go get Raeburn?' I asked.

Jack shook his head. 'He has to be able to hear that.'

But when I finally went to find him, Raeburn was sitting in the study with his legs stretched out, smoking a pipe and gazing complacently into space. Outside Ben shouted, 'Open the door, Raeburn – I know you're home – I can fucking *smell* you.'

Raeburn was wearing an expression of deep satisfaction. 'Josephine,' he greeted me.

'There's someone at the door,' I said.

'Then perhaps you should let him in.'

When I opened the door, Ben was in mid-pound and he nearly clocked me. 'Christ!' He jumped back, startled.

'It's me,' I said. 'Just me.'

Sweat stood out in beads on Ben's forehead and his long hair hung loose and wild around his flushed face. His breath formed clouds in the cold air. 'You scared me.'

'You're the one who's yelling.'

'I almost hit you.' His voice was thick with barely controlled rage and his hands were shaking. 'Go get your father. I know he's here.'

I could feel Raeburn standing behind me. When he said, 'Hello, Searles,' he sounded unusually pleasant. I could hear the smile in his voice. 'Is there something I can help you with?'

'You know damn well why I'm here,' Ben said over my shoulder. His jaw was clenched tight.

'Do I?'

'Tell your daughter to go inside,' Ben said levelly. His fists were clenched.

'Why?' Raeburn's laugh was unpleasant. 'Will it destroy her good image of you to learn that you sleep with your students?'

'No. But it might destroy her good image of you to hear that you bribe yours into lying for you.'

I thought of Margaret Revolt and began to understand.

I stepped quickly through the door and onto the porch. The melting snow was half-frozen slush beneath my socks, and the flannel shirt that I was wearing – one of Jack's – wasn't enough to keep out the cold.

'Bribery wasn't necessary,' Raeburn said.

'You unbelievable bastard.' Ben's face was white with fury.

Raeburn's eyes flicked to me. He pointed at Searles, a mirthless grin on his lips. 'Look, Josephine. Young Benjamin has discovered that life is unfair. Aren't you glad that you already know that?'

'You can't do this.' Cords stood out under the skin of Ben's neck and he said it again – 'You can't *do* this!' – only this time he screamed it, the sound harsh and furious and dying without an echo in our little clearing. It was more than rage, more than a protest at the sheer unfairness of it all; it was a denial of the very possibility of what Margaret and my father had done. Raeburn was right. Ben Searles, it was clear, lived in a world where people simply didn't do the kinds of things that my father did.

I felt sorry for him. I remembered fading in and out of consciousness with my head on his tuxedo, and the way he'd smelled like a clean forest and made light of the steaming pool of vomit on the president's rug, and I felt sorry for him.

'It's unfortunate,' Raeburn said. 'Perhaps in your next position, you'll be more careful with your female students.'

He turned around and closed the door.

I stood on the porch in my stockinged feet, and Ben looked like he was the one who was going to throw up, right now. I thought, that's only fair, and took a step towards him.

Suddenly he hurled himself at the door, pounding on it with his fists and screaming obscenities at my father through the scarred wood.

'It won't do any good,' Jack said. He was standing in the side yard in his boots; he had come around the house from the back door.

But Ben's assault was already fading into hopelessness. He gave the door one last kick and let his forehead fall onto the wood.

'It doesn't matter,' he said to the door. 'My career is over.' The despair in his voice was palpable. 'I'm thirty-two years old and my career has just been ended by a bitter old man and an eighteen-year-old girl who dresses like my grandmother.'

I reached out to touch him, and Jack said softly, 'You can get back at him.'

There was an envelope in Jack's hand and he extended it towards Ben. The young professor stared at it blankly.

I knew that Raeburn was probably standing on the other side of the door, listening. Quickly I pointed at the door, and Jack nodded.

'Please go home, Mr Searles. Please.' I tried to sound frightened and pathetic. It wasn't hard. 'Before my father gets angry.' At the same time, Jack whispered something to Ben, keeping his words under mine.

Ben's eyes widened.

They spoke quietly, Ben Searles and my brother, for only a few minutes. I didn't hear what they said. The snow, where it still lay on the porch, was up to my ankles. My toes ached with the cold.

After the motorcycle was gone in a cloud of exhaust fumes, I took careful steps through the melting snow to stand next to Jack. 'What was that?'

'A letter,' Jack said. His eyes gleamed.

'Where did you get it?'

He stuck his hands in his pockets and rocked back on his boot heels. 'Stole it from the study.'

'What was in it?'

'Margaret Revolt and our father,' Jack said. Behind us, the door opened and Raeburn came out onto the porch. He was looking at Jack but the frustration in his stance told me that he hadn't heard anything.

'You,' he said. 'What were you talking to him about?'

'Giving him directions.' Jack's face was innocent, but his eyes were shining.

Sunday night: burrowed deep beneath Jack's blankets, my icy feet tucked under his legs and his hands wrapped in my hair.

'She was smart,' he said. He was talking about Crazy Mary. 'She made up games. She'd read to me, novels about clones and Martians and space battles, and then we'd pretend to be the people in the books. She always wanted to be the alien. Or we played cards – I remember building a big house of cards, with towers as tall as I was. Once on my birthday she came up with a huge box of dominoes and we spent three days setting them up; when the box was empty, she came home with a cake and we knocked them over, and that was my birthday present.'

I was silent, waiting for him to continue.

'She was beautiful,' he said finally, and he didn't say anything else.

Eventually his breath rose and fell evenly, and I knew he was asleep.

I remember him leaving the room. I woke up enough to pull the blankets closer and go back to sleep.

Fabulous Things

The phone rang the next morning and woke me up. Raeburn answered it, which meant that it was early – he hadn't left for the college yet. The faint murmur of his voice grew louder and louder until I heard the unmistakable sound of an object hitting the wall, followed by the sound of shattering glass.

Raeburn screamed, 'Josephine! Get down here!' and I was on my feet, trembling and scrabbling for my clothes in the flat morning light.

Jack wouldn't fumble. Jack wouldn't jump. Jack wouldn't even bother going downstairs. He'd make Raeburn come to him.

I think I knew even then that he was gone.

Raeburn stood in the middle of the kitchen. His fists were tightly clenched and his face was red. The table was on its side and there was a litter of broken dishes on the floor next to it.

Through clenched teeth he said, 'Pick this garbage up.'

I moved towards the table, giving him a wide berth, and crouched down to pick up the pieces of china. My fingers shook. It was a mess. There had been orange juice in one of the broken glasses; the remnants of a fried egg were congealed on one of the plates.

I could hear him breathing heavily behind me, like an animal.

'You imbeciles,' he said. 'You stupid little ingrates.'

My hand was full of shards. I cupped them next to my body and kept picking them up as behind me, something else shattered in a brilliant burst of noise.

I didn't look around.

'Ungrateful, degenerate slut.' He was crouched down next to me now, cursing in my ear and grabbing my arm with hard, relentless fingers. I could smell the bitter stench of his breath. 'Did you help him?'

I couldn't carry any more of the shards but I was afraid to move. The garbage can was behind him.

'Did you help him? Your rotten, sneaking brother? Did you help him?' I was still crouching. He pushed hard against my shoulder. My handful of shards went flying and I lost my balance. I put a hand down to break my fall. It landed on a sharp piece of glass and I cried out.

'Idiot,' Raeburn said. He picked up a peppershaker from the floor and threw it at me. 'You can't do anything right. You're utterly incapable of the simplest – fucking – thing.'

I was crying. There was glass stuck in my palm, sharp and hot and alien. The blood was starting to drip down my wrist, but I was still trying to pick up the shards, because that was the only way this was ever going to be over.

My father towered over me, huge and powerful, his green eyes snapping like Jack's when he was angry. I flinched and tried to cover my face but Raeburn grabbed my wrists and pulled hard. I couldn't stand up. He dragged me along the floor to the overturned table, where most of the mess was.

'Quit crying!' he screamed and pushed me down into the middle of it. 'Your brother just ruined my life! Quit crying!' My arm landed hard on a piece of glass, something gave in my shoulder, and I cried out again. There were smears of blood on the floor. Some distant, removed part of me wondered how in the world I was supposed to quit crying.

'Clean it up,' he said, his voice cold and dead.

I couldn't see clearly through my tears so I had to feel around on the floor for the slimy pieces of glass – the piece embedded in my hand flaming bright and hot with every pat – and when I had gathered a handful of them I stumbled-ran past him to dump them in the garbage can, feeling myself scuttle along the floor like a bug and hating him, hating him with a hate larger than anything I had ever felt in my life. My nerves were like steel wire with current running through them; I expected him to grab or kick me every time I passed him. He didn't. He only stood, shaking and mad with fury, and watched.

'This is my house,' he said. 'You repulsive littlc creatures, you think you've taken it over. You think you count for something here. You know what you are?' he said as I crawled to the sink to get a rag to clean up the egg and the orange juice, which was mixing with my blood on the floor. 'You're like viruses. Viruses your crazy goddamned mother left behind for me to deal with.' He shook his head. 'I could have been a great scientist. I could have done miraculous things. But now what do I do? I work at a fourth-tier, *regional* private college so that I can feed the two of you, and it doesn't matter how much I try to make you something useful, to make you fucking *human*—'

And now he did grab me, lifting me off my knees by my hair. A high panicked whine came from my mouth as my feet scratched at the floor. He used his double fistful of my hair to shake me, punctuating each word. 'Everything – about you – is a *waste* – of my time.'

The pain was unbearable. I managed to get out, 'Stop,' in a thin, terrified croak, and he dropped me.

He stood over me for a moment, glaring down.

'Your piece-of-shit brother,' he said, suddenly calm. 'The one who thinks he can interfere in my business. Where is he?'

I lay collapsed on the floor, gasping with fear and aching in a dozen places. I could only shake my head.

He stared down at me a moment more. He was breathing hard. 'He left you here, didn't he?' His voice was soft. 'Left you here alone.'

I didn't look up.

'You've backed the wrong horse, my dear.' His feet, which were all that I could see of him, turned around and walked out of the kitchen.

Trembling, I brought my right hand up in front of my face. There was a shard of glass the size of a half-dollar buried in the meaty part of my palm. I took hold of it with my other hand. Slowly, slowly, I pulled it out.

When the kitchen was finally clean, I climbed the back staircase wearily. My shoulder was aching and there was an old dishtowel wrapped around my hand. The gash on my arm was less serious and had already stopped bleeding, but there was drying blood all over my hands and arms and clothes, and thick clots of it in my hair. I must have grabbed at my scalp after Raeburn let me drop. Dimly I wondered if the cut in my hand needed stitches. Jack would know, I thought. He'd even stitched up a cut for me once, when I fell through a window. We hadn't had any anaesthetic, but I had been drunk enough not to care.

My head felt hollow and sore from crying but now my eyes were dry. I couldn't keep from looking into Jack's room as I passed. His leather jacket was gone. The pile of clothes on his floor looked smaller.

Once, when we were children, I spilled chocolate milk on the Persian rug in the study and Raeburn shook me until my nose bled. Then he shoved me into the bathroom so I wouldn't bleed on anything important. Seven hours later, after Raeburn had drunk himself into a stupor and I'd cried myself out, it was Jack who prised off the bathroom doorknob with a screwdriver. That was the first time we slept in the same bed. I guess he was probably ten years old then, which would have made me eight. I remember that he put me next to the wall, let me curl up against his chest. I remember his warm body, the stretchy feeling of dried blood on my skin, and the chill of the wall against my back.

If Jack were there, he would have come to help me. But Jack was gone.

5

With Jack gone, I felt like I'd lost half my brain. I hated him for leaving me.

I figured this much out eventually: the letter that Jack gave to Searles was the same letter that Margaret Revolt had sent to the college administration, but my brother had found his copy in my father's study. I don't know how it linked Raeburn to Margaret. Maybe there were notes in the margins in his handwriting. From what I could piece together from listening to Raeburn on the phone, both Ben's future at the college and my father's hinged entirely on whether or not Margaret Revolt admitted that it had all been a hoax, that Ben Searles had never made a pass at her. It remained to be seen whether or not Margaret – Margaret the Brilliant, Margaret the Incomparable, Margaret the Deep and Profound – was also Margaret the Loyal.

When I finally met her, over a year later, I realized that Margaret had (of course) been the girl out on the porch with Jack at the Christmas party, the one with the thick glasses and bobbed hair. The one who had said that I could have gotten the alcohol anywhere because they weren't checking ID. The one with whom Jack had insisted on finishing his conversation. The one I'd forgotten to ask Jack about – or, more accurately, the one that I hadn't asked him about, because I suspected that he'd lie to me and I didn't want to hear him do it. Only then, when I met her, did it occur to me to wonder what Margaret was doing at the party, which was supposed to be faculty only.

Understand, though, that all of this was happening miles and miles below my radar. I absorbed it because it was in the same space that I was, the way that my clothes absorbed cooking smells in the kitchen. When it was all happening, I didn't really care about Raeburn or Searles or Margaret Revolt. I was too busy slowly going insane.

I guess that there must be all kinds of going crazy. Some people talk to trees; some cook compulsively; some sit and stare blankly at walls for hours on end. Most people retreat into themselves; I retreated into the world, which was as far away as I could get from my own reality. I started hitchhiking. I'd go into town during the day and wander for hours, staring in shop windows and watching the world go about its terribly normal business. For the first few months it was cold, and that's how I discovered the card store. I'd never sent or received a greeting card, with the exception of the few that arrived before Christmas every year from distant relatives or Raeburn's colleagues – but even those were the boring, generic kind sold in boxes. My favourites, I discovered, were the modern ones, intended for very specific situations: Sorry that we're getting a divorce. Congratulations on deciding to enter rehab. It's time for me to tell you I'm gay. The confessional nonpoems in these cards were stilted and sincere: 'I know that the decision that you've made was difficult for you, and I want you to know that I will always be there for you.' I read them, one after another, with a hard place in my throat.

I never found one that I could send to anyone. Sorry my father tried to ruin your life? Or, sorry my brother beat the shit out of you? Sorry I was such a pathetic daughter that you didn't want to take me with you when you left? I could never think of a good one to send to Jack. The closest I came was: I love you, I hate you, I miss you and I never want to see you again, how am I supposed to live without you?

That spring, I also discovered movies. Jack hadn't liked movies – too manipulative and common, he said – so I hadn't seen many, but there was a movie theatre downtown, and in the afternoons it was cheap. Tragedy, horror, and blow-things-up action movies, I soon discovered that I had no use for. My favourites were romantic comedies. That world, I could live in. Everyone was beautiful, everyone was rich, everyone was witty, and if anyone left the story, it was because they were mean or shallow or otherwise undeserving of the glamour of it all. Every hooker had a heart of gold, and the underdog always ended up winning.

Sometimes, after the credits rolled and the lights came up, I'd stare at the red exit sign, think about the glare of the sunlight outside, and be completely unable to move. So I'd sit through the movie again. After a few weeks, the ushers stopped asking me for money when I sat through show after show. The same was true of the woman who worked at the greeting card store. She never hassled me, no matter how many hours I spent sitting cross-legged on her carpet, reading the cards. Once, she even gave me a cup of coffee when I came in, saying that it was cold out there and I could probably use it.

During the day, I actually felt okay. But I never found a way to deal with the nights. For a while I tried going out at night and sleeping during the day, but the outside world was even scarier than the house in the wee hours of the morning. At least in the house there were walls around me. I might see weird things in the corners, but at least there were corners: places where the walls met. A limit to the space surrounding me.

One night, when I couldn't sleep, I poured a tumbler full of whiskey from the bottle in Raeburn's liquor cabinet and carried it upstairs with me. Sitting on the edge of my bed, I took steady, medicinal gulps until the walls began to spin. I wanted to be unconscious, and that's how I ended up. But in the morning I was sick, and the world was still there. I didn't do it again.

By the end of February, the situation at the college had turned into a campus-wide frenzy, complete with student petitions and strident demonstrations. Raeburn was so distracted that he hardly even seemed to notice that I was there, and that was fine with me. He didn't fly into any more rages, but I gave him no reason to. I didn't clean anything, but I didn't dirty anything either. I barely ate. There were some weekends when Raeburn and I only saw each other in passing. He'd nod at me, I'd nod at him, and we'd continue on our respective ways.

So I was surprised when he sought me out. I was standing at the front window, staring out at the dark woods; he stood behind me, his reflection ghostly in the window. He said, 'Josephine, would you like me to tell you something that will make you feel better?'

Would I like it? How would I know? 'I guess so.'

'Palomar just found a new supernova. It's less than five light-years from the edge of our solar system.' He stopped and waited, as if he expected a response.

I didn't know what to say. 'Thank you.'

'A supernova is a major cosmic event,' he said patiently, as if he were explaining to a child. 'The shock waves could disrupt the earth's orbit. Do you know what that means? It means – it *could* mean – the complete decimation of life on earth.'

Then he did something I'd never seen him do before. He winked.

'The world really doesn't deserve to survive,' he said.

From that night on, I lay in bed and imagined the supernova, millions of miles from the edge of our solar system, eating itself alive in a bright blaze, every stray molecule adrift in the lifeless vacuum being used to feed the fire. I imagined shock waves, huge and invisible, rippling through the galaxy, knocking the stars out of alignment and tearing into the thin atmospheres of any stray planets in their way. And oddly enough, it did make me feel better, because the night wasn't so empty. There was a supernova out there, and nothing was going to last much longer.

After a while I began to lose my brother.

He became a mythical figure. I had trouble remembering the days when he had been a living, breathing, talking entity in the room next door to mine; they seemed like a dream. Instead, I imagined him in scenes from the movies I watched: sitting in the corner of a bar full of glamorous people, smoking enigmatically and staring into his drink. Wandering the streets in the rain, looking for something he couldn't find. Hauling lobsters in the North Atlantic, pausing only to wipe the sweat from his brow and stare wistfully at the horizon – thinking, perhaps, of the sister he'd left behind, long ago and far away.

It must have been in early May that Ben Searles called, because when the phone rang I was standing on the porch, watching the rain falling on the elms, and the rain was warm. The phone was loud and shrill in the empty silence of the house. For some reason I thought, It's Jack, and my heart surged. The sudden wave of wanting my brother hit me viscerally, making my chest hurt and my eyes water. I think I flew into the house without once touching foot to floor; I grabbed the phone, took a deep breath, and couldn't say anything because I wanted it too badly.

'Raeburn?' a voice said. It was Ben Searles. I had forgotten about him. I slumped down to the floor, taking the phone with me.

'Josie,' I said finally.

'Josie, let me talk to your father.' He sounded cheerful and excited.

I stretched the phone cord out and let it snap back. 'He's not here.'

'Will you give him a message for me?'

I didn't answer.

'Tell him Margaret Revolt confessed,' he said. 'Taking my class, writing the letter, everything.' He started to laugh. 'She confessed. It's over.'

'No,' I said.

'What?' He sounded confused.

'I won't tell him that. He'll kill me.'

There was a pause. When Ben spoke again, his voice was kinder. 'I heard your brother is gone.'

I didn't answer.

'Why didn't you leave with him?'

I opened my mouth to tell him it was none of his business, and what came out was, 'He didn't want me to.'

There. There it was, lying baldly on the kitchen floor in front of me like a shattered mess of egg and orange juice and broken china. Jack didn't want to take me; he didn't want me to come; he didn't want me. *He didn't want me.*

Another pause. Then Ben said, 'This isn't the way the world is. People acting like this. You know that, don't you?'

'It doesn't matter,' I said. 'Nothing does.'

'Is there something you need?' Ben sounded confused and helpless. 'Is there anything I can do?'

I reached up and put the phone into its cradle.

Summer came and the semester was over. None the less, every Monday morning Raeburn threw a pile of clothes and books into the back seat of his car and drove away, just as if the college were still in session. He said he was teaching a summer class. I didn't believe him. I didn't care.

One day, I tried to climb out onto the roof, but the vast expanse of shingles was too wide, the slope was too steep, and I was too scared. After I crawled back through the dormer window into the room on the third floor, I spent a while picking desultorily through the boxes in the room. Below a layer of thick, inscrutable critical-theory texts I found a pile of composition books full of lecture notes written in a precise, delicate hand.

Mary was a margin jotter. The edges of the pages in her note-books contained her response to the entire education process in general, and each class in particular. 'WASTE of my time. Shut up, for the love of God.' Once she'd filled an entire margin by keeping careful track of how many seconds were left in the class. She hadn't managed to take any notes on the class itself, beyond the date at the top of the page and a few cryptic scribbles.

The ink of her downstrokes was thick and assertive. She'd used a fountain pen. Raeburn used one, too. I turned to another page. This was a philosophy class – part of it was about Aristotle – and it looked like she'd made it through at least half the class this time before getting bored. From that point on, the page was covered in doodles, swirls and skulls and musical notes. Except at the bottom, where she'd written 'Mary Chandler Raeburn' and then crossed it out, as if it embarrassed her.

The class notes filled a little over half the book. I didn't find any other references to my father among them. With my thumb I sent the remaining pages by in a yellowing, college-ruled blur. A musty smell rose from the pages. The paper was slightly stiff with age.

As the pages turned by on my lap, I saw a flash of blue. Quickly I flipped through the book until I found it: a page mostly ripped out, wrinkled and torn, with only a few inches remaining at the top. The preceding page had been ripped out completely; it looked very much as if someone had seized the two pages in an angry fist to tear them out, and hadn't noticed that they'd missed part of one. There were a few lines of blue ink still legible at the top of the torn page, written in a messier version of Mary's hand with a cheap ballpoint pen.

> look at her I think about how she'll grow up and meet some man who'll eat out the middle of her like a sandwich and leave the crusts to rot on the plate and

I shut the notebook. I didn't want to read any more.

Around the Fourth of July, I found a pink flier tacked to our front door, asking us to join the Citizens' Watch programme 'to help combat the crime wave that has hit our hitherto peaceful neighbourhood.'

'The police are doing nothing,' the flier read. 'It is up to Hill residents to patrol our own streets, to look out for each other, and to continue to foster the sense of community and belonging that has always set us apart from the crowd.'

I threw the flier away and started locking the doors.

Not long afterwards, Raeburn went to the campus to meet with the board of trustees, who were going to let him know the conditions they'd decided on for his return in the fall. I spent the evening in the parlour, reading a copy of *Wuthering Heights* that I'd found in one of Mary's boxes and listening to Jack's Wagner. The music was loud and encompassing and kept my attention away from the silence that had rushed like water into every part of the room.

At three o'clock in the morning I heard a noise on the front porch. I stiffened with fear. Then I heard muffled swearing and the jingling of keys at the lock.

It wouldn't be him, I told myself. It would be Raeburn in the doorway, glaring, home and drunk because the meeting had gone badly. He wouldn't explain and I wouldn't ask. I'd turn off the Wagner and go back to my book and the silence, and later on I'd go to bed, and time would continue to pass. When I woke up, my book would be sitting next to my bed and the day would be half over. Maybe I would walk to the pond.

The door opened. A single set of footsteps made its way down the hall.

And even if it was Jack — what did he think, that he could vanish, abandon me, and then drop back into my life six months later like a summer cold? That he could walk in the door and ask for a drink and a sandwich and that would be the end of it?

God, how I hoped it was him.

When Jack walked into the parlour, he was thinner than he had been — so was I, I guess — and he was wearing a navy blue shirt that I'd never seen before. His hair was longer, long enough to fall softly behind his ears, which were now pierced with small silver hoops.

For a moment we neither moved nor spoke. Looking at him was like looking at a stranger who'd somehow stolen my bone structure. There was an expression on his face that I couldn't identify, part wariness and part surprise. Who was he to be surprised? Where did he expect me to be?

And, of course, I loved him again immediately. I didn't seem to have a choice.

'Hey,' he said.

I heard myself say, 'Hey yourself.'

'Came back to get some things.' He took a step into the room and stopped. Now his face was carefully blank. I tried to remember when I'd last washed my hair.

'Oh?'

'Upstairs.'

'Oh.'

When I didn't say anything else, he said, 'I guess I'll go get them,' and turned away from me. I followed him upstairs and we stood at the door of his old room, staring through the doorway. The room was empty. The furniture was gone. A few dustballs gathered in the corners.

'Jesus,' he said. 'Guess I'm out of the family for good, huh?'

It hurt me to be so close to him. 'I saved your books,' I said. 'And some of your albums. He threw everything else away. I think some of your clothes are in my room, if you want them.' I tried a smile, to see how it felt.

It felt strained, and Jack didn't smile back. He pushed past me angrily and walked down the hall to the room where Raeburn stored most of Crazy Mary's things. The door was locked. Jack tried to kick it in, but it didn't budge.

'It's locked,' I said.

'I see that.' He pulled a pocketknife out of his jeans. In a moment he had the lock jimmied and was inside the room.

Every surface in the tiny room, which had once been our

mother's sewing room, was covered with leaning piles of boxes and old clothes. Jack went straight to the box on the table that held what was left of Crazy Mary's jewellery. He pawed at the contents for a moment. 'Do you have those pearl earrings? The ones you wore at that party?'

'They're in my room.'

'Get them for me.'

'Why?'

'Because,' he said, 'that's all we have that's worth anything. I think she took all the good stuff with her when we went to Chicago.'

My chin went up. 'They're mine. If you wanted them, you should have taken them with you when you left.'

He stuffed a handful of cheap jewellery in his pocket. 'That won't get you anywhere.'

'What won't?'

'Trying to make me feel guilty. You think I wanted to leave you here alone?'

'You must have,' I said, 'because you did. You left me here.'

After all the long months, after all the times I'd rehearsed this conversation in my head, that was all I could say. But he was there; he was finally there. He was looking at me. He was listening to me. So I said it again: 'You left me here.'

'Josie—'

'You left me here.'

He dropped the box lid and came over to me. He tried to take my shoulders. I shook him off.

'Would you just—'

'You left me.'

'Listen to me for a moment.'

'No,' I said. 'You left me.'

'Shut up!' He grabbed my upper arms, hard. 'Shut up! For God's sake, Josie, be quiet!' With each word he gave me a hard, quick shake. I let him. My head was rolling and limp.

He let me go.

'Jesus.' He frowned. 'What the hell is wrong with you?' There was a lost, confused look on his face I'd never seen before.

I shook my head.

There was a mirror over what had once been Crazy Mary's sewing table. He grabbed my arm and pulled me roughly over to stand in front of it.

'Look at yourself,' he said.

I looked at the pale skin, the greasy hair, the deep circles under my eyes. It was the same face I'd been seeing for six months.

'Look at yourself,' he said again. 'You look like a corpse and you're acting like a lobotomy patient. What the hell happened to you?'

The man standing next to the wan girl in the mirror was touching her face just as Jack was touching mine.

'Time and space,' the girl in the mirror said. The man's arm crept around her waist and his body curled against hers.

'When I was here, you were always beautiful,' he said. 'You're the only girl I've ever known who could be beautiful and hung-over at the same time.'

I watched the wan girl smile slightly.

'You were alive then.' He was crooning now, his voice low and smooth and rich. 'You were amazing. We were amazing.'

'It wasn't ever me.' My voice seemed to come from someone else.

Jack's mouth was close to my ear, against the soft place beneath my earlobe; and when he spoke, his words and his lips were like kisses. He was kissing me.

134

'My poor little sister,' he said. 'Poor, pretty little sister. What happened? What happened to you?' His hands were on my stomach, under my sweaty T-shirt, stroking the skin and my thin ribs, and I was shivering, tensing, with each touch. I turned towards him, feeling the desperation in my face and hating it.

'You did,' I said.

During the long six months that we'd spent apart, I had often lain curled in my bed at night, imagining the warmth of his body wrapped around mine – of any body wrapped around mine – trying to remember what it had been like to be a person touched by another human being. The feel of hands on my skin. The warm pulse of another heart, my ear pressed close to hear it. A body protecting me from the rest of the world.

It was a simple thing. At that moment, it was all that I wanted.

I was crying. Sitting on the floor of the hallway crying.

'Stop it,' he said.

'I'm sorry.' I wiped my running nose on the back of my wrist.

'Don't be sorry. Just quit crying.' He shook his head and stood up. 'I hate it when you cry.'

'Then quit making me,' I said softly.

He didn't answer. He ran his hands through his hair and then held them out to me. I took them and he pulled me to my feet.

'You're starting to look like you again.' He kissed my forehead absently and started checking his pockets, methodically. 'Listen, Jo, do you think you could get me those earrings?'

'Earrings?'

'The pearl ones.'

Numbly I went to get them. Jack had taken them out of my ears when I was passed out after the Christmas party. He'd left them on the dresser and I hadn't touched them since. I stood for a moment with them in my hand. Then I reached behind the head-board and took the charm bracelet out of its box.

When I came back out into the hallway he was gone and my breath caught. Then I heard the Wagner playing downstairs, in the study.

He was going through the books on the shelves, making a pile on the couch of the oldest ones with the most elaborately tooled covers. They were Raeburn's first editions. 'Thanks,' he said when I gave him the earrings, and stuck them carelessly in his pocket without looking at them or me.

'This too,' I said and held out the bracelet.

He stared at it for a moment and then reached out to touch it with one finger. 'I remember that. Where did you get that?'

'It was Mary's,' I said. 'It's mine now. You can have it.'

And I gave it to him. He touched the tiny test tube with something akin to reverence and slipped the bracelet carefully into his pocket with the earrings.

'Where have you been?' I asked softly.

He picked up a book and blew dust from its spine. 'I don't think I want to talk about that.'

'I didn't hear from you. I didn't think you were ever coming back.' He didn't answer. 'Why did you?'

'Come back? Why do you think?'

I stared at my hands. My thumbnail was ripped down to the quick. 'If I knew,' I said, 'I wouldn't have asked.'

'Fair enough.' Jack tossed the book carelessly down onto the couch. 'I came back because I needed money, and because I knew there was stuff here I could sell. I came back because I liked the idea of breaking into Raeburn's house and making off with everything that was worth more than two cents.'

'Did you do the break-ins on the Hill?' I interrupted.

'Have there been break-ins on the Hill?' he said evenly.

I looked at him for a long moment.

'Okay,' I said. 'Go on.'

'Go on? There's nothing left to tell. I came back because of you.'

'But you're not going to stay.'

He laughed. 'Are you kidding?'

'So what's the point of coming back at all?' I was getting angry.

'To get you,' he said simply. 'What did you think?'

I stared at him.

'Unless you want to stay,' he offered.

'I don't believe you.'

'Then I guess I'm lying.' He didn't seem to care. 'Come or stay. It's up to you. I won't be back again.'

'Where would we go?'

'I know people. We'll have a place to stay.'

I looked around at the study, at Raeburn's oversized chair and the ugly blue nude on the wall; at his collection of antique sextants and telescopes gathering dust on the bookshelves; at the dark wood walls and the rows of thick, tattered science books. I thought about my own room, which hadn't changed since I was two. I thought about the long, empty hours that I'd spent sitting in the kitchen, watching the shadows move as the wall clock counted away the hours. I heard Ben Searles saying, 'This isn't the way the world is. You know that, don't you?'

And then I looked at Jack.

I wrapped my arms around myself, feeling my ribs through my thin cotton shirt. I closed my eyes and thought about the supernova.

'Okay,' I said, without opening my eyes.

The car Jack was driving was an ageing black coupé with a

rosary hanging from the rearview mirror and a Saint Christopher medal pinned to the visor. It smelled strongly of coconut air freshener and cigarette smoke. I helped Jack load the books and silver into the trunk and then threw in a pillowcase that held a few pairs of my underwear and some clothes.

'Whose car is this?' I asked Jack as we worked.

'Becka's,' he said. 'You'll meet her.'

The sun was starting to come up when we hit the interstate. Not long after that, I fell asleep. When Jack woke me, we were no longer moving.

'We're here,' he said.

'Where?' My mind was groggy with sleep and driving and my ears were ringing.

'I told you. Becka's house. Erie.'

6

Whoever Becka was, she lived in a small, one-storey white box in a shabby neighbourhood. Some of the houses that lined the streets had once been perfectly respectable Cape Cods; some of them, like hers, had obviously been built after the neighbourhood had started to slip and nobody cared about the details. There were no lawns; the paint was peeling and the bricks were dirty. Becka wasn't home. The paper towels in the kitchen had ducklings printed on them and there was potpourri in the bathroom, but all of the floors were grimy and there were beer rings on the battered coffee table.

Jack saw my face and laughed. 'Nice, isn't it?'

'We were pretty squalid, sometimes.' I was looking through the pile of dishes next to the sink for a glass that looked relatively clean.

'Sure, but we're mad geniuses.' Jack threw his coat over the back of one of the chrome-and-wicker chairs in the kitchen. 'I can't help thinking that there's some merit in the fact that we spilled our ashtrays on the *Principia Mathematica* instead of *The National Enquirer.*'

'Where did you meet her?'

Jack shrugged. 'I keep telling myself this is temporary, but I haven't come up with anything better yet.'

He showed me the bedroom. There was only one, with a big, unmade bed in it. Jack's old leather jacket, the one I'd worn to the bonfire, was hanging over the back of the one chair in the room.

I touched it. 'Do you like her?'

He put his arms around my waist. 'Why do you want to know?' I didn't answer.

I met Becka an hour later, when she came home from work. She had black hair and huge brown eyes with long, curling eyelashes that she liked to flutter to punctuate her sentences. She called Jack 'sweetie' and 'honey' and said things to him like, 'I picked up some of that ice cream you like, sweetie.' She talked constantly: less than a minute after I met her, I knew that her mother's name was Susan, that she was one-eighth Iroquois and a quarter Italian, and that she was from West Virginia. Also, that it was okay for West Virginians to tell West Virginia jokes, as long as they were from the city and not from 'down the hoot 'n' holler'.

'How can you tell that the toothbrush was invented in West Virginia?' she asked me, smiling. 'Because if it was invented anywhere else, they'd have called it a *teeth*brush!'

'Funny,' I said. I was having trouble laughing, because one of the things that I'd learned from Becka was that she was 'crazy, absolutely head-over-heels hot' for my brother.

'He called me up this morning from the road and told me he wanted to bring his little sister up for a visit,' she said. 'I said sure, honey, go ahead, because I just can't say no to that man.'

'I know how you feel,' I said.

'He told me once he had a sister.' Those big brown eyes with lashes all aflutter were watching me with sharp intelligent curiosity. 'I didn't know you guys were so close though, but I guess it makes sense. Broken home and all that.' She shook her head. 'I mean, my folks are divorced, but your parents sure are a couple pieces of work, aren't they?'

I looked at Jack, who was sitting on the stained floral couch. He shrugged almost imperceptibly.

'Just my father,' I said.

'But your mother's the one who kicked you out of the house,' she said.

'Well—' I stopped.

Becka smiled. 'Oh, honey, ignore me. I didn't mean nothing. I never mean nothing. Most things that come out of my mouth you can't even listen to.'

'Hear, hear,' Jack said. He winked at me and picked up his beer. Becka moved to sit next to him.

'You know, sweetie,' she said. 'Maybe while Josie's here we oughta call up Sharon and see if her kids might want to take her out some night.'

'Who?' Jack said.

'You know Sharon.' She punched him lightly on the shoulder. 'Sharon that I work with, Sharon with the red hair.' She turned to me. 'How long were you planning on staying, Josie? Sharon's got kids your age, sixteen, seventeen.'

I wondered how old Jack had told her he was.

'Just a few days,' Jack said and reached an arm along the back of the couch, across Becka's shoulders. 'Just until everything cools off a little at home.'

She shrugged. 'Well, I'll give her a call anyway. You might like to have some fun while you're here,' she said to me.

'Sure,' I said. 'But I think right now what I really want is a nap.'

Becka told me I should go ahead and stretch out on her bed. The bedroom walls were thin, and as I lay in the bed that Jack and Becka had shared for God knows how long, I heard her say,

'Might be Becka and Jacky want to have some fun while she's here, too.'

Jack said something too low for me to hear.

'Oh, for Christ's sake.' The playful tone was gone from her voice. 'I was joking. Can't a person even tell a joke any more?'

The sheets on Becka's bed were printed with faded yellow flowers. Her green shag carpet was matted and soiled, and there was a dead fly on the windowsill. I rolled over and buried my head in the pillow, which smelled like cigarette smoke and shampoo. I didn't cry.

When I woke, the sun had gone down. Jack was sleeping in the bed next to me, wearing only his shorts, with one arm thrown over the side of the bed and the other hand on the small of my back, underneath my blouse. The night was warm, and the places where his skin touched mine were sticky with sweat. He had opened the windows and pushed my hair up and away from the back of my neck, so that it lay like a skein of dirty silk on the pillow next to me. The cool breeze from the window should have been pleasant, but I was miserable and the breeze smelled of sulphur and stale water.

I stretched slightly. The movement woke Jack. He opened his eyes and blinked.

'Well, hi, sweetie,' he said sleepily, stretching his words in an ugly parody of Becka's accent.

I rolled over so that my back was to him. Jack propped himself up on his elbow. 'What do you think of ol' Becka?' He tugged on my ear. 'Sweet li'l thing, ain't she?'

'Are we staying here?' My voice was cracked with sleep.

He sighed.

'The thing is,' he said, 'I really do need money. I can sell the stuff we brought with us, but it'll take a few days. This is a small

142

town. People get suspicious. Now, Becka' – the blouse that I was wearing didn't have any sleeves, and he slid one hand into the armhole so that he could rub the tense place next to my shoulder blade – 'Becka makes money. Tons of it. Cash.'

'How?'

'Stripping. Sleazy, but lucrative.' He half-laughed. 'After you went to sleep, her first question was whether you'd need a job and her second question was how old you were.'

'Am I old enough?'

'Nope. And it would be over my dead body, but I didn't tell her that.' As he spoke, his hand moved down my arm to cup my elbow.

'God, I missed you,' he whispered.

I pulled away.

He looked hurt and surprised. 'Ouch.'

I refused to feel guilty. Instead I said, 'What's that smell?'

'We're about half a mile from the sewage treatment plant. Welcome to Erie's low-rent district. I'll take you out to the lake sometime. You'll like that.' Now he was playing with my hair, stretching it out on the pillowcase, combing it smooth with his fingers. Despite its awful smell, the breeze felt good on my skin.

'I thought Lake Erie was toxic.'

'It was. It's better now. I think they even do some fishing in it.' Jack pulled at the back of my blouse, moving it up close to my bra strap. I felt him trace our initials on my skin.

'Just because there are fish doesn't mean you should eat them,' I said. 'Are you sleeping with her?'

He sighed and flopped over onto his back. 'What if I am? It's a roof over my head. Yours, too, now.'

I shrugged. The only sound that I could hear was Jack's shallow breathing.

'I'm glad you're here,' he said. 'I really did miss you.'

I turned to look at him. 'It's a lot. This is a lot.' In the glare from the streetlight outside, I could see him gazing thoughtfully at me.

He got to his knees on the bed. 'Take off your shirt.'

'Why?'

'Just do it.'

I let him pull the blouse over my head, leaving me in my bra. Then he knelt behind me and began to rub my back, slowly and precisely. While he kneaded my muscles and stroked the outlines of my bones, he said, 'Look, we'll get out of here soon. I promise. But Becka can't know we're planning to leave. She'll flip out, kick us both out on the street. She thinks she's my goddamned girlfriend, for Christ's sake.'

'How long?' Jack's hands were starting to make all this mess seem very far away.

'Soon.' He leaned down and kissed the skin between my shoulder blades. 'We'll go somewhere good, a big city. Get our own place, nobody to bother us. Nobody who knows anything about us. Maybe New York.' He sighed. 'I was drifting, and this was where I washed up.'

'I don't know where I am,' I said, and he said, 'You're with me.'

We were curled together, our arms and legs intertwined, like two starfish at the bottom of the ocean.

'I promise you,' my brother said. 'I'll get you out of here. I'll take care of you. I promise.'

At five in the morning, the alarm clock went off and I stumbled to the couch before Becka came home. When the front door opened, I pretended to be asleep.

When Jack left, later that morning, I stirred enough to open my eyes and see him standing at the open door, wearing jeans and a black T-shirt, staring down at his upturned palm through a pair of sunglasses. Then he closed his hand and stuffed it into his pocket. I heard the soft clink of coins sliding against one another.

The world on the other side of the door was glaring white in the sun. My heavy eyelids closed. When I woke up, he was gone and Becka was sprawled out on her bed in a bleary tangle of limbs and sheets and carbon black hair.

She cooked me breakfast after she woke up, around two: bacon, sausage, French toast soaked in egg and deep-fried in oil until it was crisp and golden. The kitchen was already thick with humidity and I'd woken with damp and prickly skin, but the hot food was good and I ate until my face was sticky with syrup and grease and my body felt heavy.

'Sweetie,' Becka said, 'you ate that like you ain't seen home-cooked food in about a million years.'

That accent is a put-on, I thought. 'It feels like it.'

She started to clear the dishes. 'Shame your brother had to run off like that this morning.'

'Where did he go?'

'Don't know. I don't bother asking any more.' She dropped the last of the dishes in the sink and let the faucet run over them for a minute. 'None of our friends are awake that early, I can tell you that much. They're mostly night people.' She was twisting her long hair into a ponytail. There was a small, spotted window above the sink and her eyes were fixed on something outside.

'Me too.'

She smiled and said, 'That so?' in a tone I didn't like. I wasn't sure how to respond, so I said, 'Well, he missed the food.'

Becka shrugged. 'Aw, he never eats my breakfasts anyway. Kind of nice to have somebody to cook for.' She fastened the ponytail with a purple barrette and shook her head to test it. Then she wheeled around to face me. The rapid switch was disconcerting. 'Jack said you didn't bring hardly any clothes with you. You want to go shopping this afternoon?'

'I don't have any money,' I said, watching her carefully.

Becka waved that away with one hand. 'Jack gave me some to spend on you, and I've got more if that's not enough. Besides, this way we girls can get to know each other. You can tell me all your brother's dirty little secrets.' She winked.

'You sure you want to know?'

'You mean, watch out what you wish for and all that?' She laughed. There was a sudden bitter edge to her voice. 'Smart girl.'

'I was just kidding.'

'I wasn't,' she said, a little shortly. Then, with another whirlwind mood change, she smiled a big, toothy smile and told me to run and get myself cleaned up, now, so that we could head on out.

Definitely a put-on, I thought.

The store where Becka took me shopping was a huge concrete building with a row of plate-glass windows facing a vast asphalt parking lot. Becka took the lot at about fifty. I just had time to read a sign taped to one of the windows, wishing the best of luck to the Erie High School Laker Band; then Becka whipped the Ford into a parking space, barely missing an abandoned shopping cart.

As soon as the key was out of the ignition I was out of the car, grateful for the solid feel of asphalt below my shoes. It took Becka another five minutes to sort out her sunglasses and check her lipstick and make sure she had her wallet. I stared at the bright sun glinting mercilessly on the other cars in the lot and began to feel awkward.

'You're just like your brother,' she said as she got out of the car. 'Everything is fast, fast, fast. At least you wait for me.' She shook her head. 'I swear, if that man weren't so damn sexy, I'd never put up with half his bullshit.'

On the sidewalk in front of the store, there was a miniature coin-operated carousel. The battered fibreglass animals were something like ducks and something like dogs; the bright colours had been faded by the weather and the red paint on the base was beginning to rust and flake off. The carousel was revolving slowly, the noise from the engine inside it all but drowning out the tinny music. There was a crying baby with food on its face clinging desperately to the back of one of the animals, while two women talked calmly over its head.

'Something wrong?' Becka asked.

I shrugged and gave her a fake, sunny smile as we passed through the automatic doors into the air-conditioned, fluorescent-lit store. 'If you were a kid, would you want anything to do with that?'

She gave me a puzzled look. 'You mean the merry-go-round?'

'I guess so. That thing outside, with the baby on it.'

'That's a weird thing to think,' she said.

The last new piece of clothing I'd had was my Christmas dress. My wardrobe back on the Hill had been a mixture of Jack's castoffs and my mother's left-behinds; that day in the store, I was wearing a cotton blouse that used to be Crazy Mary's and a cut-off pair of Jack's jeans. I didn't much care about clothes, especially *girly* clothes; so when I saw the part of the store where Becka wanted to shop, filled with row upon row of shining chrome racks hung with bright primary colours and cheerful prints, I wanted to laugh out loud. I couldn't wear this stuff. She had to be kidding.

But I soon discovered that Becka was nothing if not serious when it came to clothes, particularly trendy clothes. She gave me a bright orange dress to try on that made me feel like a traffic cone. When I looked at myself in the narrow mirror outside the dressing room, I said, without thinking, 'Well, if nothing else works out, I can always find some road construction to stand next to.'

Becka sniffed. 'I think it's adorable.'

'You don't think it's a little bright?' I stroked the stiff fabric and tried to sound as if I really valued her opinion.

'Wouldn't have picked it out if I didn't like it.' She turned away, her face expressionless. 'But maybe I don't have your educated taste.'

'No, I didn't mean—' But then I shut my mouth. I could tell by the set of her shoulders that it wouldn't matter whether I apologized or not.

Becka moved among the racks of clothes and I shuffled after her silently. I heard exchanges all around me, flowing as fluidly as water from a rainspout. Becka said to the clerk, 'How you doing today?' and the clerk said, 'Not so bad, still hotter than blazes out there?' and Becka said, 'Sure is,' and it all seemed so easy for them. Meanwhile, there I was, about as fluid as a slab of granite. It would have been funny if it hadn't been so terrifying. In the outside world, people cared about the weather; they cared about their weekends; they cared about their baseball teams. Nobody cared about the theoretical ramifications of black hole entropy. I didn't really care, either, but my world was made up of the things that Raeburn thought were necessary and true; in Becka's world, I was like a gear uncaught, and there was nothing in the whole of string theory that could make me a part of what I had been thrust into.

Becka spun a chrome rack around and pulled out another sundress, this one bright green. 'How about this one?'

'Nice,' I said.

* * *

Jack came home later that day. I was wearing one of the dresses that Becka had bought for me. I felt stupid in it and he laughed when he saw me, which didn't help my mood or hers. Finally he suggested that he and I take a drive around Erie, so that I could get my bearings, and Becka said, her voice heavy with sarcasm, 'Oh, what a nice idea.'

'The Becka Capriola mood swing is a force of nature,' Jack said when we were alone in the car. 'Watch for it. It bites.'

Becka's house was on the east side of town. Jack drove west down tree-lined streets through a neighbourhood full of Victorian houses and wide grassy lawns, and I thought, this must be how the other half lives; but a few blocks later, we were back in the land of small box houses, scrubby ill-watered lawns, and old cars with paint fading under a thick coat of dust. Closer to the water, the boxes had been painted, and sleek, expensive cars sat in front of tidy gardens. To the right of us, the bay between Presque Isle and the mainland stretched and glittered in the sun, and I thought, Of course. Now that the water's cleaner, this is hot property.

'There's not much money here,' I said.

'It's hidden. The summer people live up near the state park, on the peninsula. Gated themselves off from the highway and everything.' Jack's lip curled contemptuously. 'They're the ones who are going to buy all that stuff we took from Raeburn.'

'What are we going to do? Go door to door?'

'Becka's got a friend who can fence things for us.'

'Great. Let's meet him.'

'You really want to get out of here.'

'She doesn't like me, Jack. She doesn't want me here.'

'She wants me here,' Jack answered. 'And if she wants me, she'd damn well better be nice to you.'

That was true and we both knew it. All the same, it didn't take

149

Becka long to get sick of me. I understood. She was in love with my brother, or at least enthralled by him; I could tell because when she talked about him, her voice held the same awe as when she talked about the characters on the soap operas she watched in the afternoons. She and Jack had met in a tattoo parlour on Peach Street, she said.

'Jack doesn't have any tattoos,' I said.

'Neither do I,' Becka said. 'But one of the ink guys down there is a friend of mine. I go down to see him sometimes, on my day off.'

'What was Jack doing in a tattoo parlour?'

'Meeting me. What the hell does it matter? I went in there to talk to Mike, and there he was. He was staying with this awful girl, over on Sixteenth Street. Wasn't a week later I said to him, 'Sweetheart, you just go ahead and move your stuff in with old Becka until you decide you need to be moving on." And the rest is history.'

'And then I came along and ruined everything.' I meant it as a joke.

'Oh, *no*, honey!' Her smile was forced. 'Nothing like that! You're a cutie pie. I'm happy to have you here, just as long as you want to stay. It's exactly like having a little sister again.'

But later that night, when Jack returned from driving her to work, he was grinning. 'What did you say to our little Becka? She's been stricken with a guilty conscience. Thinks you think she hates you.'

'She's right. I do think she hates me.'

'So do I. But why is she all wrapped up about it now?'

I told him what I'd said to her that afternoon, and he said, 'My small scheming sister, you're brilliant,' and kissed me. I didn't tell him that I hadn't been scheming at all.

Later he said, 'There is a downside, however. Our guilt-stricken Becka now feels the need to prove her goodwill, so on her next day off we're all piling into the car and going to the beach. Together.'

I groaned.

'Oh, it gets better. Becka's going to bring along a friend for you.'

'No, Jack,' I said, but he put a hand on my knee and said, 'It's okay. It's the same friend I was telling you about. You'll like him. His name is Michael.'

'That's why you were in the tattoo parlour.'

He lifted an eyebrow. 'Somebody's been telling stories.'

'So who's this girl you were living with, over on – what was it – Fifteenth Street?'

'Sixteenth.'

'Sixteenth. What was her story?'

'Her name was Teri. She was a waitress. I was only there for a week or two.'

'Before that?'

'Somewhere else.'

'You won't tell me.'

'No, I won't.'

'Because I'll be jealous?'

'Because it's over,' Jack said. 'They're history.'

The next morning, Jack and I picked Becka up from work. We'd gone down to Pittsburgh to see the planetarium, which had just reopened after a renovation. The show had started at midnight, and then we had gone to a bar, so we were awake anyway. As we waited outside the club, which was a plain cinder-block building outside town, he said, 'If I had my way, I'd buy us a private island in uncharted waters and we'd never have to leave it.'

'Are there still any uncharted waters?'

'There have to be some somewhere.'

'Becka's coming,' I said.

She was walking slowly across the gravel parking lot, wearing a light pink sundress. During the night a heavy cloud cover had moved in over the lake, and the predawn light was thick and hazy. The pink sundress was virtually all that I could see of her, floating ghostlike in midair. She was walking so slowly, I saw as she came closer, because her red shoes had stiletto heels, and they were sinking into the gravel.

'Better let her sit in front,' Jack said, so I got out of the car and slid into the back seat.

When she was still about fifteen feet away from the car, she stopped to kick off her shoes and picked them up in one hand. She was singing softly to herself as she walked, and the hand holding the sandals swung cheerfully in time with her steps, but when she reached the car I thought that the heavy makeup she was wearing made her look plucked and artificial. The skin under her eyes was grey with exhaustion.

I realized that I had no idea how old she was.

'Morning.' She smiled the same tight, tired smile she usually gave me. 'How was Pittsburgh?'

'Post-industrial,' Jack said as she climbed into the car. He leaned over to kiss her, sliding one hand into her hair and twining his fingers there. The kiss lingered. I made myself look out the window until I heard him say, 'Hey, gorgeous.'

'Hey, yourself,' Becka said. I looked back at them. There was a foolish grin on her face. 'You two been having fun. This car smells like an ashtray.'

'You look tired,' Jack said.

'Quite a night,' she said. 'Feel like some food? I'll buy.'

'Sure.'

'What about you, Jo?' she called back to me, not bothering to turn around. 'Hungry?'

'Whatever.'

Jack used his right hand to work the gearshift and then rested it on Becka's knee. 'Quite a night? Is that good or bad?'

'The money was good.' She laid her hand over his. He picked it up and kissed it, then dropped it so he could shift again. 'God, I'm tired.'

We went to an all-night diner and sat in a booth. It wasn't quite seven o'clock. There were only a few other people there, and none of them seemed entirely present – they all looked either half awake, as if they'd just crawled out of bed, or drained and half asleep, like Becka. She ordered hot chocolate and a Belgian waffle with strawberry topping and extra whipped cream. I ordered coffee.

'You don't want anything to eat?' Jack said to me.

'It's too early for food.'

'Two coffees,' he said to the waitress. She nodded drowsily and shuffled off.

Becka yawned and leaned her head on Jack's shoulder. 'All I want to do is sleep for a hundred years.'

'Sleeping Beauty,' Jack said. 'I'll try to find you a hedge of thorns.'

Becka smiled sleepily and kissed his shoulder.

Our coffee came with a dish full of individual plastic cups of half-and-half. I poured two of them into my coffee and watched the white liquid swirling in the cup. When I looked up, Becka was sitting up straight. She was holding a compact mirror in front of her face and staring at me. Our eyes met and she looked quickly back into the mirror and began wiping the heavy blush from her cheeks.

'So, y'all had a good night?' she said.

'Great,' Jack said. 'You should see the planetarium. It's cool.'

'Went there on a school field trip once,' Becka said vacantly. 'Planetarium, zoo, whole nine yards.'

'I've never been on a school field trip,' I said.

'We used to go all over the damn place. Even went out to Fallingwater once. God, that was a long day. Real pretty, though.'

'It is,' I said. 'I've never seen it in the springtime, though.'

Jack continued to stir his coffee. 'Only during the winter,' I went on. 'Jack and I went when we were younger.'

'Did you.' Becka sounded uninterested.

'We went at night. It was closed. We had to sneak in.'

'That's you all over.' She glanced at Jack. 'Never do things the easy way.'

'I hate that crap, though,' he said, stretching an arm across her shoulders. 'Tours and guides and cameras and gift shops.'

'Frank Lloyd Wright desk sets and official Fallingwater coffee cups,' I added.

Becka leaned her head against Jack again and closed her eyes. He said, 'Human beings suck the life out of everything that's beautiful. The only way to keep something pure is to keep it to yourself.'

'On a private island?' I said.

Becka, close to sleep, made a small whimpering noise. One of Jack's arms went around her, his hand burying itself again in her hair. His eyes were on me as she snuggled against him. 'In uncharted waters.'

And I remembered: Josie fourteen, Jack sixteen. Pulling the

truck off the road into a clearing and hiking to the house in the darkness, afraid to use flashlights or even to get too close. The house itself was dark. A lone floodlight shone in the maintenance parking lot, where the park ranger's truck sat by itself, quiet and deserted. The house and the river that ran beneath its cantilevered platforms seemed like a single living organism crouched there in the silence. Jack and I crept around the grounds like thieves, and in whispers he pointed out the things that he found beautiful about the house: the wide terrace, with its slick, polished flagstones; the dark windows above the stucco walls, silver in the moonlight; the many-paned windows that formed a corner of the room inside, a corner that disappeared when the windows were open because by a miracle of physics it bore no weight. He kissed me by the lower falls. Then we heard a noise and we thought it was the ranger so we ran. Our boots crunching on the snow-covered twigs made so much noise that even if the ranger hadn't heard us before, he would have then, and we didn't stop running until we had our truck in sight. And I remember, when we got home, the way the attic smelled, and the silence that was the dead of winter, and the watery shadows that the icicles hanging from the eaves outside cast through the window.

The waitress dropped Becka's plate on the table and walked away without a word. Becka opened her eyes and stared at the waffle, which was covered in a drift of whipped cream and spotted with preserved strawberries gone shapeless with syrup. Dreamily, she picked up a fork, stabbed one of the globs of fruit, and put it in her mouth.

'If that's true,' she said as she chewed, 'you two are the purest people I ever met, 'cause you keep everything to yourselves.'

'Everybody's got a secret or two,' Jack said.

'Or three, or four.' Becka opened her eyes wide. 'I bet I can list everything I know about the two of you in under a minute.'

'What are we betting?' Jack asked.

'Whatever you want,' she answered.

He looked at his watch. 'All right.'

'Your father's smart, like you. But mean. I think maybe your mother is dead, but I can't tell because your story keeps changing. You have bad dreams and you don't like deep water or tight spaces. You won't come watch me dance but you don't ever ask me about it, or get jealous like some guys do. You drink too much and you drive too fast, and you're vain as hell.' She looked at me. 'And about two weeks ago, I found out you had a little sister. And the way you spend money, you must have come from it. And that's it. I don't even know how old you are, exactly.'

'Thirty seconds,' Jack said.

'Not bad,' I said, although I hadn't known about the deep water or the tight spaces.

'Now, you I don't know anything about.' She was still looking at me. 'Except that you look just like Jacky here, so I imagine he's telling the truth when he says you're brother and sister.'

'What the hell,' Jack said. 'Why would I lie about that?'

'I don't know.' She picked up her fork, stabbed the waffle through the middle, and began sawing at it with her knife. She didn't look at either of us. 'Forget it.'

'He's nineteen,' I offered.

She shrugged.

'Okay,' Jack said. 'What do you want to know?'

'Nothing.' She paused with her waffle-laden fork halfway to her mouth. A strawberry fell off and hit the table with an audible plop. 'But if you're not going to tell me about things, then don't sit here talking about them like I'm not even here. It's not polite.'

156

She shook her head and shovelled the food into her mouth. 'I get so tired of all your goddamned special little secrets.'

She dropped her fork and pushed back her plate. She stood up, took a twenty out of her pocket, and dropped it on the table.

'I'm not hungry any more,' she said and left.

Jack and I followed her.

When we got back to Becka's house, she went straight into her bedroom and closed the door behind her. It had started to rain and the inside of the house was damp. My eyes were gritty with exhaustion.

Jack drew me a bath and sat on the toilet while I soaked. I had a feeling this was something Becka would not have approved of, had she known; but she was asleep in the next room, oblivious, and it was good to soak in the warm water and pass quiet words with Jack. Afterwards he brushed his teeth in the bathroom; I crept into Becka's room and stood over her, wrapped in a pink towel. She hadn't taken off her makeup before going to bed and it had smeared. I stared down at her blurred features and had trouble remembering what she really looked like.

Becka's friend Michael knocked on the door at about two in the afternoon. Becka was still in bed and Jack was making coffee in the kitchen, so I answered the door.

He was older than I had expected; he had crow's-feet around his hazel eyes, and I wondered again how old Becka was. He was also easily the tallest person I'd ever met. He was wearing a pair of camouflage pants cut off at the knees and a sleeveless undershirt, and the parts of his arms and legs that I could see were long and spidery and covered with tattoos. His black hair was jagged and rough, as though he'd cut it himself.

He looked at me and smiled a small, private smile.

'Jack's sister.' His voice was smooth and sharp, like a knife blade.

'Michael,' I said and let him in.

'Where's Becka?'

'Still in bed,' Jack called from the kitchen. 'You want coffee?'

Michael shook his head. 'Go tell her to move her West Virginia butt. The day's wasting.'

'Hang on,' Jack said. A moment later he emerged from the kitchen and gave me a cup of coffee. 'Be your charming self while I go see what's up with Beck, will you?'

When he was gone, Michael smiled the private smile again. 'Are you charming?'

'Not yet.' I was too sleepy to be self-conscious. 'Try me again in a few hours. I haven't even brushed my teeth yet.'

'Don't let me stop you,' he said.

Standing at the basin, I could hear Jack and Becka talking in low voices in the bedroom. I wondered what was going on.

When I came out of the bathroom, combing my hair with my fingers, Michael was sitting on the couch where I'd slept the night before. He hadn't even bothered to push aside the sheet I'd used to protect myself from the rough upholstery. He was reading a paperback. He'd wrapped the front cover around the back of the book and I couldn't see the title.

There was nowhere else to sit so I sat down next to him. He didn't acknowledge me. He read his book. I examined my fingernails. We sat in silence.

After a few minutes, Jack came out of the bedroom, looking exasperated. 'Bad news,' he said.

Michael closed the paperback and stuck it in his pocket. 'Becka's bailing out on us.'

Jack nodded.

'Oh, no,' I said, without much conviction.

'She's tired. I think the two of us are going to hang out here. But' – and Jack looked at me, his eyes grimly apologetic – 'she says you two should go without us.'

'Whatever.' Michael didn't sound as if he cared much either way.

I went cold. 'Jack—'

'Go, Josie,' he said, and it was a command. 'There's no reason for you to sit around here all day.'

The closed bedroom door was mocking us. I could imagine Becka lying smugly in bed behind it, proud at having engineered an entire day without me around. At that moment, I hated her.

'Fine,' I said.

Michael drove an old Jeep with a deep dent on the front fender. The Jeep was open to the air, and the drive down Twenty-sixth Street to Presque Isle was too loud for conversation. Which was just as well, because I was furious. This girl, this *ordinary* girl, had dismissed me as easily as if I were some extraneous little tagalong sister. Worse, Jack had let her do it. I brooded so deeply over the slight that when the trip was over and Michael turned off the engine, I was surprised.

He had pulled off a narrow paved road, behind three or four other cars. The Jeep was parked on a stretch of dirt between the road and a dense forest; across the road there were trees, too, but they were sparser. In the spaces between them, I could see a thin blue line that was the water. As we sat in the car, a couple rode by on bicycles.

'Very pretty,' I said.

'If you think she planned this, you're right,' Michael said. 'She told me about it yesterday.'

'Somehow that doesn't improve my mood.'

'Not saying it should. But you can't blame her. There she was, living dumb and happy with your brother, nice enough guy, fun to look at and treats her good, mostly, and then along comes his baby sister and boom, she's like – Mom, with sixteen-year-old kids hanging around, and that guy she's so into doesn't hardly give her the time of day any more. Of course she's pissy about it.'

I stared at him. 'I'm seventeen. Not that it's any of your business. And how old do you think Jack is, anyway?'

'Oh, I'm not saying I don't have my opinions about your brother,' he said. 'I've got plenty of those. All I'm saying is that if Becka's not happy with the way things are, well, it's her house, and you've got to make do with that if you want to hang around. Which I guess you do.'

I gave him my iciest look and said, 'Exactly what *opinions* do you have about my brother?'

Michael shrugged. 'I never trust anybody with that much charm.' He pulled a pair of sunglasses from above the sun visor and put them on. 'Come on. I didn't slog all the way out here to sit in the car.'

I followed him, carrying the rubber sandals that Becka had bought me. The sand was hot and the water, once we got there, was clear and inviting.

'I thought this was a lake,' I said. 'Why are there waves?'

'It's a pretty big fucking lake.' Michael took off his shirt and draped it over a rock. 'Are you wearing a suit under that?' He gestured towards my shorts and T-shirt.

'Don't have a suit.'

'Well, it's a hot day. You'll dry. Can you swim?'

'Sure.'

He pointed at the lake. There was a cluster of rocks jutting out of the water about fifty feet from shore. 'Let's go out there and come back.'

'Why?'

'Give us something to do.'

I stared at the rocks, gauging the distance and the calm water. 'Want to race?'

Michael was wading into the lake. The water was already above his knees. 'We're doing this to kill time,' he said over his shoulder to me. 'Why rush?'

Out in the water, which was warmer than I expected, he kept to his word, stroking slowly and lazily and sometimes turning over onto his back so that he could look at me.

'Watch out for the sharks,' he called to me at one point.

'Funny,' I called back.

But the truth was, as my arms and legs stretched in the warm, glassy water, my mood was lifting. I didn't look at Michael as I swam the last few strokes to the rock. The side was too slippery and steep to climb up, so he was treading water a few feet away, his wild hair slicked down against his skull.

'Better?' he said.

'What do you care?'

Michael took a mouthful of water and spat it out. 'Don't get pissed off at me. I'm just the babysitter.' Then he dived underwater and headed back to shore. He stopped to wait for me in the shallows.

'Not fair,' I said. 'You didn't give me a chance to rest.'

'Nope.' He flopped down on the hot sand.

I flopped next to him. 'So what did Becka say when she asked you to do this?'

'Exact words?' He put on Becka's accent: ' "Mikey, sweetie, Jack's weird little sister is visiting and I need to get her out of my hair for a day or so. You think you can take her out, show her a good time?"'

I stared at my sand-covered feet. 'She called me weird?'

'She might have called you a freak. I can't remember exactly. Don't bother trying to brush that off yet. Let it dry.'

'Why are you telling me this?'

'Well, the way you've been doing things clearly isn't working,' he said. 'And I know Becka pretty well. Better for you to know where you stand.'

I had nothing to say to that. I looked at his tattoos. A huge Chinese dragon, snarling and intricate, covered his left leg; the right had his name, Michael, written down the length of it in elaborate Gothic script. One of his arms was completely covered with black and red ink, and the other had a bracelet of barbed wire drawn around his biceps. They were a little disturbing – I wasn't quite sure why – but beautiful.

'Did you do your tattoos yourself?' I asked him.

'Nope. The ones on my legs I had done in high school. The others a guy I work with does for me.'

'Why don't you do them yourself?'

'Zenon's a better artist than I am.'

'Does it hurt?'

'Get one and find out.'

'Pass.'

'I'll do it for you,' he offered. 'For free. It's not often I get to work on teenaged-girl flesh.'

I turned and stared at the waves, my cheeks burning. I was suddenly conscious of the way my wet clothes were clinging to my body. 'I think I'm going to go back in the water.'

I started to swim back out to the rocks, but I changed my mind when I was halfway there and turned around again. Michael was lying on the sandy beach, basking in the sun like a snake. He wasn't looking at me.

Jack and Becka were somewhere else, I thought. Jack is off with a woman and I'm off with a man. People who see one of us alone have no idea that the other one exists. The thought gave me a tiny, inexplicable thrill. As I swam back to the shallows, I thought, I could be any girl in the world. Michael could be my boyfriend or my brother or even a friend.

I stood up in the shallows for a moment, looking at him. His head was turned away; he couldn't see me. He wasn't handsome – his nose had a crooked place where it might have been broken and his eyes were too small. He was thin and wiry but not muscular. I found myself wondering whether he was attractive anyway.

Suddenly something sharp dug into my heel and I yelped. Michael raised his head. His impenetrable sunglasses stared out at me.

'What happened?' he called.

'I stepped on something,' I called back. 'It's okay.'

My heel was throbbing. I picked up my wounded foot and held it in my hand, turning it so that I could see the sole. The skin of my heel was wrinkled, pale, and shiny with water. There was a small dark object, smaller than my smallest fingernail, buried under the skin. As I watched, blood welled up from the dark spot and ran down my ankle in thin streams.

Michael stood up and walked towards me.

'You're bleeding pretty good,' he said. 'You want me to carry you in?'

'Just let me hang on to you while I hop,' I said.

He gave me his arm and I limped to the water's edge, where a knee-high ledge had eroded away from the shore, and sat down.

'Ouch.' I gripped my heel tightly. 'It really hurts.'

'Move your hands so I can see it.' He felt around the wound. 'There's something in there. Hang on, I've got a knife in my truck.'

'Knife?' I said, but he was already sauntering up the beach towards the road and the Jeep, and I remained at the edge of the water, bleeding into Lake Erie.

This is a place I never expected to be, I thought.

A moment later, Michael was back with a big bone-handled pocketknife. 'Lie down on your stomach. Got to dig it out.'

'I'm not squeamish.'

'I'm a tattoo artist. I know about people and pain – and tattoos don't hurt half as much as this is going to. Lie down on your stomach. The last thing I need is you jerking your foot and me cutting it off.'

I did as he said and he took my foot into his lap. My toes were pressed against his leg. The drying cotton of his trouser leg was warm against my skin. He bent over my heel and I felt the knife cut like a bright flash into the throbbing.

'Easy,' he said. 'You know, you should have taken me up on the tattoo offer. It really isn't as bad as this and you'd have artwork under your skin for ever. This way' – and the knife dug again into the meat of my heel – 'all you'll get out of it is a scar. There.'

Twisting my body around, I sat up and held out my palm. He dropped a small, bloody pebble into it. The pebble had only one sharp edge. 'You hit it just right. Bad luck.'

I threw the thing out into the water.

'You're bleeding on me,' Michael said, and I realized that my legs were still across his. I was almost in his lap. One of his hands, the one that wasn't holding the bloody knife, was resting lightly on my ankle.

'I want to rinse this off.' I moved so that I could swirl my wounded foot around in the water. 'I hope you were kidding about the sharks.'

He stood up, brought his shirt from the rock it was draped across, and handed it to me. It was a regular white sleeveless undershirt. 'Wrap this around it.'

'I'll bleed on it. It'll get ruined.'

'They're three for six dollars at the SuperMart. I can spare it.'

'Thanks.' I held it pressed to my foot all the way back to Becka's house. By the time we got there, the bleeding had slowed. Michael covered the cut with a piece of gauze from the first-aid kit in his glove box, and I put on my sandals.

For a minute we sat in the car and stared silently at the small white house. Becka's car was still parked at the kerb in front of it.

'Do you think it's safe to go inside?' I asked. He shrugged, inscrutable behind his sunglasses, and smiled his little smile. 'Guess I'll give it a shot anyway.'

'I'll hang around for a second or two just in case. Nice meeting you.'

'Likewise,' I said. 'Thanks for digging the rock out of my foot.'

I hopped out of the Jeep, feeling unexpectedly lighthearted. But the closer I got to the house, the heavier my mood grew. Jack was there, but I didn't want to go back in.

As I walked into the front room, I heard the unmistakable sounds of loud, vigorous sex coming from the bedroom. I stood for a moment, not knowing what to do.

Through the wall, Jack moaned.

The Jeep was still idling outside. 'Not safe after all?' Michael said.

'Not by a long shot.' My hands were shaking. 'Can I have a cigarette?'

'In the glove box,' he said. 'So what do you want to do for the rest of the day?'

'I don't care. Do you have anything planned?'

'Free as a bird.'

'Then take me somewhere.'

We bought strombolis and spritzers from a dingy little Italian takeout place, and then Michael took me to the park downtown. There was a university nearby, and although it was summer there were still a few young people lying around on blankets, reading books with glossy covers, oblivious to the world. We sprawled out on the soft, thick grass under a tree.

I sat cross-legged and tore idly at a fallen leaf. Michael stretched out next to me, with his head propped up on his hand. His long legs, with their dark tattoos, drew curious glances from the strollers, but he didn't seem to notice. He was watching a couple nearby, obviously college students; they were both reading, the boy lying on his back and holding a paperback book in the air over him and the girl on her stomach reading a heavy textbook. They both had highlighter pens. Sometimes, without a word, one of them would tap the other on the shoulder and they'd trade highlighters.

Michael said, 'Sex, college-style.'

'Like entropy.'

'Disintegration into chaos?' He saw my expression. 'Hey, I watch television, too, babe.'

I don't, I thought. 'Disintegration, yeah, but it's also – wasted energy, I guess. Energy that you can't actually use for anything, because it sort of – burns itself out by existing.' I pointed at the college kids. 'Like spending all of your time reading about things other people have done.'

He shook his head. 'Pass.'

'Me too.'

His eyebrows went up. 'You? Hell, you're still a baby. Who knows where you'll end up.'

I looked at the girl studying on the blanket. She was wearing a clean, pretty blouse and exactly the right amount of makeup. Then I looked at my hands. 'Not like them.'

Michael looked at me for a long moment. 'No,' he said. 'Not you. Not either of us.'

We sat in silence for a while, watching the college couple, and then I said, 'Jack says you fence things.'

Michael gazed lazily up at the tree branches moving in the breeze. 'From time to time, I am capable of finding homes for objects that have lost their way.'

'How does one get into that line of business?'

'You're asking a lot of questions.'

'You bought me alcohol, and I'm underage. And you gave me a cigarette before.'

'In for a dime, in for a dollar?'

'I suppose so.'

'I used to work in a garage,' he said. 'Made ten dollars an hour, and everything I made, Uncle Sam got fifteen per cent. So I started looking for alternative business opportunities. Started out selling inspection tags and licence plates. After a while it was spare parts – tell some rich guy he needs a new alternator and sell the old one to one of my buddies, cheap.' He shrugged. 'I only did it to the summer people. Developed into quite a little sideline.'

'So why did you quit the garage?'

'Didn't quit. Got fired.'

'For stealing?'

He smiled. 'For making personal phone calls.'

'You're kidding.'

'Nope. And now I draw tattoos on people.'

'And do you find tattooing more emotionally rewarding than working on cars?'

'Somewhat,' Michael answered, nodding gravely. Then, suddenly, he sat upright. 'Let me look at that foot.'

I extended my legs towards him and he pulled the foot into his lap. He peeled back the adhesive tape that held the gauze over the wound, and we both looked at the dark dimple on my heel. There was a little dried blood around the edge of the wound. Michael licked his finger and rubbed it away, gently. 'You'll probably live.' He pressed the adhesive tape back down to seal it; but his long, thin hand was still on my ankle, and he didn't show any inclination to move it.

He pulled my other leg into his lap and I wondered what I would do if he leaned down and kissed me. Then he actually did, and I was surprised to find that what I did was kiss him back.

For the rest of the afternoon, we lay twined in the cool shade and kissed, and never once did he slip a hand under my T-shirt or ask me to get in his Jeep with him so we could drive somewhere. There seemed to be nothing else for the two of us to do other than lie on the grass in the cool summer shade, with the breeze coming in from across the lake, and share our innocent kisses, as though we were two normal people enjoying a day off together. Instead of ourselves.

I said, 'Your eyes change colour, did you know that?'

'Yours are army green,' he said. 'They're the same colour as my pants.'

We went to the bar, which wasn't as crowded as I expected. Michael said that it would be, once the shift at the mill ended. I went into the bathroom and washed my hands; then I lifted my feet up into the basin, one at a time, and washed them, as well. I took the wad of bloody gauze and tape off my wounded foot and threw it away. The hole in my heel was still sore, but it was no longer throbbing.

When I came back, Michael was sitting at the bar, and there was a beer in front of the stool next to him. 'I told the bartender that you were twenty-one,' he said. 'So if anyone asks, that's how old you are.'

'I'll try to keep that in mind.' I picked up the beer and took a long pull.

We sat in silence. People were starting to filter into the bar. Somebody put Johnny Cash on the jukebox; it was a song Becka liked. The bartender was leaning his round stomach against a corner of the bar, talking to an old guy wearing a John Deere cap. The old guy was eating pretzels, breaking them into pieces. I could tell he had dentures by the extra movements of his mouth when he chewed.

Then Michael said, 'You're a nice person, Josie.' He wasn't looking at me.

I didn't know what to say. I said, 'Thanks,' but it didn't feel like enough.

'It surprised me,' he said. 'You being so nice. I expected you to be more like your brother.' Then he did look at me. 'From what Becka said.'

I took another drink and swallowed it before answering, 'We're not that different.'

'You're close.'

I glanced casually at him. 'Sure. Broken home and all that.'

Michael gave me an appraising look.

A little while later, when the front door opened and we were hit with a gust of hot, reeking air, sour with the smell of the lake and the car exhaust from the highway outside, Michael's hand was resting lightly on my knee. I turned and saw my brother walking through the door with Becka, one hand possessive on her shoulder, his hair freshly washed and his white T-shirt clean and soft-looking. There was a lazy, bored grin on his face that vanished when he saw us.

They headed towards us, Becka wearing a satisfied half-smile and Jack with angry eyes fixed on me despite the look of patent cool on his face. Michael sat up straighter and said, 'Hey,' as they came within earshot.

'We interrupting something?' Becka said. She was wearing thick makeup to cover a red, angry-looking mark on her upper lip. She'd been rubbed raw kissing my brother.

'The beginning of a long and drunken evening,' Michael replied. 'And that's about it.'

'Good,' Jack said. 'Because you should have seen what happened to the last guy I interrupted with my sister.' His voice was friendly, as if it were a joke.

Soon we all moved to a table. Michael took the chair across from mine; Becka sat down next to me. 'How was the beach?' she asked.

'It was the beach,' Michael said.

'It was fun,' I said. Jack's eyes were fixed on mine. 'How was your day?'

'Great,' he replied.

'That's nice,' I said. 'What'd you do?'

Becka said gaily, 'Oh, we hardly did anything at all. Sat around on our butts all day.'

'I can imagine,' I said.

Michael's eyes were on me, glittering brightly as he sat in

silence. He was smiling his private smile again. It made him look closed off and distant, and it made me uncomfortable.

'I think I'll go get another beer,' I said.

'Get a round,' Jack said.

'Want me to come with you?' Michael asked.

'No, I'm fine.'

The bar was crowded by now, as Michael had said it would be. There were men everywhere: big men in shabby work clothes, who smelled of sweat and labour, dancing with girls who were preened and pressed. I preferred the sweat to the smell of the girls' hairspray and perfume.

I glanced back at the table; Michael said something and Becka, watching him, laughed. Only Jack was looking at me. His eyes burned and his jaw was tight. He looked a little like Raeburn had, that night at the Christmas party, when Claire was teasing him.

Suddenly I was intensely unhappy: forceful, tidal-wave unhappiness, the kind that washes over you and fills your ears and your eyes and your lungs. Sometimes when I feel that way it helps to get drunk, but it's like shoring up a high-rise with playing cards. Sooner or later something happens – a word or a song or a turn of phrase or, more often, an unwelcome memory – and everything comes crashing down. This time it was remembering Raeburn that made it happen. I found myself fighting back tears.

I fought my way to the bar, pushing at people who couldn't or wouldn't let me pass. A woman carrying a glass of water bumped into me, and the water sloshed onto my shirt. It was one of the shirts that Becka had bought for me, and the cheap material instantly glued itself obscenely to my skin. The woman slurred an apology and vanished into the crowd. I made it to the bar and a man holding a beer said, 'Hey, baby, when's the wet T-shirt contest start?'

At least I'm wearing a bra, I thought. 'Shut up,' I said.

The bartender was wearing thick glasses and an ancient green T-shirt that said ERIE HOSE CO. #8 across his fleshy chest. When I finally got his attention, I tossed back my hair and told him to get me four Budweisers and a shot of Jack Daniel's. His eyes never left my chest.

I did the shot at the bar, took the four bottles between my fingers, and made my soggy way back to the table. When Jack saw me he swore. 'What the hell happened to you?'

'I got wet.' I slammed the beer bottles down.

'Oh, you poor thing.' Becka reached for one of the beers.

'I've seen uglier things happen in this place,' Michael said. 'Seen uglier things, period.'

Jack said, 'Jesus Christ, Mike.'

I half-fell back into my chair and pushed my hair out of my damp eyes. The whiskey was warm in my stomach and I knew that as soon as the beer hit my bloodstream, I'd be fine. Even when the rest of the world shook under my feet, I always had a good, solid grasp on getting drunk. 'It's hot in here anyway,' I said. 'I'll live.'

The night slipped away. My throat was telling me that I was smoking too much, and my giddy, giggly mood should have been a good indicator that I was drinking too much. I filed that information away to be examined at a later time and drank every beer that appeared in front of me. Sometimes Michael was sitting with me; sometimes it was Jack. More and more it was Jack. I found, as the evening wore on, that I had less and less to say to Michael, and he seemed to have less and less to say to me.

Eventually I was alone at the table. Jack took the chair across from me. 'Thought you were dancing,' I said.

'I stopped.'

I tried to flick my cigarette into the ashtray and almost knocked over my beer, catching it around the neck just in time.

Jack watched. 'You're cute when you're drunk,' he said. 'You've got to be the cutest drunk I've ever known.' He leaned across the table and said, suddenly serious, 'Josie, did Michael make a move on you today?'

I tried to fix him with a steely gaze. It was harder than it should have been. 'Jack, did Becka make a move on you today?'

'No,' he said. 'I made a move on her.'

'Well, then.'

'It kept her happy, didn't it? And in case you haven't noticed, it's in our best interest to keep Becka happy.'

'Of course. Our best interest.'

'Better fucking believe it.' He sat back. His eyes were sullen now.

'So what if he did,' I said.

'Did he?'

'Yes.' But that wasn't exactly true. 'No. He kissed me. But I wanted him to.'

'The guy's a freak,' he said.

'I'm a freak. Your girlfriend says so. Besides, he was nice to me. He cut a pebble out of my foot.'

Jack stared at me for another moment. Then he shook his head. 'You're drunk.'

'Dance with me,' I said. 'Will you dance with me?'

'Are you crazy?'

'Yes. No. I don't know.' My eyes were filling with tears and my T-shirt was damp and sticky and uncomfortable. 'Maybe I just want to go home.'

Suddenly Becka appeared out of nowhere and collapsed into Jack's lap. He quickly hid the disgust that crossed his face.

'Hiya, darlin',' she said.

'Where have you been?' he asked.

'Dancing with Mikey, since you abandoned me.' Her mouth formed a pretty little pout that made me want to roll my eyes. 'But now I wanna dance with you.'

Jack gave her a perfunctory smile. 'I think I'd better take Josie home.'

'Are you coming back?'

'She's drunk. I want to get her out of here. Make sure she's okay.'

'I want to stay,' Becka said firmly. 'I want to stay here.'

'So stay,' Jack said.

Her eyes narrowed dangerously. 'I want you to stay *with* me.'

'Becka, she's my sister,' he said. 'I'm taking her home and staying with her.'

Becka stood up, knocking over my beer. 'Your sister, your fucking sister. I'm sick to death of hearing about her. You want to take her home, fine. Take her all the way home, will you?' Her eyes focused on me. 'No offence, sweetie, but I didn't sign up for this and I don't want it. I'm not your fucking Girl Scout leader, okay?'

'All *right*, Becka.' Jack helped me to my feet. 'She's just a kid, for Christ's sake.'

'She's about as much a kid as I am.' Becka's hands were on her hips and her mouth was twisted.

'Jack,' I said.

'It's okay,' he said.

Becka made a disgusted sound. 'Fine. Get her out of here. I'll get a ride home with Michael. At least *he* likes me better than his sister.'

Jack wouldn't talk to me on the way home, and when we got back to Becka's he was angry and a little rough. When I woke up the next morning, thick-headed and sick, I was in Becka's bed. Jack was sitting on the edge of it with a cup of coffee.

'Becka didn't come back last night,' he said. He no longer seemed angry. His eyes were gentle but very grave. 'Here, drink this.'

I took the cup and did my best. 'I'm sorry.'

He shrugged. 'It was my fault. I shouldn't have trusted him with you,' he said, although that wasn't at all what I was apologizing for. He put his hand on my leg. 'We'll deal with her. I'll deal with her.'

I rolled over onto my side and put my head in his lap.

'I'm sorry,' I said again.

'Don't be.' We heard a car pull up in front of the house. 'You'd better get up.'

My clothes from the night before were on the bathroom floor. I put them on, wincing at the bar smell of cigarettes, alcohol, and sweat that saturated them, and then took my time washing my face and brushing my teeth. I was hoping that whatever was going to happen between Jack and Becka would happen while I couldn't hear it over the running water. But as I turned it off, I heard Becka say loudly, 'Don't you blame me, don't blame me *or* my friends if your precious innocent sister throws herself at everything with a—'

Then there was the loud sudden crack of a slap and a high female yelp of pain.

I burst out of the bathroom in time to see Becka sprawled on the floor with a pink splotch spreading on one side of her face. She leaped to her feet with a shriek of inarticulate fury and went for my brother with her nails in front of her like an irate cat. Without thinking I jumped between those bright red claws and my brother's face and threw up my arms to stop her.

'Get out of my way!' she screamed. She grabbed me by the shoulders and threw me against the nearest wall. I fell heavily and grunted in pain. Before I knew what was happening I was covered in Becka, enraged and vicious: her nails at my eyes, her hands in my hair, her tiny sharp shoes stabbing my thighs as she kicked at me.

Then Jack was on her. I heard two more slaps in quick succession, and then he tore her away from me and held her back by her upper arms.

Becka's nose was bleeding. 'I want you out of my house,' she spat at me through the blood. 'I want you out of my house *now*. This is my house.'

'Becka,' Jack said, his voice cruel and composed. 'Calm down.'

She wheeled around to face him. 'You too! Out! You think 'cause you're a good fuck I'm gonna let you walk all over me? You snake! You asshole! You *hitter*!' Her face was purple with rage.

'You're right, Becka.' Jack was still calm. 'I shouldn't have hit you. But you shouldn't have said that about Josie.'

'Oh, I know. She's just a kid, isn't she? Innocent as can be, doesn't know nothing – well, I know exactly what she knows, I know enough to know that – but *she's* just a kid, *she's* not a cheap twisted little whore—'

Then he hit her again, with his fist this time. She fell to her knees, holding her face, and burst into a storm of tears.

'No,' he said. 'She's my sister.'

Then he came over and helped me up. 'Okay?' His voice was gentle.

I rubbed my thighs where they were beginning to bruise and nodded numbly. Becka was howling, letting loose great violent wails of frustration and pain. She sounded as if her heart was breaking. Maybe it was.

'Get your stuff.' Jack's face was grim.

Becka jumped up and ran into the bathroom, slamming the door hard behind her.

'Get your stuff,' he said again.

Outside King of Prussia, Pennsylvania, the bus that we were riding to New York began to make sick coughing noises. When we got to the bus stop, a wretched little cubicle tucked away in a sprawling, almost deserted strip mall, the driver told us that we were going to have to wait for a replacement bus, which would come from Harrisburg. It might be a while, he said. It might be hours.

The dingy little waiting room had two rows of hard plastic chairs that faced each other in one corner. The air was chilly and stale with air conditioning. We sat down to wait. We'd only been sitting there a few minutes when Jack got up and went to the restroom.

When he came back, he dropped back into his chair. 'Fourteen hundred, including the three hundred Michael gave me last night.'

I knew he was talking about the fat roll of money that he'd saved while he lived with Becka. He'd gone to the bathroom to count it. 'That's not so bad,' I said.

'It is in New York,' he said. 'You know what we got the most for? That charm bracelet of yours. It was *vintage*, or something.'

'You sold it?'

Jack nodded. 'Hungry?'

I was too full of *mine it was mine you sold it and it was mine* to think about food. 'I guess so,' I said.

'Tough luck. We are embarking on hard times, my darling. You want a candy bar out of the machine?'

Mine, I thought. It was mine. 'I'll pass,' I said, 'but thanks loads.' My voice sounded normal.

'Anything for you.' He stretched out across a row of lime green chairs and rested his head on my thigh. Throwing an arm over his eyes, he didn't say anything else for a long time.

The waiting room was air-conditioned, but the sun streaming in through the smeared plate-glass windows was hot. As the afternoon wore on, the squares of sunlight on the floor came closer and closer to where I was sitting until they were directly on top of me. Soon the backs of my thighs were sticking to the plastic. I was stiff and sore where Becka had kicked me.

I wasn't sure if Jack was really asleep or pretending, so I tried to keep still. I started to count flecks. There were flecks everywhere I looked. Blue flecks in the green chairs. Yellow flecks in the orange chairs. Grey flecks in the white linoleum. The windows were streaked and spotted with brownish grime. A man in uniform came in and talked to the woman behind the counter for a long time. I listened to the way that they flattened and twisted their words out of shape, and I tried to ignore my legs.

Eventually I couldn't sit still any more. My legs were aching and buzzing for motion and I needed to move. I shook Jack's shoulder until he woke up.

Irritated, he wouldn't answer any of my questions about New York – where we were going to stay, or how long we were going to live there. I told him that his personality was improved by unconsciousness and he said, 'Next time don't fucking wake me up then.'

I quit talking to him. He stared straight ahead, out the plate-glass windows. There was a vaguely disgusted look on his face. I'd never felt so lonely.

7

Many hours later I opened my eyes and found myself staring at a half-naked, too thin girl with incredibly dirty hair that might have been blond a long time ago, when it was clean.

Ah, I thought, only a little surprised by my lack of surprise. Mirrors on the ceiling. Trust my brother.

I had only faint memories of the night before, of climbing off the bus and walking for what seemed like miles along brightly lit streets until we came to a dimly lit stairway. I remembered standing behind a man in a silver shirt and a woman whose high black boots shone as brightly as her sequined dress, and I remembered telling Jack, as we followed a soiled carpet down the hall to our room, that they must have been to a costume party that night. He told me that I had a lot to learn; I told him I'd learn it tomorrow; then I used the bathroom, took off the clothes I'd been wearing for the past thirty hours, and went to sleep.

We were in New York City, in a hotel room. The shower was running.

I sat up in bed and examined my surroundings. The shade on the room's one window was pulled all the way up, but the light in the room was dim and pale. I could barely make out the only other piece of furniture in the room, a combination TV/VCR standing on a metal cabinet. There wasn't room for anything else.

There was barely room to walk around the edges of the bed.

The shower stopped running and Jack came into the room, wrapped in a towel so small that he might as well have skipped it. 'Like the room?'

'Great.'

He sat down on the edge of the bed. Of course he did; there was nowhere else to sit. 'Don't panic. It's not permanent.'

'Great,' I said again. 'What's the permanent solution?'

'We look for a place. Like we've always talked about doing.'

'Then what?'

'Then we hope we find one before our money runs out. This place only looks cheap.'

'When we find a place. Then what?'

'Christ, Josie, don't nag,' he said. So I knew that there was no 'then what'.

'I'm going to take a shower,' I said.

Jack was propped up against the wall, with his legs sprawling and the towel cast casually across his lap. He picked up the remote control and said nothing.

There was an impressive collection of small plastic bottles lined up on the side of the bathtub. Although there were several brightly coloured bottles of massage oil and lubricant to choose from, there was no shampoo, so I washed my hair with bubble bath, which didn't work very well but was better than nothing. My wet hair smelled like the lake, which made me think of Michael. When I walked back into the bedroom, Jack had the TV on and was watching languidly while three grainy women standing by a grainy swimming pool peeled their clothes off. 'Look at that pool,' he said as I wrapped myself in the towel and sat down on the edge of the bed. 'We should have gone to Los Angeles.'

The three naked women on the videotape were surprised by a

workman, presumably there to clean the pool. There was hardly time for introductions before the workman slipped and fell into the crystal blue water, forcing the three women to fish him out and take off all his clothes.

'Classy,' I said.

'Comes free with the room.' Jack and I watched as the three women started to lick at the pool man's wet body, which was skinny and too pale.

I felt a finger slide up my spine and the TV said, 'There, aren't you glad we got you out of those wet clothes?'

Later Jack and I sat together in a diner booth, our cheeseburgers pushed to one side as we pored over the apartment ads in the free newspaper spread out on the table in front of us.

'Here,' I said. ' "Beautiful two-bedroom in East Village. High ceilings, great light." That sounds okay.'

'Josie. We have no jobs, no friends, and less than a thousand dollars to our collective name. Deduce.'

'No beautiful two-bedroom in the East Village?'

'Clever sister.'

'I thought we had more than that.'

'Hotel room is two-fifty a night,' Jack said absently and turned the page.

'That is the most depressing thing I've ever heard.'

'Here.' He slid the paper over to me.

The ad that his finger pointed to said only that there was an apartment available immediately and listed a phone number. No high ceilings, no great light.

'That's good?'

'Very good.' He dropped a ten on the table to pay for our meal.

Nine hundred, I thought, give or take.

Jack called the number from a pay phone and got the address. During the hour-long walk, I kept expecting to be impressed and excited by New York, and at first I was. We walked through a part of the city where the buildings were tall and beautifully wrought, covered in fine carved stonework or gleaming glass that reflected the clear summer sky. The people around us walked fast; they wore tailored suits and talked into wires that snaked from their ears to the sleek mobile phones they held in their hands. All of it, the buildings and the people and the limousines idling in the street, seemed part of something indefinable yet vitally important. Making my way through the crowds with my brother, I felt blissfully anonymous.

But as we walked, the buildings became smaller and the people slower. The fast walkers were still there, but now they looked overdressed and uncomfortable, and they were interspersed with people who ambled slowly and obliviously along, as if there was nothing in life that was worth hurrying to do. There was too much traffic, and everything was too loud. I kept a tight grip on Jack's hand. I expected him to complain about it but he never did.

By the time we found the apartment building, the bottoms of my feet were burning and sore. The front door was propped open, so we didn't bother ringing. The inside of the building was dark and stiflingly hot. The black and white ceramic tiles on the floor, the carved banisters, and the moulding near the ceiling were regal in a dingy, exiled sort of way, but the paint was flaking and there was broken glass mixed with the small drifts of mysterious filth collecting in the corners. The apartment was on the fourth floor, the door painted bright blue. When Jack knocked, it was opened immediately by an impossibly tiny girl with tawny skin and a metal stud in the middle of her lower lip.

'Where the hell have you been?' she greeted us, fluttering brightly striped eyelids in consternation. 'I expected you to be here, like, half an hour ago. I'm going to be late for work. What did you do, *walk* here from midtown?'

I felt Jack's grip on my hand tighten, but he only smiled his winning Jack smile. 'Actually, we did.'

'It's such a nice day,' I said like an idiot, standing in the oven-heat of the hallway in my sweat-soaked clothes.

The girl made a disdainful face and moved back to let us into the apartment. 'Yeah, whatever. Here it is.' She made a sweeping gesture with her arm that managed to convey her contempt for the apartment, the world in general, and us in particular. 'Look fast. I gotta get to work.'

While we checked the place out, she dashed around angrily, pulling pieces of clothing from corners and covering her lips with coat after coat of thick red paste. The rug on the floor was worn but brightly patterned; the walls were painted a deep rich red and mostly hidden behind huge canvases with blackish purple bruises smeared across their surfaces. The cabinets in the tiny kitchenette were the same bright sky blue as the door. There was only one window, which opened onto a brick wall and was covered in iron bars. Someone – presumably the artist-girl – had candy-striped the bars with red and sky blue paint and woven a string of white Christmas lights through them.

'Are you on the lease?' Jack asked her.

'Fuck no.'

'Who is?'

'Like I give a shit. I give my rent to the guy downstairs. Nobody's ever come to evict me.'

'How much?'

'Six hundred. Look, I've got to get to work. You want the place,

183

I'll be out tomorrow and I'll tell Louis you're coming.'

I looked around at the cramped one-room apartment and hoped Jack would say no.

'Yes,' he said.

'Fine,' the girl said. 'I'll throw in the futon for an extra fifty. You want it, pay me now. Otherwise, rent was due on the first, so you're late.'

'But it's the eleventh,' I said.

She shrugged. 'Louis is a nice enough guy. Plus, we sleep together sometimes. So why pay if I'm moving out?'

That night, Jack wanted to celebrate. He bought a cheap bottle of champagne, which we drank in the hotel room out of plastic hotel cups. We watched another porn video. It was even cruder than the first one had been. We could laugh at it this time.

'I'm glad you came with me,' Jack said, dipping his finger in champagne and tracing our initials lazily on my stomach. 'I guess I can be a pretty lousy brother. But I need you. You're good.'

He bent over me and slowly licked the liquid from my skin. His tongue sliding across me was hot and alive.

If I'd been unenthusiastic about the apartment that first day, I loathed it the following afternoon. Without the paintings, the colourful rug, and the Christmas lights in the security gate on the window, the apartment seemed a lot less bohemian and a lot more like a prison cell decorated by the criminally insane. The mysterious filth in the corners of the hallway outside had escaped from the artist-girl's rug, I guess, because there were places on the apartment floor where it was an inch thick.

The cheerful blue cabinets were cheerful, all right, but they were also painted shut. When Jack finally managed to cut one of them open with a razor blade (slicing his thumb badly in the process), we were greeted by a burst of hot, stale air, massive quantities of mouse droppings, and two cans of what we guessed was tuna fish. We had to guess, because the labels had been chewed off long ago.

'How long do you think this has been sealed up?' I asked, trying to keep my face out of the stench of the cabinet and sweep mouse droppings into a garbage bag at the same time.

'Don't ask,' Jack said grimly, sucking on his cut thumb. He threw down the T-shirt he was using as a rag. His face and shoulders were coated with a thick layer of sweat and grime. Last night's good humour had vanished. He walked over to the window, which was standing open against the heat, and slumped down below it with his head in his hands.

I watched him. I didn't like what I saw. 'It's not that bad.'

'It is.' Jack rubbed his face hopelessly with both hands. 'It absolutely fucking is.'

I scraped the last of the mouse droppings into the garbage with a folded newspaper and sat down next to him, trying not to touch anything, including myself.

'It'll get better,' I said.

He surveyed the room with revulsion and shook his head. 'You know, last night I actually thought the red paint on the walls was kind of sexy.'

'If slaughterhouses turn you on.'

'Christ,' he said. 'We've got to sleep here tonight.'

I looked at the floor, which was still streaked with dirt after three rounds with the mop we'd bought that afternoon, and shuddered. The artist-girl had taken the futon with her. She'd taken our fifty dollars, too.

By the time we had taken care of the most obvious mess, it was after midnight. Jack managed to convince the man behind the counter at the corner store to reopen the deli counter and make us some sandwiches, which seemed, in my exhausted state, a miracle on a par with the loaves and the fishes.

On our way back into the building, we passed a young, black-haired man with olive skin coming out. We'd seen him earlier that day, on one of our many paper-towel-buying trips. He had stopped in the hall to watch us go by, staring frankly at us out of dark curious eyes. He hadn't spoken to us and we hadn't spoken to him, but now he lifted his chin in a sort of half-nod.

Jack, noncommittal, said, 'Hey.' I said nothing.

Upstairs, we spread the sandwiches out on the floor. Jack only made it through half of his before he was up on his feet, pacing.

Finally he put on a clean shirt. 'I'm going out.'

'Where?' I asked, a bit incredulously, through a mouthful of ham and cheese. It wasn't so much that I thought there was nowhere to go, in this huge city; but with so many places to go, where were you supposed to begin?

'For a walk. I'll be right back,' he said and left.

Along with the sandwiches, Jack had bought an incomplete Sunday paper at half price. I spread it out in a thin mat on the grungy floor and covered the mat with the one blanket that we owned. Then I lay down. Our clothes were in plastic shopping bags, piled in the corner. Staring at them, I had a mental image of the artist-girl getting ready for work and tearing through piles of clothing. I had thought it was bohemian eccentricity. I'd been wrong. No closets.

It took me an hour of puttering around the apartment to realize that Jack wasn't going to be right back, a conclusion I accepted with more calm than I would have thought possible a year before. He had only one shirt and not very much money, so I knew he'd be back eventually. There was nothing in the apartment that I hadn't already tried to clean that day, so I folded back the blanket and read the newspaper. In the science section, I found a headline that read, 'Dying star gives space telescope a chance to shine.' The article said, 'A recent supernova, discovered at the Palomar Observatory in southern California, is expected to provide scientists with some of the most detailed photographs ever taken of the death of a star.' And, buried deep in the article: 'The supernova is not expected to pose any danger to Earth. "Earth is in constant danger from interstellar objects and events – like asteroids and supernovas and solar flares – but the chance of a catastrophic event actually occurring during the span of human life on earth is infinitesimally small," said one leading scientist. "In interstellar time, it would be like a blip within a blip."'

I turned the page.

By the third hour I was hungry again. I ate the other half of Jack's sandwich, but it didn't help for long. I had Jack's bankroll, so there was really nothing to stop me from walking down to the corner store and buying a loaf of bread or a can of soup. Considering this fully, with all of its various ramifications, took another half-hour or so. Once I even put my sandals on and stood up to leave, but I kicked them off at the door. I didn't have keys, I told myself, which would mean leaving the apartment unlocked, which couldn't be a very good idea. Besides, just because the outside door had been propped open all day didn't mean it would stay that way all night. What if I went to the store and in the meantime somebody came along and closed the door? Better to stay and wait. Jack would be home soon, I told myself. By morning, anyway.

Sometime near dawn, the scratchy wool blanket pushed to the side and the newspaper thoroughly perused, I fell into a sort of half-sleep and dreamed that I was reading the cartoons in colour

187

but all of the colours were wrong and I couldn't figure out what went where. The sounds of the street outside wove in and out of the dream like the artist-girl's Christmas lights in the barred window. Someone was singing, in Greek, on the sidewalk, and the dream shifted. Raeburn was reading Euclid aloud, which he had done a lot that summer when I was six. Then he made toast for me, which, as far as I could remember, was something that he had never done.

September came and went in a hot, disoriented blur. The headlines at the newsstands screamed BAKED APPLE! and HOT HOT HOT! Even now I can only remember flashes of that month, like a slide show, and I can see the images but it's hard for me to believe that I was actually there, acting and being and doing. And time must have passed, because one day I reached up to touch my collarbone and discovered that its edge stood out more than I remembered, as if I'd spent that month eroding.

One afternoon, when the humidity was obscene and being in New York was like being in a diseased lung, we spent two hours in the rainforest enclosure at the Central Park Zoo, where the automatic misters made the air dewy and cool. The park, with its wide green lawns and tree-lined avenues, was the only part of the city that didn't make me feel desperate and alone. When we emerged, Jack's shirt was clinging to his shoulders and my hair was curling and damp at the ends. In no particular rush, we made our way slowly across Central Park South, which was choked with people going home from work and movies and sightseeing. Jack took my hand so we wouldn't be separated. I felt distinct from the rest of the world, as though I'd come from another time. I could see and hear and feel every detail with startling clarity: the heat in the air, the cool clamminess of the ersatz rainforest still clinging to our clothes, the way the thick silver chain that Jack wore lay against his throat, the sun going down, the musicians and street performers, the carriage drivers sweating in top hats, telling me that I should make my fella take me for a ride through the park, love. Everything fell into place like cards in a shuffled deck, making perfect and profound sense.

Most of the time, of course, nothing made sense at all. As the hot spell broke but our money continued to melt away, Jack grew petulant and unpredictable. He told me a thousand times and occasionally in tears that our lives weren't the way he'd planned them, but I still found myself watching him too carefully and working too hard to predict his reactions. If I'd stopped to think about it, I would have realized that all of that work was more than a little like living with Raeburn again, except this time I didn't have my brother to catch me when I fell down on the job. But I didn't stop to think about it. Sometimes he said that coming to get me was the best thing he'd ever done and sometimes he said it was the worst. I was never afraid of him the way I was of Raeburn. He was just angry, and I was just in the way.

One night, when our bankroll had shrunk to a couple of crumpled bills at the bottom of a coffee can, Jack brought home a bottle of cheap rotgut whiskey. He drank his straight; I mixed mine with watery lemonade from a plastic jug. After I'd had two drinks and Jack had slugged most of the rest straight from the bottle, he watched as I took a used coffee stirrer and mixed round three in a plastic cup.

'How the hell can you drink that?' he asked.

'There's pretty much nothing I can do to it that will make it taste any worse than it does on its own.' I wasn't really complaining, but Jack was drunk, and snide.

'Sorry,' he said. 'Sorry we can't afford Chivas this week, prima donna.'

'Relax. We'll drink Chivas next week.'

'How magnanimous of you, princess.' He took the bottle back from me.

I stared at him. In my plastic cup, the yellow liquid swirled and sloshed. 'You're the one who wanted to come here,' I said.

'Not like I had a whole hell of a lot of options, having to drag you around with me, did I? In fact' – his voice grew fake-bright – 'I seem to remember that it wasn't until I went and got you that my problems started.'

Sure, shacking up with Becka was the high life, I wanted to say. Instead I said, 'Come on, Jack,' and threw the stirrer out the open window.

Without speaking, he stood up and went to the sink. The apartment was stifling and hot. He turned on the water, leaned over, and splashed handful after handful on the back of his neck. Outside, there were car horns honking and people shouting.

I rose as quietly as I could and went to him. But when I tried to touch his shoulder he wheeled around and slapped my hand away, hard.

'Say it, little sister. Fucking say it.' He was livid. 'I came along and ruined your life, didn't I? You were happy as a little princess with Daddy on the Hill and I waltzed in and now you're living in squalor. And that's all my fault, isn't it?' Water stood out in beads on his skin. He pushed past me and grabbed the whiskey bottle again.

'Prima donna,' he muttered. He tipped the bottle to his lips, found it empty, and hurled it against the wall. It didn't break. 'Fucking prima donna.'

My hands clenched into fists. 'Okay,' I said, 'you ruined my life.

But all you ever talk about is how great life was when you were on your own – how easy and fun it all was, how many girls you had – so I guess I ruined your life, too, didn't I? You ruined mine, I ruined yours, and it's all my fault. Except for the fact that it wasn't me that moved in with Becka Capriola, and it wasn't me who got us kicked out.'

'You didn't help.'

'I didn't beat her up, either,' I said, and he hit me.

It was only a slap across the face. It stung but it wasn't even hard enough to unbalance me. Wildly, I thought, is this real? Did that happen? Is this real?

Jack was staring at the hot place on the side of my face. Suddenly he sprang back as if he were the one who'd been slapped. 'Oh, sure. I'm the violent son of a bitch who beats up his poor little sister. Everything that's wrong with the world is my fault.' Veins stood out in cords on his wrists; he didn't seem to see me any more. His eyes were alive with rage. I realized that Jack was in a different world now. Whatever was wrong with him, I had to get out of his way until it was over, so I ran.

I had never needed to run from my brother before. For two hours I walked aimlessly past streetlights and police cars and panhandlers, past arguing couples and kissing couples. I saw them, registered them as obstacles, and avoided them, but my mind was caught on things like the keys I'd left behind, and why we had only one set, and why I hadn't had my own set made. Towels. Why didn't we have more than one towel? We should have more towels, and sheets, too. Even though we didn't have a bed yet. We would someday, and we'd need sheets. We had separate toothbrushes, but only one pillow. We weren't prepared for this at all. Of course, we hadn't exactly planned anything. Why hadn't we planned anything?

I turned a corner and found myself facing a broad highway. Across it, the lights of New Jersey sparkled in the Hudson River. I'd walked all the way across the island. I stared at the dark water for a long time. Then I turned my back on it and kept walking.

A week later Jack and I were standing under an awning at the corner of Thirty-fifth Street and Park Avenue while soft, heavy drops of rain fell onto the sidewalk. Jack had decided that we were going to be criminals.

He was holding a crisp new fifty-dollar bill against the wall of the nearest building. The fifty, along with the $7.61 in my pocket, was all the money we had in the world. We were in trouble.

'O ye of little faith,' he said and showed me the bill, on which he'd written, 'Happy Birthday Josie!!! from your Loving Aunt Becka,' in a looping feminine script.

'Very funny,' I said. 'This isn't going to work.'

'You have a better idea?' I didn't and we both knew it. He put the bill in his pocket and told me to follow him. 'We've got to keep close, but not look like we're together.'

I did as he said, following him into a well-lit coffee shop down the street. The shop was packed with people on their lunch breaks. Jack went ahead of me and bought a sandwich, which had to be made up behind the counter. I took my time at the refrigerator case next to the register, picking up cartons of yogurt and reading the nutrition information until his sandwich was wrapped and on the counter in front of him. Then I grabbed a carton at random and joined the line, two or three customers behind him.

The girl at the counter was busy and frazzled. Jack used the marked fifty to pay for his sandwich, and then walked out of the store without looking at me, heading towards the river and the park where we'd agreed to meet. I would pay for my purchases with the five I had in my pocket, and then tell the clerk that I'd given her the fifty with the phony birthday message on it. The bill would be in her drawer; she'd have no reason not to believe in my Loving Aunt Becka, so she'd give me change for the fifty and I'd leave more than forty-five dollars ahead.

Jack had come up with the idea. I thought it was absurd. Worse than absurd: it was reckless and doomed to fail, and it reeked of desperation. But that stench had been too strong lately, so Jack's plan had to work. And because I was younger, and a girl, and more innocent-seeming, I had to make it work.

The cashier took the five from my shaking hand and made change without ever really looking at me. I was grateful for that.

'Next,' she said.

I stared into my hand for a second, as Jack had told me to, and then smiled sheepishly and said, 'Excuse me,' thinking, this is insane, this isn't going to work, why am I the one who has to do this?

The cashier was ringing up the next customer. Stuffing the change from the five into my pocket and walking out would have been the easiest thing in the world. I would tell Jack that I hadn't been able to convince her that the fifty was mine.

'Excuse me,' I said again, louder. 'I gave you a fifty.'

The girl glanced up briefly. 'You gave me a five.'

'Look,' I said, 'I'm sorry, but I'm sure it was a fifty.'

Finally she looked at me. Her hair, which had obviously been twisted up neatly and with great care that morning, was falling around her ears.

'You gave me a five, miss,' she said.

'You put it under your cash tray.' I tried the embarrassed smile again and said, 'This is stupid, but my aunt sent it to me. I think she wrote a message on it – happy birthday or something. Take a look.'

She jerked the cash tray roughly out of the drawer. There were three fifties sitting there, one of which was Jack's.

'She always uses purple ink,' I said.

She swore under her breath, quickly counted out forty-five dollars from the tray, and shoved the wad of cash towards me.

'Sorry about that. Next,' she said with finality.

'No problem,' I said, and a few steps later I was outside. A man in a suit was holding the door open for me, waiting impatiently for me to step out so he could enter. The drizzle had stopped. It was over. I'd done it.

I half-ran the few blocks to the deserted playground where Jack sat in the shelter of a wooden climbing structure, waiting for me next to a sign that said, 'Adults are not allowed beyond this point unless accompanied by a child.' Half of his sandwich was sitting neatly on its paper in front of him. He grinned when he saw me and I felt myself smile back. It had worked. We had money. Jack was going to be impressed. More than impressed: proud.

'Here,' he said and pushed the sandwich towards me. I ducked under the structure, just as a voice over my shoulder said, 'That was dumb.'

I turned.

The girl standing behind me had a wide mouth painted bright red and tiny ferretlike ears. The pale blond hair that curled behind them obviously hadn't been that colour to begin with, and her brilliant eyes matched her high black boots. She was wearing a ridiculous raincoat – clear plastic with silver glitter embedded in it – over something fuzzy and pink.

Jack's eyes widened slightly. Then he gave the girl a sleepy, innocent look. 'What?'

'Stupid,' the girl said. 'I saw the ink when you paid. You shouldn't have used purple – too bright.' Her tone said, quite clearly, that she would have caught us; we never would have gotten past her.

'Leave us alone, why don't you,' I said.

Her eyes measured me coolly. Then she stepped forward. Ducking, she joined us under the structure. Jack moved to make room for her.

'Why should I?' She shook the rain from her sparkly raincoat.

I looked her over, from the tips of her bleached hair to the pinched toes of her expensive boots. There was nothing I liked about her.

But Jack was smiling and he said admonishingly, 'Be nice, Jo.'

'Don't be an idiot.' I was trying to warn him.

'That's not being very nice, Jo,' the girl said, in the same tone Jack had used.

I moved to my brother's side and touched the small of his back unobtrusively. 'Jack, let's go. Let's get out of here.'

'Jack,' the girl said, and then said it again, slowly, as if she were holding his name in her mouth and waiting for it to dissolve like candy. She stepped forward, held out one slender, white, carefully manicured hand. 'I'm Lily, Jack.'

I said, 'Can we go?' and Jack said, folding his tanned hand over hers, 'I'm Jack, Lily.'

My brother had beautiful hands. They were slender and long-fingered, with strong bones hidden under the skin like roots in the earth. His hands adjusted spark plugs, solved equations in Greek letters, and lifted bottles to his lips with the same uncanny grace – as though they were independent and alive, moving like caged things, like beasts. I have a catalogue of mental snapshots of my brother that I flip through when the world seems too alien;

I think of his hands, and thinking of his hands always leads to that humid, drizzling day and his hand closing over Lily's like a sea creature over its small, defenceless prey.

Jack and Lily were the same kind of animal. Watching them together was like watching two cats that haven't decided whether to fight or mate. When she took us to dinner that night, she took the best table, right in front, without waiting for the waiter to lead us there, and ordered wine by the label without even looking at the list. It was a good restaurant; I was wearing my newest-looking sundress and my sandals, the nicest clothes I had, and I felt cheap and shabby. Jack was wearing a T-shirt and jeans and he looked wonderful.

'You should have the sea bass in peanut sauce,' she said to me, leaning in as though we were girls sharing secrets. We'd spent most of the day sitting in coffee shops with formless, atonal music and fabric-covered walls. Once she knew that Jack was my brother, she started to treat me as his harmless little sister instead of a threat. I'd made no such decision about her. But Jack had asked me very nicely while she was getting more steamed milk for her latte if I didn't think I could be a little bit less of a hostile bitch. I was trying.

Now she tapped the menu with one glossy, white-tipped fingernail. 'It's not on the menu. Or, rather, it is, but with chicken. It's better with sea bass.'

'Will they do that?'

'Of course they will. I don't eat chicken, anyway. No chickens, no pigs, no cows, no ducks.'

'But you'll eat sea bass,' Jack said.

Her scarlet lips curled in a coy smile. 'I've eaten fish while they were still flopping. Fish don't feel pain.' She stared at him over the rim of her wine glass.

I said, 'That can't be true. I don't think that's true.'

There was a thin silver case sitting on the table. She took a cigarette from it and lit it, letting the match burn all the way to her fingers and taking a long, deep drag before answering me.

'Of course it's true.' She sounded bored and petulant. Twin wisps of smoke drifted from her nostrils. She seemed to smoke solely for punctuation. 'They're too stupid.'

After dinner, we went to a bar where everyone seemed to be a friend or a friend of a friend of Lily's, and then to another bar, and then another. All of them were dimly lit and crowded and all the friends and friends of friends drank bright pink cosmopolitans with yellow lemon peels in them like floating scabs, and after half a dozen drinks I stopped noticing when we moved on. Lily seemed to have friends everywhere, but maybe we only went to the places where she had friends. Everywhere we went, she took my brother's hand and whisked him off to meet somebody or other, and I followed. Jack was charming, I was ignored, and very quickly I was drunk.

Eventually we ended up at a party in a crowded apartment that stands out in my memory because the giant tarantula sealed in glass on the wall was like the one in our old parlour. A boy with long blond sideburns asked me how we knew Lily. Eventually I'd learn that this was a New York expression: not where did you meet, but how do you know. Histories don't matter, but connections do. Nobody in New York has a history. But you might be somebody important, right now.

'We met her this afternoon,' I told the boy who'd asked. He wore a T-shirt that said NEVER in glow-in-the-dark letters.

'Lily does that,' the boy said.

'Does what?'

'Meets people. I never meet anyone. All day, every day.

Nobody.' He sighed a long, dramatic sigh. 'Just so I know. For my personal edification. How did Lily "meet" you?'

'My brother and I were robbing a coffee shop.'

The boy only laughed. 'He's your brother. That makes more sense. I was wondering exactly what the hell Lily was doing.'

A pretty girl within earshot said, 'Lily can handle anything,' and Never said, 'Well, that's what Lilys do. They handle things.'

'What kind of things?' I asked.

'This kind of thing,' Never answered, with a nebulous gesture at the party around us. 'Fabulous things.'

Across the room, Jack was leaning against a wall, and Lily was leaning against Jack. His hands were on her waist. My brother, in the smoky half-light, was beautiful, with eyelashes and cheekbones and all the rest. Lily had those things, too, but I thought there was something sly and shallow in her face that spoiled them. The tarantula hung over their heads like a furry arachnid star-of-Bethlehem.

'Evidently,' I heard Never say, 'at the moment she's handling fabulous things like your brother.'

He was offering me a cigarette. I took it. He said, 'What do you do?'

The pretty girl, still watching Jack, said, 'Fabulous things, indeed.'

'Nothing,' I said and smiled at him.

Never prattled on about some art exhibit he'd seen; trying to impress me, I thought. After a while I noticed that Jack and Lily were no longer standing beneath the tarantula. When Never suggested gracelessly that we disappear, too, I let him lead me into a corner, but after a few minutes of his fumbling kisses on my neck I pushed him away and fled back to the crowd. I spent the rest of the night sitting by myself on a low table in the corner.

Never stood across the room, glowering. Hours seemed to pass until, finally, Jack came to me, slightly rumpled, and said that we could go home.

Lily didn't leave the party with us. Outside, the streets were empty, peacefully silent, wet and clean from the rain that afternoon. The air was cool and dewy on my skin, which felt coated in cigarette ash. My ears were ringing and I was having trouble walking. Jack had his arm around me, mostly to hold me up. He was humming something Wagnerian.

My stomach roiled and twisted. 'Jack, I feel sick.'

He held me over the gutter, supporting me with one arm and holding my hair back with the other while I retched. When I couldn't bring anything else up, he told me to stick my fingers down my throat or I'd be sorry the next day. He was still humming.

My cosmopolitans and my Thai sea bass lay in a murky pink puddle in the gutter. Jack asked me if I could stand and somehow got me home. Once we were inside the apartment, he undressed me, and then himself, and we lay there in the semidarkness, with the streetlights flooding the room through the window.

As I was sinking into sleep, I wanted to ask him a question, but all I got out was, 'Lily?'

'I like her,' Jack said.

8

All at once, Jack had money. I guessed that it came from Lily, just as I guessed that the long red scratches on his shoulders came from Lily. He spent his nights with her and his days sleeping at the apartment. I slept whenever and spent my nights chain-smoking on the fire escape in the smothering heat, watching the street.

During the day, the noise from the street was so loud that being inside the apartment felt like standing on the street corner: delivery trucks with battered exhausts and shouting drivers who leaned on their horns; dogfights; twice a day, screeching groups of kids on their way to or from the public school at the end of the block; and at least once an hour, the wail and whine of sirens in the distance. Jack wore earplugs to sleep, but he could always sleep anywhere.

At night, though, it was quiet. We were four floors above the street. The people who passed beneath me as I sat on the fire escape at three and four in the morning were tired or drunk or crazy. None of them ever looked up.

One night when the air was still and dense with humidity, I let my burning cigarette drop from my fingers and watched it fall in a long slow arc to the street. It almost hit a dark-haired man standing on the front step of our building. He was digging in his pocket – for keys, maybe. The butt fell inches from his face and hit the concrete step at his feet with a tired burst of orange sparks.

He tilted his head back to look up at me. In the glow of the streetlight, I recognized him. He was the man Jack and I had met in the hallway that first day.

I raised my hand in the darkness, hoping that if he saw it he would take it for an apology.

He raised his hand, too, in an obscene gesture. Then he went inside.

I lit another cigarette.

The next day, while Jack was off somewhere with Lily, I strapped on my sandals to go buy some food, and ran into the man in the hallway. When he saw me, he cocked a finger at me and smiled. 'Hey, you dropped a cigarette on me last night.'

'I know,' I said. 'I'm sorry, I didn't mean to.'

'It's okay. I was a little drunk. You living in Tade's place?' He pronounced it 'TAH-day'. It was the name on the mailbox, the one we never checked.

'Was she the artist?'

He nodded. 'If you call what she did art,' he said. 'Looked to me like she just spilled paint on everything.' He put out his hand, and this time it wasn't making an obscene gesture. 'I'm Louis.'

I shook his hand awkwardly and then remembered and said, 'Oh.'

He grinned. 'Don't believe nothing you heard about me. None of that stuff's true.'

It sounded like, 'Nunna dat stuff's true.' I smiled.

'I take care of this place,' he went on. 'That's my door you slip the rent under – you need anything, just knock.'

'Thanks,' I said.

He nodded. 'That guy you live with, he your boyfriend?'

'My brother.'

'Your brother?' Louis raised his eyebrows. 'Yeah, you look alike. I've seen him around.' His eyes were careful. 'He a nice guy?'

'Of course he is,' I said.

He asked me my name and I told him. 'You need anything, Josie, you knock,' he said again.

A few days later, just before nightfall, the bare light bulb in our kitchen flashed, popped, and went out. Jack wasn't home. After standing and debating for a few minutes, I slipped on my shoes, went downstairs, and knocked on Louis's door. When he opened it, he had a beer in one hand. I could see a little of his apartment over his shoulder; it looked tidy and had clean, white walls.

'Got a ladder?' I said.

There was one in the basement, and it took both of us to lug it up the five flights to our apartment. I held the ladder steady while Louis fiddled with the light fixture.

After a moment, he made a disgusted noise. 'Look at this. Wiring's all fucked up.' Then he looked down at me, grinned, and said, 'Oh, sorry.'

'Why are you apologizing?'

'Shouldn't talk that way around a lady,' he said cheerfully.

'Please.'

'You never know. Some people get offended.'

'Not me,' I said.

He brought a new fixture up from the basement. As he clipped the wires together, I said, 'Did Tade get offended?'

Louis laughed. 'You didn't know Tade, babe.'

Just then the door opened and Jack came in. His eyes were shining and he was carrying a plastic bag full of takeout food.

When he saw Louis, his expression went blank. He put the bag on the counter. 'What's going on?'

Louis didn't look at Jack. He appeared to be concentrating on the light fixture.

'What's going on?' Jack said again, without taking his eyes off Louis.

'The light went out,' I said, and when that didn't seem to be enough, 'This is Louis. He's fixing it.'

'Is he,' Jack said.

Louis stepped down from the ladder. 'Not no more. I'm done.'

'Want me to help you with the ladder?' I said.

'I can get it.' Then, for the first time since Jack came in, Louis looked directly at me. 'I'll see you.'

'Thanks for fixing the light,' I said.

When he was gone, Jack took a beer from the fridge. 'Why did you let him in here?'

'Because I wasn't sure you were coming home, and I didn't feel like sitting alone in the dark all night.'

Jack's eyes snapped but he didn't raise his voice. 'Next time, wait. I'll let you know if I'm not going to be home.'

'How?' There was a phone jack in the wall but we'd never done anything about it.

'I'll let you know beforehand.'

'You will?' I said, dubious.

'I said I would.'

He didn't. I don't think I'd really expected him to.

That Saturday Jack asked me if I wanted to come out and have drinks with him and Lily and her friends. I said no. 'What the hell else do you have to do?' he said, but I wouldn't go. Eventually he left without me.

Fabulous Things

A few minutes later there was a knock on the door. It was Louis, holding a plate covered in aluminium foil.

'Hey,' he said. 'I went to my mom's house today. She always makes too much food. You want some?'

'Sure.' Whatever was hidden under the foil smelled wonderfully spicy.

'You're too skinny,' Louis said. 'I told my mom there was this sweet girl who lived in the building who was too damn skinny, she said I had to bring you some of her chicken and rice, fatten you up. Hey, where's your brother?'

I shrugged. 'With his girlfriend,' I said, and we stood there, awkwardly. I knew that I should invite him in, but I wasn't sure I wanted to. Besides, there was nowhere for him to sit.

'Well, then, why don't you come downstairs? Eat with me,' he said.

Why didn't I? 'I shouldn't. My brother will be home soon. He'll worry if I'm not here.'

Louis's dark eyes shone at me. 'Leave him a note.' But before I could answer, he waved a hand in the air. 'Yeah, well, if you change your mind, come on downstairs.' He turned to leave and then stopped. 'Hey, I got this old mattress down in the basement. I thought maybe you might want it. I don't mean *old*,' he said, quickly. 'It was mine. I got a new one, like, a couple months ago. So it's not like it's been down there with rats living in it or anything. You want it?'

'Are you kidding?' I said. 'I'd love it.'

'Be good to get it out of the basement, anyway,' Louis said. 'I'll bring it up for you tomorrow.'

'That'd be great.' I meant it.

He nodded. 'You think your brother'll mind?'

'Why should he?' ·

'He don't seem to like me too much.'

I shrugged. 'He doesn't like anybody.'

Louis shrugged. 'Some people are like that. They like to keep things to themselves.' He hesitated. 'Enjoy the food,' he said and left.

I let him go.

The next day, Jack came home with money and we went to the grocery store. On the way downstairs, I stopped at Louis's apartment to return his plate. While I knocked, Jack stood on the other side of the hallway, scowling.

Louis opened the door, his eyes flicking to Jack and then resting on me, calm and friendly. He didn't look in my brother's direction again.

'You like it?' he asked, taking the plate back from me.

'It was great.'

'She does good work, my mom,' Louis said, just as Jack said, 'Josie, let's go,' from behind me.

When we were outside, Jack said, 'I don't like that guy.'

'He's okay.'

Jack was walking quickly, looking straight ahead with narrowed eyes. 'I mean it, Jo.'

'Mean what?'

He stopped short and grabbed my arm. 'Stay away from him. Don't go looking for him, don't let him in, don't take his damn food.'

'Okay,' I said and pulled away. 'Christ. Okay.'

His saying that all but guaranteed that I would spend my nights on the fire escape thinking about going downstairs to visit Louis. Sometimes it seemed idiotic – it wasn't Louis that I was interested in, not really – but other, lonelier times I promised myself I'd do it the next day. Then it was October, and our rent was due, and

I couldn't have gone down, even if I'd wanted to. He'd want money, and we had none left to give him.

I reminded Jack about the rent one night before he went out. He nodded and said that he'd take care of it. I spent the day reading a copy of *The Red and the Black* that I'd bought on the street for a dollar; I was nearing the end of it when I heard the key in the lock. Jack was home.

'You're early,' I said, surprised.

He was wearing a new shirt and a satisfied smile. 'Success, sister mine. The rent is no longer an issue.' When I asked him what that meant, he said, 'Christ, Josie, what do you think? She wants us to come stay with her. What do you think I've been doing for the last two weeks?'

'Lily?' I said. I was sitting cross-legged on the mattress Louis had brought up for me. Jack had smiled when he'd seen the mattress, and frowned when he'd heard where it came from. He had said, darkly, that the last Louis had better see of my mattress was bringing it up.

'Now, now.' He started stuffing our clothes into plastic bags. 'Don't snap at brother. He's only doing what's best for both of us.'

'Gruelling work. Poor brother.'

He crouched down in front of me and put one hand on my knee. 'Josie.' His voice was serious. 'I've been working up to this for two weeks. We're having trouble making the rent and she wants me close; I told her I don't go anywhere without my sister. She doesn't care.' He laughed. 'She says she feels sorry for you.'

'She's a liar.'

'Sure she is. Who cares? She's got a two-bedroom place on the Upper West Side, and the rent comes out of her trust fund. You think I can't keep her on the line until we get tired of her? Hell, she's so high half the time she doesn't know whether she's coming or going.'

'Or coming?' I said blithely, but the words had a spiteful undertone and I thought, my God, I sound like Jack.

'Clever. Now get your stuff. I want to get the fuck out of here.'

'I'm not so sure, Jack.'

He sighed and sat down next to me. Then he reached up, pushed a stray hair from my forehead, and placed one finger lightly on the tip of my nose. 'Beloved smaller sister. Tell me what there is not to be sure about.'

Lily's apartment was in one of those beautiful old pre-war buildings, and everything in it had the kind of clean, simple lines that could only have been exorbitantly expensive. The main part of the apartment was an enormous open room. In one area, two long white couches faced each other over sleek glass coffee tables; in another part, a matching table and chairs served as the dining room. The space behind one of the couches formed a corridor leading to three closed doors, which opened on the bedrooms and the bathroom. The layout wouldn't have worked if the apartment had been any smaller; as it was, the room was like a decorator's display, the kind of place where the empty space was as important as the furniture. There were vast expanses of white silk-covered walls and thick white-on-white rugs; the only colour in the room came from the thick green leaves and the pale pink throats of the huge, waxy flowers that sat in crystal bowls and vases on every available surface. The air was filled with their strong sweet smell.

'Lilies, obviously,' Lily said proudly and pointed at each vase in turn. 'Santa Barbara, Madonna, All-in. My florist downtown makes sure I always have fresh ones.'

'They're lovely,' I said.

'My favourites are in here.' She led me to the kitchen – chrome and steel, but the pristine marble counters and the tiles on the wall were, of course, white. She pointed to a small round globe about twice the size of my fist, like a miniature fishbowl, that sat on top of the island bar. It was tightly packed with glossy green leaves and short stalks of creamy white bells, dangling all in a row down the length of the stalk, like hanging pearls. There was an identical globe on the other end of the island.

'Lilies of the valley,' she said. 'They're not really lilies at all, or so my flower guy says. But the name works.'

'They're beautiful.' I touched one of the green stalks. The delicate bells hanging from it trembled slightly.

'They're damned expensive, is what they are. You wouldn't believe. They're weeds, really. My parents' summer place in Maine has an entire flower bed covered in them. That's where they got my name,' she added offhandedly.

Jack was standing in the living room watching us, a faint smile on his face.

'The others I rotate, but I always have lilies of the valley,' Lily continued. 'When I was a kid I had a cat that died from eating them. Sad.' She shrugged and went to Jack, who slung an arm across her shoulders. Looking up into his face, she giggled. 'This will be so much fun. Just like a slumber party.' She kissed my brother and then smiled at me, revealing even rows of white teeth. Then she reached out to me with an alabaster hand. Her nails shone like glass.

'I bet you've never even been to a slumber party, have you, Jo?' She gave me a sympathetic look. 'Jack told me all about your father, keeping you locked up in that crazy old house all by yourself. It's so *Flowers in the Attic*. And I thought my childhood was creepy.' She laughed again, as if she'd made a joke. 'It's a wonder you two turned out as normal as you did.'

'We're not that normal,' Jack said and winked lasciviously.

She smiled. 'Forgive me if I hold out a shred of hope for your sister.'

'Her? She's the sick one. Far worse than me.'

I drifted over to a window, pulled aside one of the sheer white curtains, and looked outside. The sky was clear and blue, and down the street to my left, the Hudson glinted on the far side of a lush green park. We'd had trees in Alphabet City, but they were withered, scraggly things that starved in holes cut for them in the sidewalk, fenced in by low concrete borders decorated by neighbourhood artists and bums with beer cans and bits of cut glass. In Lily's neighbourhood, the trees had leaves; six storeys below me, the street was shady and lined on both sides with proud buildings and sleek, shiny cars. It felt like an entirely different city from the one that Jack and I had been living in for the last month.

I heard my name and let the curtain drop. Lily was standing behind me, obviously waiting. Jack's arms were wrapped around her shoulders and her arms were crossed over his, her small, perfect hands on his wrists.

'I said, do you want to see your room?' Lily pointed to one of the closed doors. 'It's that one. It's not much. It's where my parents stay, when they come.'

I looked inside at the big bed and the lacy curtains. There were no flowers here; the only lilies were pale watercolours hung on the walls, trapped in silver frames.

'It's all yours.' She shrugged. 'What there is of it.'

'It's great. Thanks.'

'No problem.' She smiled broadly.

We went out that night, just the three of us. By the time I was actually able to crawl into that white-on-white bed, I was exhausted, but the mattress was soft and welcoming and the sheets were clean. I still couldn't bring myself to trust Lily, but I didn't much miss Alphabet City.

The next morning, after we'd all eaten our bagels and Lily had gone to work (she worked at a fashion magazine, but I got the impression that she didn't work very hard; her father was on the publishing company's board of directors), Jack grabbed me by the waist and spun me in the air like a child. The new cologne that Lily had bought for him was strong in my nostrils.

'Beloved sister,' he said. 'My sister, my dear, my darling love, my angelically beautiful sibling: is your brother not brilliant, and are you not blissfully happy?'

His smile was wide and his green eyes were happy and relaxed. Suddenly, despite the new haircut and the expensive clothes – both Lily's work – he was my Jack again. The past two miserable months vanished into memory. I thought, there are people who live their entire lives and never know this kind of love. This will work out. This will be okay.

'Blissfully,' I said.

That evening, I was washing dishes and Jack was sitting on the white marble counter watching me, when we heard the door open. Lily called out, 'Jack? Are you there?' and came into the kitchen a moment later, wearing a white leather jacket and pearly blue boots that peeked out from the hem of her jeans. I became acutely aware of my cheap plastic sandals.

Jack held his arms out to her and she stood on tiptoe to kiss him.

'Good day?' he said.

'Every Friday is a good day.' She patted his chest. 'You want to go out for dinner tonight?'

'Sounds great.'

Then Lily looked at me. I was wearing a T-shirt and cutoffs. There were huge water splotches from the sink on my stomach and my hair was falling down around my face.

'We'll have to do something about you,' she said. 'Let's have a look at your clothes.'

I followed her into the bedroom where I'd slept the night before and dumped both of the shopping bags that held my clothes onto the bed. She poked the pile once or twice, a look of vague distaste on her face, and then shook her head.

'You'll have to borrow something of mine.' She looked critically at me. 'You're a little shorter than me. We could do a skirt. What do you have in the way of shoes?' Lily led me into her bedroom. Another globe of lilies of the valley sat on her dark wood dresser, and two lilies of a deep, vivid scarlet sat in crystal vases on the small tables next to her bed. They stood out like twin drops of blood in the white room. The smell of the flowers was lighter here than in the rest of the apartment, although I was growing used to it. I'd opened a window earlier and the fresh air had been a shock.

'Well,' I said and closed my mouth.

'I should have guessed.' She sighed and threw her closet doors open wide. 'Your brother wasn't much better at first. He's got a great sense of style, though. He always knows exactly what he wants, and it's always the right thing.' Her clothes were lined up by colour, like a pale, expensive rainbow, the lightest silver on one side and the lightest pink on the other. There was a pocket of black and a pocket of greys next to that, and on the other side of the greys were two or three men's shirts in dark colours.

They looked a lot like the one Jack was wearing that day.

'Red lilies,' I said.

'Bright red for danger.' She laughed. 'You know what those are called? Science-fiction lilies. I'm not kidding.' She pulled two hangers from the closet. 'When in doubt in New York, wear black.' She handed me the hangers and ordered me to get dressed while she took a shower. I heard the bathroom door open and shut. The water started, and then the door opened and shut again and I heard voices.

That would be Jack.

Lily's clothes felt thick and luxurious between my fingers. She had given me a black turtleneck sweater and a longish black skirt, both made of the same smooth wool. I put them on and looked at myself in the mirror. The dark material made my skin look pale and greenish. Even my hair looked sick. It was falling out of the ponytail I'd yanked it into that morning, and bits stood out from my head like straw.

I look like an overdressed scarecrow, I thought, and sighed. Then I picked up Lily's hairbrush and went to work.

The water shut off and I heard Lily laugh. She came into the bedroom, wrapped in a towel and a cloud of sweet-scented steam.

'Where's Jack?' I asked, working the brush through the split and ragged ends of my hair in front of her mirror.

'He went to have a smoke,' she said, watching me. Her wet hair fell in thick, healthy chunks over her eyes.

My own hair felt like a wig in my hands. Lily's mirror was wide and clear and honest. When Jack and I had lived with Raeburn, my hair had always been thick and shiny. Jack used to beg me to let him brush it, or at least let him watch as I did. Now it was Lily who watched me, wrapped in a towel and dripping on the white-on-white lilies woven into her imported French rug.

At least it still grows, I thought of my hair. At least it's long.

'Hold on,' Lily said suddenly and disappeared.

She was back in a second, carrying a plastic spray bottle and a small jar. Tucking the towel more firmly around herself, she took the hairbrush away from me, lifted my hair, and sprayed it with water until it was soaked through. Then she opened the jar, scooped out two fingerfuls of the pale yellow cream inside, and rubbed it between her hands. She ran her fingers through my hair, over and over again, and a sweet, rich smell, like caramel, surrounded me. I watched in the mirror, fascinated.

Finally she stopped and wiped her hands on her towel. The little beads of moisture on her shoulders had dried. 'There,' she said. 'That'll help. Go dry it. My hair dryer is under the basin.'

'Thanks.' I didn't know what else to say.

She waved dismissively. 'You'd have pretty hair if you bothered to take care of it.'

I stood where I was a moment more, awkwardly, staring at her.

'Can I get dressed now?' she asked finally.

'Sorry,' I said and fled to the bathroom.

The cream made my hair silky again. I twisted it into two long plaits and tied them with bits of black ribbon that I'd found in a drawer in the bathroom. When Lily came out of her bedroom, wearing the blue boots and a matching dress, she handed me a pair of clunky Mary Janes and said I looked cute. We went to a restaurant that served delicate Italian food, completely unlike the heavy pasta in red sauce I was used to eating. Then Lily led us to a bar downtown where the only light came from spotlights that shone on single roses in bud vases. She bought us cosmopolitans. We got very, very drunk.

At 4 a.m., when they turned on the lights in the bar, we

stumbled our way out to the street and into a cab. Jack sat in the middle and said that he was surrounded by beautiful women. 'How am I supposed to choose?' he said, touching my hair and kissing Lily.

'Well, one of us is your sister,' she said pointedly.

He pulled me close on one side, kissed her again on the other. 'True, very true. Now if I can only remember which one.'

'Here's a hint,' Lily said. 'She's the one that doesn't have her tongue in your ear.'

He laughed and bent to kiss her neck while the hand at my shoulder found one of my plaits and stroked it. The cab swerved and dodged in and out of the traffic on Broadway, and silver light from the bars and restaurants and streetlights moved through the windows as we passed.

Back in the apartment, Lily said, 'This way a sec, darling?' and pulled Jack into their bedroom. The door closed behind them and for a moment I sat on the couch where I'd fallen. There were noises from behind the door: Lily's squealing, Jack's laughter, low and rich and teasing.

I forced myself up and made my way unsteadily to my room. Lily's turtleneck went carefully back on its hanger. There was a mirror hanging over the low dresser, and I stood in front of it in my bra and pulled the black ribbons from the ends of my plaits. Lily's cream had done miracles, I thought as I started to work through the plaits with my fingers. I let myself take a small drunken pleasure in the soft feel of the hair in my hands: satiny, gentle, mine.

I heard Lily's door open and the bathroom door shut. Then I felt somebody watching me. I turned around.

Jack stood in the doorway. His expression was intent.

'Hey.' I turned back to the mirror.

He moved behind me and then his arms were around my shoulders and his hands were on top of mine on my plait.

I let my hands fall.

His fingers began to move on the rope of hair, stroking it, his fingers probing into the twisted strands and unweaving them. In the mirror, his fierce green eyes were fixed on me and I couldn't look away. The locks of hair that he'd freed brushed against my bare skin, moving gently with the motion of his hands. There was a rushing in my ears, from the alcohol in my blood and the music in the bar and the warmth of him next to my naked back. He lifted my hair, running his fingers through the length of it and letting it fall like water onto my shoulders.

I shivered.

The toilet flushed; the bathroom door opened; Lily's voice, confused, called, 'Jack?'

His hands lingered on my hair and then slid around my waist. He kissed the back of my neck.

'Coming,' he called to her and left me.

I went to bed with my skin singing. When I closed my eyes I saw the two science-fiction lilies next to her bed like two red flags, and between them her white satin sheets were like the golden pale of his skin and the pink pale of hers.

Lying in bed, I remembered sitting at the kitchen table while Raeburn explained atomic bonds to me. On a subatomic level, electrons are drawn to the atoms that need them. If an atom is unbalanced, with more protons in the nucleus than electrons in orbit around it or vice versa, it will seek out another atom with the opposite condition, and thus find balance. My brother was like those electrons, filling an infinitesimal void that people like Lily and Becka didn't even know existed. It was a talent that I wished was genetic, as I tried to fall asleep in that wide, unfamiliar bed. There was always someone who needed Jack. He was never alone.

When I woke up the next morning, the sun was streaming through my window. It was a beautiful fall day, warm and friendly and relaxed. The three of us bought coffee on the corner and sat in the park until late afternoon, Jack and Lily twined together on a blanket, me next to them. Separate, but not alone. In all of my time in New York, that was my favourite day.

Being with Lily felt like being with a movie star. Everything in her world glittered fabulously. Neither of us had the kind of clothes she wanted us to wear, so she took us shopping. It turned out that she was right about Jack; he had the instinct for it, which surprised me because back on the Hill, Jack had never given a damn about clothes. Lily figured out pretty quickly that I couldn't be trusted to choose my own clothes, and I suspect that she liked dressing me up. The things she bought me were completely different from those she bought for herself. All of my clothes were black.

She bought Jack a new leather jacket – 'And let's burn the old one, shall we?' – and then spent an extravagant amount of money on a pair of high black leather boots for me. 'You can more or less get away with only one pair of shoes in New York, as long as they're fabulous drop-fucking-dead boots,' she said, but when we returned to the apartment she also gave me the black Mary Janes that she'd loaned me that first night, and a long black skirt that she said she was tired of. She made me try it on right then, watching me turn in front of the mirror with a small satisfied gleam in her eyes.

She said, 'You and your brother. It's unfair.'

'What is?'

'Your goddamned cheekbones.' She smiled. 'What I wouldn't give.'

Jack wore the new jacket as often as he could get away with it. It was black and beautifully cut and the soft leather gleamed. Between the new clothes and the way his hair was always artfully swept back from his face, he was indistinguishable from one of her crowd. Late one night, I took his battered old jacket, the one with the sheepskin lining that I'd worn to the bonfire so long ago, and hung it in the closet in my room, behind Lily's spring dresses. He never asked about it. Our old clothes, the ones we'd worn when we left the Hill and the ones Becka had bought for me, were stuffed into plastic bags on the closet floor. For some reason I was reluctant to get rid of them.

Lily had high standards. She smoked only French cigarettes; she wore only designer clothes; she drank only cosmopolitans, and she drank them only in bars where they cost ten dollars or more. She liked to have her hairdresser dye little coloured streaks into her blond hair, frosty blue or frosty pink, to let people know what a free spirit she was. She and her inner circle (a nebulous social body with a rotating membership, where the faces weren't always the same but might as well have been) spent all their days planning their nights. Every day was a whirlwind of phone calls about who was going to be where and when and for how long, and whether a certain bar was worth going to after midnight or if all the truly trendy people would already be at the truly trendy clubs. Every night there was a planned itinerary that was set in stone until it was changed with the flip of a cell phone.

In the beginning, Jack and I went everywhere with her.

All her friends loved him. Being pulled aside by one or another of Lily's drunken girlfriends and hearing a confession of her secret passion for my brother – always with the stern exhortation that I was not to tell Lily – was the rule rather than the exception for me. The next day, I would mimic the girl's voice and gestures for Jack, which he found hilarious.

Before long Lily decided that she didn't like our being a threesome. 'It throws off the dynamic,' she said, and thus began a parade of her male friends, showing up dutifully at bars and parties and parties in bars. Each of them was highly polished, skilfully groomed, and more beautiful than the last, and I had nothing to say to any of them. Afterwards she would extol the virtues of the various Davids and Andrews and Jasons at great length, telling me how much this one or that one had liked me and what complimentary things they had said about me. I didn't think any of them could hold a candle to Jack, which was undoubtedly why Lily was on his arm and not theirs. Finally, when she figured out that I really couldn't be bothered, she paired me off with her 'very best college friend', Carmichael. He was very tall, very thin, and very gay – or so Jack claimed. It was all the same to me. I didn't care and neither, apparently, did Carmichael. I can't say that we ever had a conversation – he rarely tried to talk to me – but he seemed content to sit next to me in bars and stand next to me at parties whenever it was required.

One night he came up to the apartment for drinks, and after Jack and Lily had disappeared into her bedroom, as was inevitable, he asked me dispassionately if I wanted to fuck.

'I don't think so, thanks,' I said.

He shrugged. 'Suit yourself,' he said, and we continued sipping our drinks as if the subject had never come up. I wondered why he would want to have sex with someone he wasn't even interested in talking to, and the more I thought about it, the more absurd it became. Meanwhile, Jack and Lily were clearly trying to be quiet in the next room, but occasional moans and thumps still reached us. By the time Carmichael left, I was shaking with suppressed laughter. Neither of us ever brought up sex again.

Every week, Lily's florist came to deliver fresh flowers. After a few weeks the scent of lilies was so deeply impregnated in my skin that I could smell it anywhere: on the street, in a bar, in cabs and coffee shops.

The night I saw Never again, Lily had taken us to a party in TriBeCa. I was getting a glass of red wine from the bartender – it was the kind of party where there was a bartender – when a familiar voice next to me said, rather nastily, 'I hear you made it in.'

I turned. At first I didn't recognize him because he wasn't wearing the glow-in-the-dark T-shirt. 'Made it in what?' I said.

'That's the question, isn't it?' he said and grinned. 'Maris says Lily pulled you and your life-of-the-party brother out of nowhere. She says you're her latest bit of window-dressing.'

Maris. It took me a moment to match a face to the name. Red hair, dour expression. Worked with Lily. Her thing was buying drinks; she was one of those people who always picked up a round. I hadn't known she disliked us.

Never's eyes were bleary and I realized that he was drunk.

'She and my brother have a thing going on,' I said carefully.

He didn't seem to hear me. 'Is that why you blew me off that night? Because I don't have a trust fund for the two of you to live off?' He leaned in close and there was glee in his eyes as he stage-whispered, 'What are you going to do when she drops you?'

I stared at him. 'Is that what she did to you?'

He called me a freeloading low-life bitch and walked away. The bartender gave me my wine. I felt remote and unaffected.

Later I pointed him out to Carmichael, who shrugged and

looked bored. 'Mark something,' he said. 'Pet roach. If you offered to fuck him he wouldn't say no, no matter what he called you.'

'Pet roach?'

'One of those obnoxious New York fads back in the eighties. Some designer started gluing cockroaches to chains with pins attached, so you could wear them pinned to your clothes like jewellery. I've never actually seen one, if you don't count the human kind. Don't worry about him,' he said.

The next morning, as we walked to the coffee shop on Broadway, I told Jack about Never and what Carmichael had said. Jack's lip curled ever so slightly, but he said that we weren't cockroaches and told me that I shouldn't look gift Lilys in the mouth.

'I wasn't talking about us,' I said. But in my more bitter moments I started to think of us that way: Lily's pet roaches. Which, I'm sure, was what Carmichael had intended.

That night, after Jack and Lily went to bed, the noises coming through the wall were different. Jack's voice was low and growling, and Lily's answering cries of passion sounded desperate and painful. A week or so later I came upon her wet and dripping in the living room with a towel wrapped around her, and there was a deep red bruise on her arm that looked as if someone had grabbed her, hard. I looked quickly at Jack and then at her, but they both ignored me.

After that, though, when the three of us were home alone together, Lily wore sheer, delicate tank tops or sweaters with wide necks that fell off one shoulder, and the creamy pale skin revealed was, more often than not, marked with purple bruises or ugly bite marks. When we went out, they were always carefully covered.

In the beginning I had marvelled at Lily's ability to go, go, go, no matter how early she'd gotten up for work; there were nights when we drifted in at 6 a.m. and she was up and gone by nine-thirty. I made some comment about it to Jack and he said, 'Fairy dust and amphetamines. Check out the drawer in her nightstand sometime.'

The late nights, the more-fabulous-than-thou parties, and the crowded bars – they began to wear on me. All that we ever did was go out at night and sleep it off the next day. My brain felt slow and stupid. Time began to blur.

The weather was turning cool then, and Jack wore his new jacket everywhere because it was the only one he had. Each morning, after Lily left for work, he woke me up by crawling into my bed, and each night when I went to sleep I knew that he would come to me during the night, shaking with the aftershocks of one of his nightmares. During the day, he was never far from me: holding my hand, stroking my hair, pulling me into his lap. At the same time, he grew rougher with Lily, even when I was around. Once in the kitchen I saw him push her, hard, so that she lost her balance and came close to falling onto the stove, but then he kissed her and she was kissing him back wildly, gripping the back of his head with her hands.

She started staying home more. Her exuberant glamour began to seem forced. When we did go out into the dark glitter of the city, there were times when her eyes shone with a desperate need. At home she treated me with a formal politeness that let me know clearly that she didn't want me around any more: she didn't want me living with her, she didn't want me watching her, she didn't want me seeing her.

One night, at a bar in SoHo, I opened the bathroom door and found Lily leaning against the basin and Maris standing beside her. Lily was saying, angrily, 'It's none of your goddamned—'

But then she saw me, stopped talking, and turned her face away.

Maris saw my reflection in the mirror. 'Do you mind?'

'Sorry,' I said.

Lily gave me a strained smile and pushed past me, back into the bar. Her eyes were wet and shining.

Maris fixed me with a bitter, steely glare.

'I know what you're doing,' she said. 'You and your creep brother. Nobody's fooled, okay?'

Then she walked out.

Sometimes, when Jack was asleep and Lily was gone, I would open my closet door softly and take out Jack's old leather jacket. When I buried my face in it I imagined that I could smell the morning air in Jack's bedroom on the Hill. Whiskey, cigarettes, freedom.

Near the end of October, Carmichael sent out black roses and invitations to a Halloween party. It wasn't long afterwards that Lily told us, as she was getting ready for work, that she was going to Paris for a long weekend in November.

She was standing in front of the mirror in her living room, making sure that her lipstick was perfect. Jack was standing near her; I was sitting on the couch, with my knees pulled up to my chest. The apartment was chilly; Lily didn't like to turn on the heat because it wilted the lilies. I could see her porcelain face reflected in the mirror.

'The weather will be horrible,' she said, frosting her lips over with pale pink lipstick, 'but it'll be horrible here, too, and I might as well suffer in Paris.'

'Okay,' Jack said. He was leaning against the wall next to Lily, watching her. His voice was smooth and easy but his eyes on her were hard.

Lily met them without flinching. She snapped the top back onto her tube of lipstick and ran her finger along the edge of her lower lip. 'I'll only be gone for five days. You guys can take care of things here, right?'

'Like it was our own,' Jack said.

Lily's dark eyes glanced up at him in the mirror. Her expression was almost a glare. 'But it's not.'

Jack stuck his hands in his pockets and walked away from her. He came over to the couch and sat down next to me. Picked up a magazine.

'It's too damn early for this,' Lily said and went into the kitchen. She took a container of yogurt from the refrigerator and dropped it into her bag.

Then she sighed. 'Look, I'm just tired. I need to get out of this damn city.'

'No damage,' Jack said without looking up from his magazine.

She gazed at him. I couldn't read the expression on her face.

'All right,' she said and left.

Jack didn't look at me, but I could see the tension in his shoulders. 'Everything okay?'

He shrugged. 'She goes every year. She was talking about taking us – or at least me – with her this year.'

Leaving me by myself again, I thought. I looked at the floor. 'Are you disappointed?'

'At missing the chance to spend five days in a foreign country with only Lily to talk to? I'd kill her.' He shook his head. 'I don't care about the trip. But I'm not sure I know what's going on with her any more. I don't like it.'

I laid a hand on the back of his neck. 'It'll be okay.' I ran my fingers up and down the smooth skin that covered his vertebrae. 'She's moody, you know that. By the time she gets home tonight she'll be so perky we'll want to bash her head in again.' He didn't answer. 'She wouldn't be leaving us here alone if things weren't cool, would she?'

Jack leaned his head back against my hand. 'Could be. I don't know, Jo. I don't like it.'

And sure enough, when Lily breezed through the door that night with an armful of shopping bags, she was full of good cheer again. 'My costume for Carmichael's party,' she said, holding up the bags, and giggled. 'Wait until you see it. It's fabulous.' She kissed the air in Jack's general direction and disappeared into her bedroom.

'See?' I said. 'Fine.'

'Maybe,' Jack answered.

The noises from their bedroom kept me awake for a long time that night. Everything seemed to be fine after all.

Jack and I were at a loss when it came to Halloween costumes. When we asked Lily for suggestions, she said, 'I can't tell you what to wear. You have to pick your own costume.' Her costume, of course, was fabulous. We didn't see it until the night of the party. A long dark wig covered her pale hair, and she wore a short black dress with a ragged hem made of many layers of diaphanous material. Gauzy black wings dusted with silver glitter sprouted from her shoulder blades; her arms were bare and dusted with more glitter, and she spent an hour forming cobwebs on her temples with tiny black crystals and eyelash glue. Her lips were a bruised purple and her kohl-lined eyes glittered with something feral. 'I'm a fairy,' she said. 'The fairy of death.'

Jack decided to go as a priest, wearing black and pinning a piece of white cardboard to his collar. I raided Lily's closet, went to a few thrift shops, and ended up with a conglomeration of brightly coloured scarves and junk jewellery. I added a brightly patterned skirt and an old peasant blouse of Lily's.

When she saw me, she shook her head.

'You're the world's only blond gypsy,' she said.

'I'm the world's only many things,' I answered. I was finding the whole costume-party concept annoying. My first and favourite impulse had been to pull out one of Jack's old T-shirts and some cutoff jeans and go as Josie Raeburn. I'd discarded the idea without genuinely considering it, sensing that it would cause more trouble than it was worth. Still, it would have felt good.

New York City on Halloween: half the population was out on the streets, and in the ten blocks between Lily's apartment and Carmichael's, we saw satyrs, politicians, pixies and fairy princesses, devils in red satin, witches in black tulle, and giant carrots wearing sneakers. Children were dressed as goblins, birthday cakes, mice, tomatoes; their adult escorts were tigers, pirates, and tired-looking moms and dads in comfortable shoes. Lily was in high spirits as we walked. She would leave for Paris in the morning.

There was the usual complement of sexy witches and space aliens at Carmichael's, but for the most part his guests' tastes in costumes ran more towards the obscure and the ironic. One of Lily's friends from the fashion magazine had come in a three-piece suit; 'I'm boring,' he said when people asked him what he was. Maris, who rarely wore any combination of clothing worth less than five hundred dollars, was wearing jeans and a T-shirt and holding a disposable camera. She said she was a tourist and pointed out her practical sneakers, which she had borrowed from her roommate. Another crony – one of the candidates in Lily's man-parade, actually – was there in khakis and a polo shirt. He was supposed to be a Republican.

We were all crammed into two rooms. The lucky ones had found places to sit, on couches or tables or windowsills or radiators. Everyone knew Lily was leaving the next day and she was beset by people wishing her bon voyage. Jack's eyes were guarded and grim, but he stood his ground in his priest's collar, like a good pet roach. I felt no such obligation and staked out a safe spot in a corner.

Carmichael found me and brought me red wine in a plastic cup. He was dressed as a vampire, his dark hair slicked back from his bony face and a red jewel sparkling in one of his buttonholes. He was drunk.

'Like my fangs?' he said and grinned lasciviously. His eyeteeth were long and pointed.

'They look real.'

'Caps. There's a place down on St Mark's that makes them. They take impressions and everything.'

'Do they come off?'

'Eventually. Lily looks gorgeous, doesn't she?' He scanned me from head to toe and said, 'What are you supposed to be?'

'Gypsy,' I said. 'I guess.'

He laughed. 'Interesting choice. I guess Lily didn't tell you, did she?'

'Tell me what?'

'That's what I thought. Well, you look cute, anyway.' He saw someone across the crowd and lifted a hand. 'Hey, you made it!' he called and was gone.

I stayed where I was. That was the party strategy that I had developed: I picked a spot and stuck to it. Anyone who drifted within conversational distance, I'd talk to, provided they started the conversation and I felt like keeping up my half. At this party, at least, there were interesting things to look at. I watched as a thin girl wrapped in hundreds of feet of fluorescent pink tubing passed me, and then Jack was at my elbow.

'What the hell do you think that was?' he said.

'No clue. You know, I think I like these people a lot more when they're not dressed as themselves. At least they're fun to look at.'

'Trust me,' he said, 'they're no better to talk to. Christ, get me out of here.'

'What's up with Lily?'

'Fuck knows. She's running hot and cold. Where'd you find that drink?'

'Carmichael brought it to me.'

'That doesn't help.' Jack scanned the crowd. 'I need something potent. Listen, if you want to play sick and go home early, I'm game.' He tugged at the scarf in my hair and disappeared into the crowd.

I drank my wine, which was warm and bitter, and stood for a while watching the party move around me like a carousel. Then I went to find another drink. The apartment was small; I expected to turn a corner and find Jack at any moment. Instead I found Carmichael, standing with Maris and a man I didn't know in the hallway outside the bathroom door.

'Line starts behind me,' Maris said.

'I'm actually looking for a drink,' I said.

'I'll get you one,' the man said. He was wearing a crumpled top hat and a rusty black tailcoat, his face covered in black smudges.

Carmichael put an arm across my shoulders and said, 'Jo, meet my downstairs neighbour – Joe.'

Maris laughed. Her eyes were red and I realized that she was drunk, or high, or both. 'That's funny,' she said. 'Jo, meet Joe. Joe, meet Jo.'

'Greetings,' the man said. He had broad, muscular shoulders

that strained the seams of his black suit. When he reached out to shake my hand, I caught a whiff of his cologne. It had a sharp chemical smell.

'What are you?' I said.

Joe tipped his hat and said, with a bad cockney accent, 'Why, I'm ye old chimney sweep, ain't I, miss?'

Somebody in the crowd called out, 'Hey, the psychic's here!' and Carmichael excused himself. Maris gave Joe and me a knowing look and said, 'Think I'll go help Carmichael,' and then I was alone with the chimney sweep, standing in the hallway.

'So,' he said. 'You're Lily Carter's newest protégée, huh?'

'No,' I said.

'Funny, Carmichael told me you and your brother were living with her.'

'She and my brother have a thing going on. I sleep in the spare room.'

'But you don't work.'

'I'm only seventeen.'

His eyes widened slightly. 'You're seventeen?'

Then the bathroom door opened and a ghost in a white sheet pushed past us.

'You want to come in?' Joe said.

I looked at the open bathroom door. I looked at him. 'With you?'

'Sure.'

Past him, on the bathroom counter, I saw a glass full of cut drinking straws and a small mirror next to the faucet.

'Think I'll pass,' I said.

'Whatever you say.' Joe reached out and touched the tip of my nose lightly. I shrank back instantly. That was something Jack did. 'I'll find you later. I still owe you that drink.'

The bathroom door closed. Then the music stopped abruptly and I heard Carmichael shouting, 'Everyone! The fortune-teller is here!'

The crowd made appreciative noises and headed towards the sound of his voice. Somebody took hold of my arms. It was Lily, her eyes too bright. I wondered if she'd been in the bathroom.

'Josie first!' she called, steering me through the crowd.

Carmichael, standing on a chair, saw us coming. 'Oh, absolutely,' he said, and then I found myself standing in front of a heavy woman with a hairy upper lip and massive upper arms. She was wearing a sleeveless blouse and a long skirt; her dark, snapping eyes took in my garish costume and grew contemptuous.

'Ladies and gentlemen!' Carmichael cried. 'For your tarot-rific Halloween entertainment, my very own neighbourhood storefront psychic – Madame Olinka!'

Madame Olinka was rummaging in an immense leather bag. She brought out a greasy deck of cards and began to shuffle them on a small table. Her chunky fingers were graceful as they deftly tapped the cards back into an even deck.

'Pay first,' she said.

Carmichael grimaced and took out his wallet.

'See?' he said as he counted out twenties and pointed to me. 'We've got our own gypsy here.'

Madame Olinka looked at me. 'So I see.' I felt myself blush. She pointed to the chair that Carmichael had been standing on. 'Bring that chair. Sit down.'

'No,' I said.

But Lily was still at my back. She grabbed the chair, plonked it down inches from Madame Olinka's massive knees, and pushed me into it. 'Get your fortune told. Maybe you'll learn something useful.'

Meanwhile, Madame Olinka had laid three greasy cards face-down between us. The pattern on the backs looked like stained glass, angular and cleanly drawn. She gestured at the cards. 'Frank Lloyd Wright tarot. Very modern.'

The crowd laughed and Carmichael said, 'Only the best for my parties, people!'

Madame Olinka shrugged. 'Modern world, modern tarot.' She bent over the cards with an air of great concentration. 'I do three-card spread.' Her English was unaccented and economical. 'First card tells the past – tells how you got here, to be where you are. Second tells where you are now, what you got to do to make things right, if they're not right; and if they are right, it tells you how to keep them that way. Third card tells about the future – but just possibilities,' she added, as an afterthought. 'Not what will be, necessarily, but what could be, if nothing you do changes. Future isn't in anybody's hands but your own.'

'Sure.' Somebody put another glass of wine into my field of vision. I looked up, thinking it must be Jack. Joe the chimney sweep winked down at me.

'Ask if there are going to be any tall dark strangers in your life tonight,' he said, putting his hand on my shoulder. It reeked of his cologne. Somewhere in the crowd gathered around us, I heard Lily laugh.

Madame Olinka's eyes flickered. 'I think there already is one, right?' Everybody laughed again. Where was Jack? 'First card,' she said and turned it over. The card showed the silhouette of a man framed by a stylized window. It was hard to tell whether he was part of the window or standing in front of it, because his body was cut into pieces like stained glass. 'The Hermit.'

'That's her, all right,' I heard Lily say.

The fortune-teller ignored her. 'There's a big difference

between the outside world and the world inside your head. So you trying to make sense of things, and now, you got a better sense of time, what it do to you.'

'I do?' I said.

Madame Olinka shrugged. 'This card tells where you come from. Seems to me you got a nasty shock sometime, things aren't what you expected. Now, next card, you see, is the devil.' The card showed a woman wearing a long black dress standing on a white hill against a deep blue sky.

'The devil is a woman?' I said.

'Is she ever,' Joe said from behind me and squeezed my shoulders. I tried to shrug him away, but when his hands left my shoulders they moved to my hair.

'Sometimes she is.' Madame Olinka looked at the cards. 'Not so bad. Sounds worse than it is. You surrounded by bad feelings right now. All it means is, you got to be careful. You got to try and think clearly. Don't get all caught up in plans and schemes. Logic, right? Logic is what the devil likes most. You stay away, think with your heart. But,' and she pointed a warning finger at me, 'this all going on right now. You don't make a choice now, you maybe never get a chance to choose again.'

'Choose what?' I said.

'Choose what you gonna do.' She sounded a little exasperated. 'Choose whether you gonna believe those bad feelings swirling around you like smoke, or you gonna see the world the way it is.' Madame Olinka's eyes flickered up to the crowd and she shifted uncomfortably in her chair.

'Lots of people here,' she muttered. 'More than I thought. Got to hurry. Last card now.'

The last card she turned up showed a circle cut into pieces like a pie. The letters under the picture said 'Wheel of Fortune'.

Madame Olinka, unsmiling, tapped the card. 'But there you go. No matter what you do, things gonna be okay. You gonna end up with no worries and no tears and no questions.'

'Sounds like death,' I said.

Madame Olinka sat back in her chair, losing interest. 'What I tell you. Tarot doesn't tell the future. Could be death. Or could be happiness.'

'My turn,' a pink pixie said. I moved quickly to let her sit down. When I stood up, Joe's arm was across my shoulder. I stepped away quickly.

Lily appeared in front of me. 'Solve all your problems?' Her blackish lips were curled slightly, and her eyes glittered with that feral look again.

'Sure. Lily, have you seen Jack?'

She was staring, distracted, into the crowd. 'He's around. I'll go find him for you.' She vanished, leaving me standing stupidly, holding the wine that Joe had given me. For want of anything better to do, I took a sip.

'There you are,' Joe's voice said from behind me, and I felt his arm snake around my waist. 'How's that wine?'

The party had lost focus. Where was my brother? I moved through the crowd like a ghost. Every face I saw was a stranger's. None of them was Jack. I wanted to go home.

Then I was in the hallway outside the apartment. Carmichael was at one shoulder, Joe at the other. They were holding me up.

'Where are we going?' I said. My tongue felt foreign in my mouth and the walls around me wouldn't stay where they belonged. The men carried me down a flight of stairs. My feet didn't touch the steps.

'Joe's place,' Carmichael said. We went through a door and Joe fumbled with keys. 'You drank too much. You need to lie down.'

'Where's my brother?' They carried me through a door and I felt myself fall onto a big, soft bed. I could feel the smooth cotton bedspread under my hand.

'He's upstairs,' Joe said. I heard the sound of a zipper. One of my boots was gone. Then the other. 'He knows you're here. It's okay.'

'He told us to bring you down here,' Carmichael said from somewhere above my head.

'Where – where is he?' The room was spinning.

'He knows you're with us,' Joe said. 'It's okay.'

My limbs were leaden as the two men lifted my arms and pulled my blouse over my head.

'Jack,' I heard myself mumble. I was shivering.

'Jack says it's okay,' Joe said gently. 'Don't worry about Jack.'

'Jack—'

'Jack told us to take care of you,' I heard Carmichael say. 'Jack said we could.'

9

Everything was still. My head felt thick and sore and so did my body, but the room had stopped moving. Carmichael was gone; Joe was sitting on the bed next to me, smoking a cigarette. He was naked. I realized that I was naked, too.

The air smelled bad.

Joe looked down at me and said something about being sexy and seventeen.

'Bathroom,' I said. Croaked.

He pointed down the hallway with his cigarette.

I tried to stand up. My legs were wobbly. Somehow, I made it. I washed my hands and my face and then I looked in the mirror.

There was makeup smeared under my eyes. My hair was a tangled mess and my eyes were red. There was stubble burn on my cheeks and my chin and my breasts, and the hair between my legs was sticky and hard. My scalp was sore, as if my hair had been pulled hard.

My skin smelled of Joe's cologne.

I splashed some water on my face and then took a towel from the rack on the wall and wrapped it around myself. Things were still dim around the edges, and on my way back to the bedroom I made a wrong turn and found myself staring at a human-sized cage made from chicken wire and splintering wood. It was filled with excited, darting things, all bright little eyes and pointed little ears and snaky little backs.

Paralysed with horror, I couldn't breathe.

'You like my ferrets?' Joe emerged from the bedroom, wearing only a pair of tight blue briefs.

'No.' The cage reeked of urine-soaked wood and rodent dirt. It was the source of the bad smell in the air. The mass of ferrets inside it writhed malevolently.

Joe opened the cage and pulled one of them out. It moved sinuously up his arm and curled around his neck. 'You want to hold her?'

'No,' I said. I couldn't stop shuddering. The ferret's black eyes glittered at me from his shoulder.

'You want to know their names?' Joe pointed at each of the ferrets in turn and said, in a singsong voice, 'Lust, Sloth, Gluttony, Envy, Anger, Greed, Pride; and this little darling here is Ingrid.' He reached up behind his head and stroked the ferret's long body. Grinning, he said, 'Here, hold her,' and put the ferret on my shoulder. Its tiny claws dug into my bare skin as it sniffed at my ear and I felt its fur bristle as it investigated the back of my neck.

Then it was in my hair. My mouth opened and I heard myself scream.

The noise was loud and shrill and broke through my daze. I beat at the hissing mass of fur with my hands, still screaming, and then there was a sudden sharp pain on the side of my hand. Joe was shouting, 'Don't hurt her! Don't hurt her!' and he grabbed me and pushed me fiercely against the wall. He pinned me there with a forearm across my breastbone while he gently pulled strands of my hair away from the ferret. When she was free he lifted her back to his shoulder. She hissed at me again and he held me by the arm and slapped me, twice, hard.

'You stupid bitch. You fucking hurt her,' he said and let his arm fall.

My legs gave out and I slid down, crumpling in a heap at the base of the wall. Joe stalked into the bedroom, the ferret twined around his neck, and came back a moment later carrying my clothes.

He threw them at my face. 'Here. Get dressed and get the fuck out of here.'

The ferret blinked at me from his shoulder.

I found my underwear in the pile and pulled them on. There were long smears of blood down the length of my thighs.

'It bit me,' I said. 'My hand is bleeding.' I held it up.

'Get out of here,' Joe said again and shook his head in disgust. 'Fucking pathetic.'

Outside, it was early morning. There was a thick fog clinging to the empty streets and the air was cool and damp in my lungs. I'd wrapped my bleeding hand in one of my gypsy scarves and was clutching it to my chest. My tights had disappeared and my boots were rubbing painfully against my legs.

Every muscle in my body was tired or sore. My stomach hurt and my head was fuzzy.

Jack says it's okay. Jack said we could.

No. Obviously that hadn't been true. I had been calling for my brother; that's why they'd said that. Because Jack would never.

The doorman in Lily's building was asleep in a chair in the lobby. I rode the elevator up and let myself in. The apartment was dark. I tripped over Lily's suitcases. So she hadn't left yet.

I went to the bathroom and turned the bathtub faucet on, peeling the gypsy costume off as I went and kicking it into the corner. There was rubbing alcohol in the cabinet; holding my hand over the sink, I poured some directly into the ferret bite. It burned. I hissed and swore.

'You're back,' Jack said from the doorway.

'I'm back.' I kept my head down. My face was starting to bruise where Joe had hit me. If I turned that side of my face away from Jack, he'd see it in the mirror. If I turned it away from the mirror, it would be facing him.

'We tried to find you before we left.' He moved into the bathroom and closed the door. 'Maris said you went off with Carmichael. Lily was thrilled.'

'I want to take a bath,' I said. 'Can you leave me alone, please?'

Jack didn't leave. 'Did you go off with him?'

'I want to take a bath,' I said again.

Jack moved forward quickly and grabbed my shoulder, turning me around to face him. His hair was wild and there were deep bags under his eyes. He stared at me.

'What happened to your face?' His voice was emotionless.

I didn't trust myself to speak. The bathroom was filling with steam that made my eyes water. 'Same thing that happened to the rest of me,' I managed to say. 'I got hit by a truck.'

We stared at each other for a long moment, and a memory drifted into my mind.

Does your brother do this?

'Some truck,' he said finally and let me go. 'Do you want me to stay?'

I told him to go back to bed and sat in the bathtub for a long time, ignoring the sting of the hot water on my hand. Finally I climbed out, dried myself on one of Lily's thick white towels, and went to bed. The sheets felt clean and smooth on my skin, and the pillowcase was cool under my head. I didn't sleep.

A few hours later, I heard voices in the living room. Lily was leaving. Not long afterwards the door opened and Jack slid into bed with me. I buried my face in the pillow. He didn't try to touch me.

Jack said, 'She's gone.'

I didn't say anything.

'I couldn't read her last night. She was so drunk.' He half-laughed and said, 'She said she loved me, do you believe that shit?'

'No,' I said.

I felt him shift.

'I don't believe it either. You know why?'

I closed my eyes tight.

'Because you're the only one who's ever loved me,' he said. 'That's why. You're the only one who's ever loved me and I'm the only one who's ever loved you.' His hand slipped under my neck and pulled me into the crook of his arm. I let myself be pulled. 'That's all there is. That's all that's true. Nothing else matters.'

For a long time I didn't trust myself to say anything.

'Are you okay?' he said.

Does your brother do this?

Jack said we could.

But Jack would never.

'No,' I said. 'I'm not.' My throat felt cracked and raw.

'You will be.' His voice was confident and sure. 'You just have to move past it. Let it go.'

I wanted to scream.

'I was calling for you,' I said. 'You should have been there. Where were you?'

I felt his arm tighten around me and then relax. 'Smaller sister,' he said. 'I'm here now.'

* * *

Jack's cure for my ills was the same as it had always been: get good and drunk. But for the first time in my life I didn't have much appetite for drinking. The smell of alcohol made me think of ferrets. Most things made me think of ferrets. I had nightmares about ferrets, moving over me in a furry grey wave, poking and prodding and biting me.

Two days passed and the nightmares got worse. My hand wasn't healing the way it should; the initial sharp pain had dulled to a constant hot throb. The edges of the wound were inflamed. When I poured rubbing alcohol into it, it was like putting my hand in fire.

The television weathermen were predicting a heavy snowstorm coming in from the west; it would be the first one of the year. A night, a day, a night, another day passed, and no snow.

One night we sat on Lily's roof terrace, wrapped in coats and scarves from her closet. Jack said, 'It's nice to be alone again, isn't it?'

I didn't answer. I cradled my wounded hand and stared out at the cold dreary city.

'She'll go on more vacations,' he said. His breath made fog in the air. 'Hell, I shouldn't complain. We have everything we want.'

'We have everything she lets us have.'

Jack put his arm around my shoulder and pulled me close. 'Why the dire thoughts, little sister?'

My gaze was fixed on the skyline. 'Must be the storm coming.'

The street below us was empty. Maybe people were staying indoors, waiting for the snow.

Jack tried to make his breath form a ring and failed.

'No snow yet,' he said.

By nightfall, there was still no snow, but the sky hung low over the city, heavy with cloud cover. The meteorologists assured us that the snow was coming, it was only a matter of time. My sleep, when it came, was fitful. Jack slept next to me but it didn't help.

When the sun came up on the third day, it was raining. After the rain stopped, Jack found a pair of ice skates in Lily's closet and decided we'd go skating in the park. They were girl's skates, with smooth white boots and clean laces. The blades were still sharp and they fit me perfectly.

But the rink was too crowded. The line at the rental counter looped all the way around the rink and people were standing four deep at the rink's edge. I shook my head. So we walked around the park instead, buying hot chocolate from the snack bar by the zoo. Jack had a little flask that he'd found somewhere and taken to carrying, filled with vodka. He put a little into his cocoa and I slung the skates over my shoulder, tied by the laces. Jack watched me fumble with the knot. 'We look like we've gone, anyway. Does your hand still hurt?'

The throbbing pain in my hand had become a familiar companion. The pain burned steadily at night, when Jack's breathing was soft in sleep, and was still there when I woke up in the morning. I'd been keeping it to myself. It had to get better eventually. 'It's fine,' I said.

We walked towards the Ramble, where our stroll turned into a hike. The rain that had come instead of snow had made the steep hills treacherous. Last summer I'd liked the Ramble; if you ignored the dog walkers and the joggers and the distant sound of traffic, it was a little like walking in the woods on the Hill. In the summer, there was the rich green light and the low humming of insects in the air; there were the rough, unpaved paths looping back on themselves and making that part of the park seem larger than it really was. Sometimes it was hard to find the right path out of the woods.

But that afternoon, the leaves were off the trees, the buildings on Central Park West were all too visible through the bare branches, and the Ramble seemed stark and sinister, with its twisted switchback paths that came to sudden dead ends in pockets of marsh. After a few minutes it began to feel like a bad dream, as if we were trying to perform some simple task like crossing the street and couldn't figure out how to do it. My hand ached, and the skates that I'd slung jauntily over my shoulder were banging heavily against my rib cage.

Jack took my good hand in his.

We turned a corner and found ourselves on a small stone ledge overlooking one of the marshy parts of the lake. In the summer it would have been buzzing with insects. Now it was empty and lifeless. The water was as smooth as glass. The clouds overhead drained the scenery of colour. None of the other paths were visible from where we were standing.

My brother stared out over the water. He was wearing the leather jacket that Lily had bought for him. His hands were jammed in the pockets and his eyes were far away.

'Jack,' I said.

He looked at me.

'Did you talk to Carmichael and Joe that night? Did you – did you say anything to them?'

'No,' he said. 'I never even met Joe.' He shook his head. 'Every time I look at your face, I want to kill them. You know that.'

I lifted a hand to the side of my face where it was still bruised and sore. I shivered.

'You know I could never stand for anyone else to touch you. Even in Erie. That Michael guy,' he said. 'You know I'd do anything for you. I'd kill those guys, if you wanted me to. Even that.'

I shook my head.

His eyes snapped. 'I would. I'd do it. You only have to say the word.'

I wondered. Joe and Carmichael were Lily's friends. 'It wouldn't change anything,' I said.

When we got back, there was a postcard from Lily in the mailbox, an arty black-and-white shot of misty steps and bare trees against a winter sky. On the back, she'd written, 'This is exactly what I needed. Hope the two of you are having as much fun as I am!'

'What do you want?' Jack asked me the next day, over coffee and rolls at the diner down the street. 'What do you want, more than anything else in the world?'

The fingers of my right hand were stiff and uncooperative. I had trouble tearing open the packet of sugar for my coffee. 'To leave New York,' I said, and it was true: what I wanted more than anything else in the world was to leave the city and never come back to it. Once, I had found the anonymity of the crowded city comforting. Now I felt as if I were constantly biting back screams that would force people to turn and stare at me, to acknowledge that I was there.

'Leave?' he said. 'Why the hell would you want to leave?'

Because there is a searing pain in the only part of me that was ever truly mine. Because someday I'll go to a bar and sit next to Carmichael, and you'll sit across the table from me and smile. I said, 'Because it's expensive, and difficult, and we don't have any money—'

He gave me a pained look. 'Since when have we ever worried about money?'

I didn't answer.

'You really want to give up everything we've worked for here,' he said, 'everything we've managed to do, because of one bad night.'

One bad night, I thought. 'Never mind, Jack,' I said.

'At least we're not in goddamned Janesville,' Jack said. 'You know what Crazy Mary used to say when something went wrong? She'd say, "We'll fix it. We'll figure out a way, Jacky. The greatest force in the universe is the power to think for yourself." And when I asked her what that meant, she'd say, "It means, at least we're not in goddamned Janesville."' The light in his eyes faded a little. 'No worries, young sister. Things will end in happy places. They always do with us.'

I thought of Lily's apartment, a cold, charmless pocket in a tall building that was a hive of cold, charmless pockets, and said nothing.

Jack signalled to the waitress for more coffee. I said, 'Did you know that ferrets are illegal in New York City?' I had learned this from a flier posted in the window of the local pet shop.

'No. So are mountain lions. So what?'

'Mountain lions are big, though. Why would ferrets be illegal? They're like guinea pigs.'

'It's too easy for them to survive here,' the waitress said as she poured our coffee. 'Give them a month or so, we'd have ferrets instead of rats in the subways.'

I imagined it: standing in the subway with Jack, waiting for the No. 2 train. Winter. A flash of tawny pelt on the tracks. Rustling in the litter at the end of the platform. They're everywhere, even crouched at the foot of the stairs. We're surrounded.

The night Lily was due back, Jack and I lay side by side in bed, not touching.

'You fall off a horse, you get back on,' said Jack, who had never been on a horse in his life, to the ceiling.

Next to him in the darkness, sore and silent, I said nothing, and soon he fell asleep. I wasn't really sleeping at all any more, just dozing and dreaming thin pain-dreams that seemed real. Eventually I was aware of the pale winter sun coming through the window. I was alone in the bed. Lily was laughing in the living room.

When I saw her curled up like a spoiled Persian cat in the armchair, with her bronzed skin and her newly dyed brown hair, I realized that I hated her. Listening to her chatter set my teeth on edge. After spending a day with her friends in Paris, they had all decided 'on a whim' to go off to Greece for the rest of her time abroad, and she'd had such a wonderful time and met so many wonderful people, and it had all been so rejuvenating, so incredibly fabulous – the food, and the music, and the beaches, and the parties, and the scenery! I sat there on the couch in the endless blur of her prattling, empty of everything except the throbbing in my arm and my seething rage.

Lily's eyes widened when she saw the bruises on my face, which had faded to a dull yellow. She glanced quickly at Jack, who sat next to me on the couch with one of his arms flung across the back of it, his fingers barely touching the back of my neck. He was smiling but his eyes were grim.

'And you two,' she said, pulling up one trim leather trouser leg so that she could unzip her high black boots. 'You had a good time?'

'It was fine,' Jack said. 'We didn't do much.'

'As long as you enjoyed it.' Lily peeled away the cashmere socks underneath her boots to reveal tanned, pedicured feet. There was a silver ring on one of her toes.

Jack said, 'Let's go have dinner.' He stood up as he talked, went to the closet, and took out his black leather coat.

Lily stretched her legs out and gazed at her glossy, shell-pink toenails. 'Maybe.' She swung her legs up over the side of the armchair. 'But first I want to take a nap. I cannot *wait* to sleep in my own bed.' In one motion, she sat up, swung her legs down to the floor, and stood up. She yawned prettily. 'I'm exhausted. Can you try not to wake me up?'

Her bedroom door closed with a small, smug noise and Jack and I were left together in the silence that fell instantly over the rest of the apartment. He came to me and we stood together.

When Lily awoke, she expressed concern about my arm, which was swollen and angry-looking up to the elbow by then. I told her that I'd cut it opening a can of olives.

She told Jack to forget about dinner, to take me to the emergency room.

'Josie's okay, aren't you, Jo?' he said. I wasn't; I could hardly bend my wrist, and I couldn't move my fingers at all. But I nodded.

'I'll take you tomorrow if it's not better,' he told me. 'Just not' – his eyes flicked to Lily – 'now.'

When he was out of the room Lily sat down next to me and said, 'What about your face?'

'Born with it. Nothing to be done.'

She gazed steadily at me for a moment. 'Did Jack do it?'

'Jack would never hurt me,' I said.

'I know what he can be like,' she said evenly. 'I know how he can get.'

'The difference between you and me, Lily, is that I don't get off on it,' I said, instead of telling her that it was none of her goddamned business. I sounded so much like Jack that my stomach lurched.

She didn't blush and she didn't look away. Her dark eyes were serious, for once.

'You're smarter than that, Josie,' was all she said.

That night, her first night back, she went out for a drink with Maris and came back late. I went to bed early and sank immediately into the familiar dream-haunted, fitful sleep. I was aware of Jack lying down next to me and getting up again, as restless as I was.

He was sitting on the edge of my bed when we heard Lily's key in the lock. It was only after he went to greet her that I realized that he was wearing only his underwear. I wondered what she would think, and why I didn't care.

No noises came through the wall that night. All I heard were voices, Lily's and Jack's, rising and falling and rising again. More than once I was pulled out of a half-sleep by Jack's angry voice, but I couldn't ever make out the words. Then Lily, quiet and sibilant, hushing him, calming him.

Finally I woke with a start to find my room filled with bright light and swirling cigarette smoke. Jack was sitting next to me, propped up against the white headboard. There was a cigarette in his hand and a highball glass full of butts on the table next to him. His gaze was fixed blankly on the wall but the set of his mouth was angry.

'We have to leave.' His voice was toneless. 'She wants us out.'

Still not fully awake, I asked, 'When did this happen?'

'Last night,' he said in the same cheerless monotone. 'She said she decided while she was away. She's going to her parents' house in Maine Saturday morning. She wants us gone by then.'

'Is that what you were fighting about last night?'

'I let her win. Told her she was right, after all.' Then he turned to look at me, and his green eyes were as cold and expressionless as his voice. 'You always hated her, didn't you?'

I shrugged. I didn't care.

'I've always hated her, too,' he said. 'From the moment I saw her.'

On Friday, Lily made herself scarce. Jack brooded, and smoked, and drank. Once I said, 'Something will come up. It always does,' and he said, 'Sure it will.'

'We'll go to California. Like you said when we first got here.'

'Maybe.'

'Or anywhere else you want.'

Slowly, he turned his head and looked at me.

'Josie,' he said. 'Little sister. Quit trying to make me feel better.'

She came home that night, holding two shopping bags in each hand. A blood-coloured scarf edged in black embroidery was wrapped jauntily around her neck. The scarf blazed against her new dark hair. One of the bags held a bottle of champagne, already chilled, and a bottle of pear brandy. 'A going-away party,' she said gaily, 'for all three of us, and if we don't all set off with hangovers tomorrow I'll turn in my Holly Hostess badge and join a leper colony.' She dropped the bags on the island in the kitchen and looked around. Her eyes skipped nervously over my brother, who was standing in a corner of the kitchen, watching her sullenly.

'I went to see my decorator today,' she said, starting to dig around in the shopping bags. She pulled out plastic bags of tomatoes and garlic and boxes of pasta. 'I think I'm going to have this place redone, get rid of all this damn white. André has some beautiful tapestries in his show room. I'm thinking reds and purples, maybe some indigo.' She gave us a dazzling smile. 'Doesn't that sound gorgeous? You'll have to come back for a visit when it's done.'

Jack pointed at the two bottles on the counter. 'What are we supposed to do with these?'

'First, open them,' she said. 'Then, drink them.'

'Chick drinks,' Jack said as Lily poured generous shots of brandy into three wine glasses and topped them off with champagne.

Now he looked at her intently. She didn't seem to notice.

'A festive drink for a festive evening.' She handed us our glasses with a flourish. 'Voilà. Mimosa à la Lily. Now, what should we drink to?'

Jack said, 'Whatever you want.'

'To the future, then,' she said, and we drank.

Once you've decided to tell the truth, it's hard not to qualify it. The facts are the easy part. The sky is blue. Fire is hot. He hit her. The problem is that it's so often tempting to qualify those facts: *It sounds worse than it was. It sounds terrible when I say it like that.* Or there's the other way out: rationalization as absolution. *It was awful, I shouldn't have done it. I wasn't thinking. You have to understand how I was feeling, what I'd been through.*

Either way: I didn't do it. But I didn't stop him.

We were drunk. Something different.

Lily and I were each stretched out on one of her two white couches, laughing. I told myself that it was all a sham, that I was only acting cheerful, but the truth was that this was the last night that I would ever spend in Lily's apartment. We would leave the next morning; I didn't know where we would go, but it would be somewhere else. That was enough for now.

Jack brooded in the background. Once, while Lily was in the bathroom, he came to me and let his head drop into my lap, whining, 'I hate her. I hate her. I hate her.' He sounded like a child. I wondered why leaving Lily was so different from leaving Raeburn or Becka, but she came back into the room before I could ask him.

Lily told us a story about a friend of hers who had been cheated by every tour guide and shopkeeper in Athens. By the third time the friend paid fifty dollars for a ten-minute cab ride, I was laughing, and so was Lily. Next to me on the couch I felt Jack grow more and more rigid until finally he said, 'For the love of Christ, would the two of you please shut *up.*'

Lily fixed him with a pitying gaze and said, 'So very, very grouchy.'

In response, Jack jumped to his feet and threw his full glass of champagne at Lily's pure white wall, leaving an ugly wet splotch.

Lily's eyes widened and she laughed. Her laugh was high and uneasy. I laughed, too – I couldn't help it. His gesture was so melodramatic and self-indulgent and I was giddy with alcohol and fever and nervous tension. When Jack walked around to the back of the couch and stepped on the stem of the glass, it snapped with a noise like a tree branch breaking and I giggled again.

'Fuck both of you,' he said.

Lily beamed up at him drunkenly. 'But darling, you already have.'

Time froze. Across the room Jack was looking at Lily with new eyes, ablaze with green fire. I felt as though one of the walls of the room had collapsed, like the bombed buildings in war photos, with the inhabitants' lives exposed: this is how they lived, this is what they ate, this is how they loved.

Her eyes glittering, she looked at Jack, who was standing between the couch and the wall, then at me. 'I'm right, aren't I?' She clapped her hands and laughed wildly. 'I knew it. I knew it! Carmichael had his suspicions, and I knew, of course I knew, but I didn't *know*.'

'Lily,' Jack said. His voice was low and dangerous.

She jumped to her feet. Her eyes shone. 'Oh, I'm not judging. I think it's kind of romantic. A little sick, maybe, but who isn't a little sick sometimes?'

'Lily,' I said. I thought that I should probably put myself between her and Jack, but I couldn't make my feet move, and in addition to the alcohol and the fever and the fear, there was a burgeoning excitement in me that was a little terrifying. I saw Jack move towards her.

Lily kept talking.

'How long?' she said. She had raised herself up and was half sitting, half standing, with one knee bent under her and her body twisted around to face Jack over the high plush back of the couch. It was a childish, gleeful pose, as if she were too excited to sit all the way down. 'I bet you were kids when you started. It's like one of those British novels. Kids in those books are always fucking each other. Was it like that?'

I saw my brother reach over the back of the couch and put his hands on Lily's shoulders. He told me later that he only meant to push her down, to make her shut up, but then she said, 'To tell you the truth, those books always kind of turned me on,' and Jack's hands moved so quickly that I saw only a blur. One hand went over her eyes and the other over her mouth, and with a mighty jerk he pulled her by her head over the back of the couch.

Her dark red lips opened to cry out once, and then I couldn't see her any more.

Jack had one of the heavy glass vases from the side table in his hand and I saw his arm move downward fast, once, twice, three times. By the time I made it to the other side of the couch Lily was lying crumpled on the floor. Her blood was mixing with the water on the floor and there were pale blue lilies and deep red liquid everywhere. It was too late.

We put her in the coat closet. Neither of us could think with her lying there like that. Then we cleaned up the blood and the glass, changed our clothes, and threw the ones we had been wearing into the incinerator. The clothes that we put on were our old clothes from Janesville, which I had been keeping in plastic bags on my closet floor. Just in case.

We did all of this silently, speaking only when it was absolutely necessary. It was like cleaning the house in the old days, after a week of tearing it apart: see what has to be done, do it.

Her foot – I see it – got her? – no, wait –

Jack and I worked as if we were one person.

When it was done, we collapsed onto Lily's big bed and slept in the same clothes we'd worn when we'd fled our father together. We slept holding hands.

When I woke up the next morning, my hand felt like it was on fire. Jack asked me if I thought I'd better see a doctor.

I was too tired to dissemble. 'I don't know,' I said.

He held my hot hand and felt gently around the wound. 'It looks bad. Should I take you to a doctor?' he asked again. I was having trouble standing, so we went to the emergency room. The waiting room had the same hard plastic chairs as the bus station we'd waited in during the long trip to New York. It all began to seem unreal, the chairs and the waiting and the dead girl at home in the closet. My mind drifted and I let myself imagine that we were still on that trip. We still had all the long months in the city ahead of us. There was still time.

10

The doctor took one look at my arm and said, 'That doesn't look good. We'll have to admit you for that.' I told the admitting nurse that my name was Lily Carter and that no, I didn't have any health insurance. I gave them her address. The nurse checked a box on a form. 'Sign here,' she said tersely.

They put me in a bed and plugged an IV into my arm. A female nurse with immense hips and a flat, pasty face was making adjustments to the IV drip. Jack sat beside the bed.

There was another bed in the room. The girl in the bed was a few years older than I was and looked far sicker. The only sounds she made were her raspy breathing and her thick cough.

'I can only stay for a while,' Jack said. 'I have to think.'

The hospital was anonymous and reassuring. The clean white sheets, the impersonal nightgown, and the scentless pillow were soft and thin with use. Even the pain and stiffness in my arm were welcome: a tangible problem that was being countered by a tangible solution, the saline spiked with antibiotics that was slowly dripping into my arm. It was comforting, somehow. Everybody seemed to know exactly where they should be and what they should be doing. The doctors came in on schedule, asked the same questions, made – presumably – the same notes. The thin doctor with the gleaming scalp was the one I liked best.

He was the one who talked to me about rabies, and how they were going to have to treat me as if I was infected unless I could remember where I'd gotten my ferret bite.

I found this amusing. 'Are there ferret control police?' I said. 'A ferret elimination task force, perhaps?' It was my second day in the hospital. Tepid Josie Raeburn no longer, I had become Lily Carter, and I was the life of the party.

The doctor smiled a perfunctory professional smile. 'If we can talk to the owner of the ferret – if it's been vaccinated or if we can have it tested for rabies – then we can assume that you're safe. Otherwise, we have to treat you as if you're infected.'

He had explained to me that the rabies treatment would involve six extraordinarily expensive shots in four weeks. I saw no reason to be concerned about the cost; after all, since when had Lily Carter ever worried about money? 'How do you test it for rabies?'

'We don't,' he answered. 'Animal Control does. This isn't really my area of expertise.' He sneaked a look at his watch. 'But I think they just observe it for a while. Make sure it doesn't act strange.'

'Really? I thought they cut off its head.'

He ran his hand over the shiny skin where his hair used to be, a tired, for-God's-sake gesture that made me a little sorry I was teasing him. 'Maybe they do, if they seem sick. I don't really know.'

An unfamiliar nurse came in to check on the girl next to me, putting a thermometer in her mouth. I said, 'If I act strange, will you cut off my head?' The nurse glanced at us as she left, her eyes curious. The doctor grinned wryly.

'No, Alice, we're not going to chop off your head,' he said.

'My name's not Alice.'

'Off with her head,' he said. 'Get it? Alice in Wonderland,' and when I still didn't react, 'The children's book. Down the rabbit hole?'

'I never read it. I didn't know it was about decapitation.'

'You've never read Alice in Wonderland.' It was somewhere between a statement and a question, and I shook my head. He rolled his eyes, looking a little more human, and said, 'What is the world coming to?' as he left.

They gave me the first rabies shots anyway: one in the arm and another in my right hand, where the bite was. The girl in the next bed lay there, her breathing still laboured. She never looked at any of the doctors and nurses coming and going from the room, but stared straight ahead, feverish and unseeing. Her eyes were burning hollows in her face.

Later, the nurse returned to change the bag on my IV. She checked the tape holding the needle in the back of my hand. Reaching across and picking up my hand, she said, 'Didn't they wash your hands when they admitted you? Your fingernails are filthy.'

The dark crust underneath my fingernails was mostly Lily's blood. I shrugged.

The nurse leaned down to get a closer look at my nails. 'That looks like blood,' she said. 'Is it blood?'

'I bled a lot when the ferret bit me,' I said and held up my bad hand. 'I can't clean it with my hand like this.'

She grinned, friendly now. 'I wouldn't worry too much about it. I haven't lost a patient yet to dirty fingernails.'

She left and the wheezing girl and I lay there like two dolls forgotten under a bed. I pretended it was a game: the first one to move lost.

When the balding doctor showed up again, there was no hint of his wry grin. 'Boyfriend been by today?'

He meant Jack. 'Later,' I said. 'He just called.'

'Good,' the doctor said and pulled up a chair next to my bed.

'You've come to chop off my head, after all,' I said.

'Not exactly. I've got some news for you.'

'You're letting me go.' My hand felt much better. The swelling had gone down and it no longer hurt to move it.

'Soon.' He was studying my chart. 'Lily, when was your last period?'

I stared at him. 'You're joking.'

'I'm afraid not,' the doctor said. 'How old are you, Lily?'

'Eighteen.' I would be eighteen in January. Jack had warned me to tell them I already was so that there wouldn't be any questions about the hospital forms.

He was watching me carefully. 'You seem surprised. Have you been using birth control?'

I didn't answer.

He smiled. It was a gentle smile, and kind, but there was anger there, too. 'Then why are you surprised?'

I pinched a piece of the industrial bedsheet with the fingers of my good hand, leaving a crease, and then rubbed the crease smooth again. The giddy pseudo-Lily vanished; Josie was back, limp and exhausted and only able to function because of the plastic tube snaking into her arm. The last person who slept in these sheets, I thought, was probably a good person. Sick, but healthy. In my head, a voice said: We're different from the rest of them.

'You must think I'm pretty stupid,' I said. The words tasted bitter on my lips.

The doctor sighed. 'That's not at all the sense I get. Although I don't quite know what to make of a kid that's never read Alice in Wonderland.' He cleared his throat. 'Which reminds me, I picked this up for you at the gift shop. Thought it might cheer you up.'

He handed me a brightly coloured paperback with a little girl in an apron on the cover. There was a formal, absent look on her face that I liked. I turned the book over in my hands, smelled the spicy, wholesome scent of its pages, and thought, I don't deserve this.

'Is that what I am?' I said. 'A kid?'

'Not a kid,' he said awkwardly. 'Young, maybe. Although,' he looked at me carefully, 'I don't imagine you feel very young at the moment.'

'You don't know the half of it.'

'I imagine not.' Then there were a few moments of silence as we both waited for something else to happen: the gawky doctor with his hands stuffed in his pockets, me lying shell-shocked on the bed, the book in my lap and the girl on its cover staring impassively up at me.

'Thank you for the book,' I said. 'I'll tell you where the ferrets are, if you want.'

'It's okay,' he said. 'But you need to think about what you want to do. Maybe your parents can help you.' The expression on my face must have discouraged him, because he sighed again and said, 'Well, talk to your boyfriend when he gets here. I'll be back later. Okay?'

'Okay,' I said.

A few minutes later, the wide-hipped nurse came in with a lunch tray. 'Poor dear,' she said. 'Well, it's a life lesson. It'll all turn out all right, though, don't you worry. Nature usually has her way in the end.'

I stared at the unappetizing food on the tray. A plain chicken breast, mushy peas, dry rice. Suddenly I wanted to stuff it down the nurse's throat. I could practically hear the noises she'd make, see her face turning purple as she choked to death.

No. That wasn't me. I shut my eyes to make the image go away and said, 'Yeah, well, nature has a pretty sick sense of humour.'

Time passed. I spent most of it reading Alice in Wonderland and reflecting with cynical amusement on all of the bottles I'd sipped from in my time, none of which had been labelled drink me and none of which had succeeded in turning me into anyone other than the person that I was. Eventually I heard the lively jumble of voices in the hallway outside that meant that the day nurses were leaving and the night shift was coming on. The night nurse that I knew best was skinny, with wispy grey hair and surprisingly strong arms. I was waiting for her to come in when the nurse who had changed my IV bag appeared in the door. She was wearing a black leather jacket over her purple uniform and carrying a worn denim bag.

'Hey.' She sat down on the edge of my bed without asking.

'Hi,' I said, confused.

'You want me to do your nails?' she asked, taking a small zippered case out of her bag.

'What?'

'I'm on my way home, but it won't take long.' She opened the zippered case and out came a sharp-looking silver instrument. She didn't wait for my consent. 'One thing my mother always told us was keep your nails nice,' she said, picking up my hand. 'You keep your nails nice, you can get away with almost anything.'

I smiled. It felt almost natural. 'Is that the secret? If only I'd known.'

'You stay away from those ferrets,' she said. 'You'll be okay.'

That was all she said. We sat in silence, both staring at my hands, as she cleaned my fingernails, trimmed and filed them, and then buffed them down with a flat rubber stick. She was sure and fast. When she was done, my hands looked like they belonged to someone else.

'That's amazing,' I said.

'That's seven months of beauty school.' She grinned at me as she zipped her tools back into their case.

I grinned back. 'Whatever it is, it's impressive.'

'Doing my nails always makes me feel better,' she said.

And it helped. I didn't think it would, but it did.

When I woke up the next morning, my pale roommate was gone and Jack was stretched out on her newly made bed. I woke him up, told him what the doctor had said, and asked him what I should do. He rolled his eyes and said, 'Can't they take care of it?'

I said, 'I suppose.'

He seemed restless and didn't stay long. When he was gone, and the wide-hipped nurse came in, I asked her what had happened to my roommate. She clucked her tongue. 'Poor thing. We took her up to the isolation ward this morning.'

'What was it?' I said.

'TB,' she said. 'The doctors never even thought about it. She wasn't the type.'

'How'd she get it?'

The nurse shook her head.

'Some outlandish college trip she took last year – Bangladesh or Sri Lanka or somewhere. If her mother hadn't mentioned it on the phone, we would never have known. We'll probably be able to control it, but what an awful disease. Such a pretty thing, too.' She gazed at me for a moment, and then said, 'You, too.' She patted my arm. 'Well, you're young yet.'

I stretched the fingers on my right hand experimentally and watched the way the light shone on my fingernails. The only thing that hurt was the needle in my hand. Even the ferret bite was beginning to heal.

When Jack came to get me later that morning, he brought me some of Lily's clothes and the high leather boots she'd bought for me. The other bed was still empty and he sat on its edge as I put my old clothes into the plastic I ♥ NY bag that Lily's things had been in. As I packed, he talked. He seemed jumpy; his hands moved constantly, plucking at his shirt, pushing his hair back behind his ears.

He wanted to rent a car, he said, but he had realized that we'd need Lily's driving licence for that. Besides, it left too many traces. So instead we were going to take a bus somewhere. 'I wish it were more glamorous, but every other way we could do it leaves too much of a trail. What do you think?' He leaned over and ran his hand down the side of my throat and said, practically purred, 'Is your brother an evil genius, or what?'

I could see the quick beat of the pulse fluttering in his neck and a fine sheen of sweat on his forehead. 'You've been taking Lily's pills, haven't you?'

'I needed to stay awake and think. Haven't slept since it happened.' I stared at him, taking in the bright green eyes and the fine high cheekbones as if for the first time. 'I needed to take care of you.' He touched my nose lightly with the tip of one finger and said, 'We've gotten away with it, little sister. What do you think of that?' There was pride in his voice.

'I think the girl who was in that bed had TB,' I said.

He jerked away and jumped to his feet.

'Jesus, Josie,' he said and shuddered.

Before they let me go, one of the nurses gave me another rabies shot and talked to me interminably about future appointments that I had no intention of keeping: one follow-up, three more rabies vaccinations, and a TB test (in April, because the sallow girl might have infected me). Downstairs, I had another endless conversation – this time with a sour-looking woman – about bills I did not intend to pay and payment plans I planned to ignore. By the time they put me in a wheelchair, I felt adrift in lies, as if there were a fathomless ocean of untruth surging beneath me and I was in a tiny boat with no sails. Jack would approve, I thought.

We both had to sign forms before they'd let me leave. As I signed Lily's name, I thought, no EAT ME or DRINK ME required; with a flash of ferret teeth and the flourish of a pen, I had become someone else. When I glanced at Jack's form, I saw that he had written 'Carmichael Barrett'. Our eyes met. He gave me a barely perceptible shrug. I had never known Carmichael's last name.

Jack had Lily's ATM card and he used it to get cash. We took a cab back to the apartment. In the back seat, I watched dispassionately as he filed the money away in his wallet, thinking vaguely of the time earlier that year when pulling five hundred dollars out of a cash machine would have sustained the two of us for months. And there was a time before that when we hardly thought about money at all. On the Hill, we'd only thought about each other.

Jack had Lily's ATM card. What did I have? I had her driving licence. Her identity felt like a prize that I had won, through all the weeks of tense borrowed luxury that I'd lived in her apartment, through all the long months of loneliness with Jack and without him before that, and all the long years of Raeburn's housekeepers and geometry lessons before that. Because Lily had not worked for what she had, and I had done nothing but work in one way or another all my life, and what did I win? A healing ferret bite, a copy of Alice in Wonderland, and two weeks' worth of antibiotic pills the size of walnuts.

We drove through the park. As the cab threaded its way between the stone retaining walls of the Seventy-second Street Transverse – walls I'd always liked, because of their age and dignity – Jack told me that the only thing that he would miss was the leather jacket that Lily had bought him. It was hanging in the coat closet. I told him I liked his old one better anyway.

My brother. I had my brother.

And I had the twisted version of family that we'd built together, and I had a pair of fabulous drop-dead boots. I had Lily's jewellery, her diamond solitaire necklace and the blue topaz ring, and Jack told me that I could keep them or sell them, whichever I wanted. For now, they were in the pocket of my jeans. So I had them, too.

Lily, on the other hand – I told myself – had lazed her way through life in a manner befitting her elegant surroundings, and if the thought had ever occurred to her that money came from work and not from accountants, it hadn't stayed long. She'd spent her short, luxurious life doing nothing, and now she was in a closet. There were a multitude of other Lilys living in the city. Perhaps one among the many wouldn't be missed.

So, really – I told myself – things weren't so bad. We were moving again, and we were finally going to leave New York. In the cab, Jack was singing softly along with the radio. I told myself that the good times he'd promised when we left the Hill were finally coming, that we'd have money and a place of our own. We'd be safe.

But I was also thinking, as we headed back towards Lily's apartment and the locked closet door, that things that should have been very difficult – like lying, like stealing, like killing – had become very easy very quickly. My eyes kept moving between my beautiful brother and my own faint reflection in the window. We were very much alike, Jack and I.

Something stirred deep inside me.

Lily's apartment was cool and the scent of lilies of the valley was thick in the air. The florist must have come while I was in the hospital. I wondered what Jack had told him.

As we walked in the door, the phone was ringing. We ignored it. 'Has it been doing that a lot?' I asked.

'Afraid so. I talked to your old friend Carmichael, told him that she'd left for Maine already. Then I stopped answering it.' He shrugged. 'Her parents left a message on the machine.'

'That's a problem.'

'Not really. I guess they're in Florida. They didn't know until the last minute that she was headed up to the house in Maine.'

Jack had prepared for my homecoming. There was soft music playing in the background, airy and dark and a long way from his adored Wagner. He had also moved one of Lily's overstuffed white armchairs against the closet door, placing the tall lamp on one side of it and one of the glass occasional tables on the other. The closet was tucked away in the corner; it looked as though someone had deliberately created a cosy little nook, maybe for reading.

'I've got wine chilling,' Jack said. 'I thought we'd go all out, this one last night.' He placed a bottle of wine on the centre island and then went to the cupboard and brought down two of Lily's crystal wine glasses. There was a conspicuous gap in the cupboard where one of the glasses was missing.

I stood on the other side of the island and watched him. 'This one last night before what?'

265

'Before we hit the road.'

'And then what?'

'You,' he said, coming around the island and putting his hands on my shoulders. 'You never trust me.' He kissed my forehead tenderly. 'We have this conversation every time we do anything new. You always have to know where we're going, what we're doing – I thought you wanted to leave the city. Haven't we always come out all right in the end?'

'We're not at the end of this yet.'

Jack stood back. He gave me a long, hard look. Finally he reached for me.

I stiffened.

His hand fell on top of my head and he shook my head back and forth, softly, as though I were a dog that he was reassuring.

'Close enough,' he said. He began to take pots and pans out of the cupboard. 'Poor little Josie. Always so serious. Tell me this, young sister: where do you *want* to go? We're free as birds and we have all the money we could possibly want. Pasta okay?'

'You're high,' I said. 'It'll be easy enough to trace us with the camera from that ATM machine, and you want us to keep using the card? Why don't we carry her down to the police station now and throw her on the front desk? Say, "Here, looky what we did?"' Distantly, I thought, I would *never* have spoken to my brother like this. I would never have needed to. I would never have wanted to. I would never have dared to.

For a moment Jack didn't answer. He put the big pot in the sink and turned on the faucet. As he stared down at it, watching it fill, all I could see of his eyes were his long, thick lashes. 'First of all, it's not what *we* did. It's what *I* did. Second of all, I did it for you.'

Now he looked at me. The pot was overflowing. 'I told her, if she wanted to watch me fuck another girl, I'd do it. But not you.'

I walked around the island, reached out, and turned off the taps.

'Why not?' I said, and his eyes flashed.

'You know why not.'

'Do I?'

'Because nobody else has what we have,' he said. 'Because we belong to each other in a way that nobody else will ever understand, and I refuse to share that. I refuse to share you.'

I turned away from him, lifted the pot out of the sink, and carried it to the stove.

Jack followed me. 'We'll sell her stuff. This place is a gold mine. We'll loot her and run, and we won't ever have to think about her again. It'll all be over.'

'Is there sauce,' I asked, knowing that it would never be over, 'or should I go ahead and make some?'

'It was just because I love you,' he said. 'That's all it was.'

There was no bottled sauce, but I found a plastic container in the refrigerator that contained the leftovers of the sauce that Lily had made the night she died. There was almost enough, but not quite. I would have to make more.

I cut up the last clove of garlic, dumped it in the frying pan with some olive oil, and watched as it sizzled and snapped.

The two vases of lilies of the valley sat on the island bar, as they always did.

The old questions were chasing themselves around and around in my head. Where would we go? What would we do? How would we survive? Jack was right, there was enough loot in Lily's apartment to keep us for quite a while, and if we sold a little here and there as we travelled, it wouldn't really be traceable. But we couldn't run for ever, and the money from Lily's jewellery and crystal and silver would run out eventually.

And then where would we go?

What would we do?

How would we survive?

They'd find us. I didn't believe for a minute that they wouldn't find us.

I dumped the leftover sauce in the pan and tossed its plastic container in the sink, considering these questions as if they were a maths problem and all the variables waited only for the application of the right theorem.

He had done it for me.

There was a can of crushed tomatoes in the cupboard. I opened it and mixed the contents with the bubbling sauce on the stove.

Nobody else has what we have.

Jack was moving around in the other room. He was already sweating and unable to sit still, but he had taken another one of Lily's pills as he carried a glass of wine – his third – from the living room to the kitchen and back again. A small pile of jewellery and trinkets was amassing on the coffee table. I knew that he was trying to find things that we could sneak past the doorman without arousing any more suspicion than we already had. So that we could sell them as we fled, and have some money when we got to the next city, the next apartment, the next girl – or maybe it would be a guy, and it would be my turn again, as it had been in the beginning, with Kevin McNerny. Because, I realized, *that* was what was going to happen, over and over again. That was what our life would be.

I chopped onions and sprinkled them over the surface of the sauce. I took pasta from its jar on the counter and put it in the pot of water Jack had filled, which was boiling on the stove.

When I looked up, Jack was gazing at me across the room.

'You're beautiful,' he said.

I smiled. It was almost painful.

He came to stand behind me, put his arms around my waist, and kissed the side of my neck. 'We're not doing so badly for two crazy kids against the world, are we?'

I didn't answer.

'Say something,' he said. His voice was desperate now. I had never heard him sound like that. He buried his face in the hollow of my shoulder and I felt his breath, warm and moist, against my skin. In my head, a younger Jack, supremely confident and not at all desperate, said, 'We're not like them,' echoing Raeburn. I was thinking of the pond, of the warm sun on the rocks. Jack's wet, cool hands on my back. 'We'll never be like them.'

A vision of a sun-dappled park, green and shady and cool, came to me. Tattooed legs stretched out in the thick grass. Other hands in my hair and uncomplicated kisses that were nothing more; the couple with the highlighters looking back at us as we kissed, thinking, 'Look at that girl and her boyfriend, look at that couple.'

Jack took plates from the cupboards and cutlery from the drawers and went to set Lily's glass-topped table.

When I was a kid I had a cat that died from eating them.

In a flash, I saw again, clearly, how everything that I had been through, everything that I had done, would repeat itself. Because of Jack: because of the way he was, and because he was right – he was the only person who loved me. His love was written indelibly on what was left of my soul.

Suddenly, although I knew that it was far too soon, I felt the still-living thing beating inside me like a second heart.

Watching Jack steadily, I took the fresh lilies of the valley from the two crystal fishbowls and carried them dripping to the cutting board. I chopped them, quickly, with the big knife.

My brother finished setting the table and lit a cigarette.

'When you and I get our place,' he called to me, 'I don't want to have anything white in it at all. Not even white sheets.'

'Fine,' I said and laid the fragrant and mutilated flowers in a soft sinking heap on top of the sauce. I picked up a wooden spoon and stirred them in, watching as the remains of the white bells disappeared into the red sauce and the glossy green leaves softened. Soon there was no trace of them.

For a moment, I thought I saw the words EAT ME floating among the tomato and onion. I tasted; the sauce burned going down. A sprinkle of red chili flakes took care of that. Jack liked spicy food. We would eat heartily.

'Let that simmer,' I said to him as I rinsed the scent of the lilies from my hands. 'Don't stir it.'

We sat together over twin plates of pasta piled high with sauce. There was good wine. Candlelight played romantically over the polished silver; it cast interesting shadows around my brother's jaw and cheekbones, making him look dramatic and other-worldly. He told me that he was glad that we were still together, that he had never regretted rescuing me from our father's house, and that he couldn't imagine life without me.

I said, 'Me too,' and stared at my first forkful of pasta, with its hot, glistening strands wrapped round and round in a neat knot. The fork seemed to float independently in midair, unrelated to the hand holding it or the person to whom that hand belonged.

I could not bring myself to put the food in my mouth.

No. That's not the truth. The truth is that I chose not to eat it. The truth is that when Jack put the first bite into his mouth, I felt some dark place in me *opening*, some place that had never seen sun, never felt fresh air.

When I put my fork down, Jack said, 'Are you still feeling bad?'

'A little,' I said.

He gave me a sympathetic look and took another bite.

I didn't eat anything. Jack ate everything on his plate.

I told him I was tired and we went to bed. The sheets were cold and we huddled together under the blankets. Jack fell asleep quickly, as he always had, his arm draped over me.

I thought I wouldn't sleep, but I must have. I woke up to the sound of the toilet flushing and Jack crawling back into bed. His skin was clammy and he was trembling.

'I think I'm sick.' His voice was weak.

'What's wrong?'

'Everything,' he said and fell back into a fitful sleep.

It didn't last. Within fifteen minutes he was awake again, groaning and panting. I laid my hand on his forehead. The pulse in his temple fluttered under my fingers. I turned on the bedside lamp and I could see that his colour wasn't good.

I touched his sweaty forehead. 'Is there anything I can do?'

'Stay up with me,' he said.

I rose and went to the kitchen. There was some ginger ale in the refrigerator; I poured some into a glass and brought it back to him. He was curled up in a tight ball on the bed with his eyes squeezed shut. When he heard me come near he opened them and they were dark and haunted.

'Maybe you've been taking too many pills,' I said.

He shook his head. 'The sauce must have been bad. It's all I can think of.'

I lay next to him in bed and stroked his hair while he tried to sleep. His body was warm and comforting against mine. Once he opened his eyes and said, 'Jesus, I can hardly see.'

'It'll be over by morning,' I said. 'Food poisoning doesn't last.'

He smiled weakly. 'Think I'll live?'

I gave him a critical once-over. 'Doubtful.' He laughed painfully.

As time passed, he started to complain of a sharp pain in his gut. Around three o'clock, he asked me to read to him. I found the copy of Alice in Wonderland that the doctor had given to me, and I read to him until four, when he said that he needed to use the bathroom. When he finally made it to his feet, he couldn't walk without help.

By the time he went back to bed, he was panting and exhausted. I picked the book up to read to him again and he put his hand on my wrist. 'Don't, Josie,' he said. 'My head is splitting.'

He put his head in my lap and closed his eyes.

He slept restlessly until the sun came up and the light in Lily's bedroom grew brighter. He didn't seem to know where he was. He asked me what time Raeburn was going to be home and I said, 'No, Jack, we're in New York. We're at Lily's.'

He nodded. 'Of course we are. Is she here?'

'No, Jack. Lily's dead.'

He gazed up at me for a moment with his beautiful green eyes and their long, long lashes. 'Josie?'

'Yes, Jack?'

'Just checking.'

'Who did you think I was?'

'Mary,' he said simply.

Then he fell asleep again.

I took his steel watch from the nightstand and put it on, so I know that at exactly ten minutes past nine my brother's breathing began to come in short pants. I'd been stroking his hair and suddenly my hand was covered in his sweat.

His eyes opened. My eyes were wet, but I felt a great calm as I stroked his forehead and murmured soothing things. I told him everything would be okay. I told him he would feel better soon. I told him that we'd find a new, better life to live somewhere else. I told him that I loved him. Suddenly he opened his eyes wide and seemed to see me, really *see* me, and he opened his mouth as if he were going to speak. He took a breath – a deep, rattling gasp – and let it go. He did not take another one.

For a long time I sat frozen on the edge of the bed and stared at him, trying to memorize his face, his eyes, the smell of him. He was my brother. He was the pivot around which my life had revolved. He was the only person who had ever loved me.

When I moved, it was as if I were moving through thick water. The silence was heavy in my ears. I took his old leather jacket and the high black boots that Lily had bought for me. I took his wallet and the copy of Alice in Wonderland. I left Lily's credit cards. I left her jewellery.

The doorman was dozing when I left. I caught a cab at the corner and took it to the bus station. I bought a ticket. Every step was uncertainty and agony, but soon enough I was out of the city and onto the highway, and it was easier.

I left New York.

My brother stayed behind.

Epilogue

Twelve hours later I stood on the front porch. The door was closed, its chipped paint at once familiar and strange. The elms overhead were bare; the snow was deep and the woods were muffled and quiet. I'd crossed three states on a bus. The air was so clean and sharp that I felt I'd just emerged from a loud, dark tunnel.

There was a new housing development going up. I'd passed it on the way. It had happened before, but never on our side of the Hill. It meant that somebody had died; the houses themselves were protected by historical designation, but the grounds were up for grabs as soon as the dirt hit the coffin. The trees were already a little thinner in that direction. Soon, I thought, the cushion of thick growth that had protected us from the world would be gone. When new houses went up on the cleared lots, they'd be visible from the porch even in the summer, when the leaves were at their most dense.

I knocked.

I'd gotten off the bus in Harrisburg and caught another one to Carlisle. I'd hitched to the house from the bus station. I was tired and it was cold, but Jack's leather jacket had kept me warm. When I buried my face in the sheepskin collar, I could smell the last year of my life: lilies, mostly; cigarette smoke; and underneath it all, the sweet, spicy scent of Jack's cologne, and the close air in his room. The lack of him beat within me like a new heart.

His, plus mine, plus the other, made three.

I would think about that later, I decided.

The door opened.

A girl in thick glasses, her dark hair cut in a smooth, severe bob, stood in front of me. She was wearing a long shapeless skirt and a sweater that I recognized as my father's. 'Yes?' she said.

And then she whispered, 'Josephine.'

'Margaret Revolt,' I said.

My father and I sat at opposite sides of the kitchen table. I'd already gone upstairs and retrieved my birth certificate from underneath my mattress, and it was safe in my pocket. The kitchen was smaller and dingier than I remembered. There was one patch of sunlight in the room that fell on a long, deep scratch in the floor. It seemed inconceivable that I had ever lived here.

'College was pointless anyway,' Margaret Revolt had told me. 'The only reason I stayed as long as I did was so that I could keep taking Joseph's classes.' She said that she was still learning, that my father was teaching her more than college ever could. Then she had lamely offered me orange juice and I had refused. Now she was hovering uncertainly in the background. It was easy for me to ignore her.

Raeburn's shirt was clean and so was his hair, which looked as if it had been recently cut. He had new glasses and I thought he'd lost weight. He looked ten years younger than he had the last time I had seen him.

'Where's your brother?' he finally said.

I shook my head.

Margaret started to speak and Raeburn quelled her with a look.

'He abandoned you. I could have told you that would happen. You're better off without him.'

'I didn't mean that,' I said. 'I meant, don't ask me. I won't tell you.'

Raeburn's eyes gauged me for a moment. 'Before she had children, your mother possessed the most brilliant mind I'd ever seen – until Margaret, of course.' He leaned in, close and conspiratorial. 'I see her in you. I see her in *both* of you.'

Margaret Revolt moved uncomfortably in the background.

'It was you children who drove her over the edge,' he said.

'No.' My voice was clear and strong. 'It wasn't.'

Raeburn's eyes shifted from me to the table, and back again. He said nothing.

'Are you staying?' Margaret said.

I looked at Raeburn and realized that I was utterly without fear of him. I was smiling. It felt like the first real smile in years. 'Not here.'

My father barked out a short, contemptuous laugh. 'Where will you go?'

'Anywhere I want.'

Raeburn took a drink from the glass of whiskey in front of him. He swirled the liquid around in his mouth. His eyes were wary.

'Something's different,' he said. 'What has your brother done to you?'

'It was me,' I said. 'I did it. Not him.'

Acknowledgements

I owe a particular debt to Dr James C. M. Brust, M.D., who could always be counted upon for answers, no matter how strange the question. Binnie Kirshenbaum, Nicholas Christopher, Lauren Grodstein, and Gordon Haber read this book in its nascent stages and told me to keep going. Emily Gohn lived with me through the first six drafts and is still my best friend; Owen King lived with me through the last three and will always be my superhero. Al Sanfilippo, Marvin Frankel, and Nicolaus Mills were lampposts along the way. And, of course, the incomparable Julie Barer and Elaine Pfefferblit helped the story inside my head find its way more fully to the page. Without their faith, talent, and hard work, this book might still exist – but it wouldn't be nearly as good.

Finally, with much love and gratitude, I would like to thank my family, especially Esther Long and Mary Lou Roe. And, of course, my endless appreciation goes to my mother, Theresa Braffet, whose hands are always full of books, and my father, Jim Braffet, whose head is always full of stories. All of this is yours.